A Date with Darkness

A Novel of the Theological College of St. Van Helsing

Vanessa Knipe

BooksForABuck.com
2011

Vanessa Knipe

BooksForABuck.com
July 2011
ISBN: 978-1-60215-149-9

Chapter One

Sally stepped on her brake halfway into the parking space. A dead bird lay, wings spread, on the tarmac in front of her bumper. No wonder the van in front of them had slowed then driven on.

'What is it, Mummy?' Timmy leaned forward through the seats to look.

'Nothing.' Sally edged over the carcass. Surely those weren't chalk markings around the bird? Well, this parking space was as close as it got to the entrance today. She had no time to be squeamish; the road works on the A64 had made them late.

'Look at the roller coaster!' Timmy pointed through the windscreen at the rails running high over the entrance block to Toowich Park.

'That's too high for you.' She grabbed her newspaper—needed to identify them to the person they were here to meet. 'There'll have age and height restrictions.' And if there weren't any rules, Sally was going to invent them to keep her five-year-old son off the dangerous rides.

A van circled round. The passenger stared at her, and then hit the driver who also turned to look. Sally glared back: why should she care what they thought about respect for dead birds? The van drove along the rows, and then hovered, as if waiting for another car to move.

Timmy bounced in his booster seat, trying to get his seat belt unfastened.

Sally opened the car door. As her foot touched the tarmac, a loud cawing sounded in the trees on the far side of the car park. A murder of crows burst out of the branches and flew towards York, chased by a squall line of bruise-colored clouds. Momentarily the clouds covered the washed-out October sun and red light flowed across the car park.

Sally watched for a moment longer then climbed out of her car. She reached out to close the door.

A burst of static stung her hand. Reflex jerked it away. She paused, and then prodded the door with her index finger. Nothing, the static had grounded. She rubbed her hand to ease the itching then shut her door.

Timmy banged on his door. 'Let me out.'

Something splattered on the car window. She straightened and a red spot stained her hand. Automatically, she pulled a tissue from her pocket and dabbed at her nose. No blood dripped from her nostrils. Another red spot plopped on the car, clashing with the scarlet paint. It slid down the car like red syrup.

She raised the paper to cover her hair and the weird rain made little popping noises. Pollution? Algae? She heard that they had red rain in India, but that sort of thing didn't happened in Yorkshire.

Well, they maybe late, but she wasn't allowing Timmy to get covered in this gloopy red rain. She turned back to the car, when out of nowhere a gust of wind snatched her copy of the newspaper. It fluttered away.

'Hoy!' she shouted, as if the wind could understand. 'I need that edition.' – Even with its misleading report of calm, dry weather.

She abandoned her car to chase the paper, fallen leaves scuttling alongside it. The wind dropped and Sally stamped, catching her paper underfoot. Another squall roared through the trees, forcing her further away from her waiting son. Turning her face to one side, she managed to snatch a breath.

The wind pushed against her as she tried to retreat to the refuge of her car.

'Sally!' shouted a female voice across the car park. 'Mike! Do something!'

Picking her hair out of her eyes and mouth, Sally scanned the car park. Her friend Gail—one person she had wanted to avoid today—stood several rows away, eyes fixed on something above Sally's head.

Sally glanced up.

A lamp cover teetered on top of the matt-gray pole. The wind holding Sally was the only support for the swinging cover. The gust began to fail. She felt dizzy, as if she was falling into the sky. The rushing beat of blood in her ears almost drowned the hammering of running feet.

Hands grabbed her waist, dragging her to the tarmac, knocking the wind out of her.

Pain stung her shoulder and cheek as they scraped on the gravel: the dark smell of oil and dust on the ground near her nose.

She and whoever had grabbed her rolled, until her back slammed against a car: her head and face protected by his shoulder. Something clattered near her ear, then a crash like a hundred golf balls hitting greenhouses.

Peering out, she saw fragments of the smashed globe radiating out from the spot where she had been standing. Sally gulped for air; she would not remember five years ago. She pressed her hands over her eyes,

4

refusing to let the memory of blood be smeared over this lot of shattered glass—like the shattered windscreen five years ago.

She felt her shoulders being shaken and her wrists tugged, as her rescuer tried to pry her hands away.

'Are you hurt?'

His voice sounded familiar—over the sound of glass breaking in her head.

'Sally!'

Gail dropped to the ground by the 4X4. Sally wrenched away from the man and burrowed into her friend's comforting hug.

'Sally, it's all right now.' Gail stroked Sally's shoulder-length hair, fingers tangling in the blonde curls.

'Is that really Sally Neville?' the man asked.

'Cartwright. I'm sure I told you that, Mike,' Gail said.

'Mike Rider.' Sally looked up, a smile hovering on her lips. He had come back. For a moment she was eighteen again, sharing their first kiss.

'I forgot,' Mike said. His smile slid away and he watched her with cold eyes.

Her smile died as her memory returned. Humiliation flared. Seducer! *He seduced me and ran. Where is your pride woman? He broke his promise.*

'Mummy! Mummy!'

Grateful for Timmy's interruption, Sally shuffled round to face her car. The boy elbowed Gail aside as he flung his arms around his mother's neck. Sally rubbed her tears on his brown hair.

'Timmy, darling, Mummy's safe. But mind the glass.'

The quiet struck her. She lifted her head from where it lay against Timmy's. Her paper lay as if she had dropped it. Mike squatted to retrieve a hiking stick from under the 4X4. Black Doc Martin boots crunched on the broken glass.

'What happened to the wind?'

'What wind?' Gail said, sitting back on her heels, ready to jump in and comfort her friend if necessary.

'The wind that had me chasing my paper all over the blasted car park.'

Happy shrieks sounded, accompanied by wheels running over a track. Not even a breeze puffed.

With worried eyes, Sally looked at Mike.

Ignoring her, Mike leaned on the hiking stick, frowning at the sky.

Sally looked up to see what he was staring at. The squall line of clouds slunk away, jostling each other like guilty children trying to hide behind each other; they faded into wisps and vanished.

He turned back to Sally.

'There's no wind, you must have imagined it in the shock of the lamp cover falling on you.'

Fresh scuffmarks marred the finish of his black leather trench coat, tugging at her gratitude. That patronizing tone in his voice was new. It acted like weed-killer on her appreciation, destroying it before it took root.

'What's he doing here, anyway?' Sally said, watching Gail get to her feet and brush the dirt from her boot-cut jeans. 'I thought we'd lost him for good in the delights of the Big City.'

Gail sighed. Sally bit back the next cheap shot she had thought out. There was no point in annoying her friend despite her awful brother.

Timmy pulled away from Sally's cuddle; reassured his mother was all right, he looked hopefully at the entrance to Toowich Park.

'There's a whole load of people running from the ticket stands,' he said.

Mike followed Timmy's pointing finger. 'You need to get up,' he said, offering his hand. 'There's a delegation of Toowich Park security jogging over here.'

Feeling a bit weak, Sally grabbed his wrist. Again static flashed. Sally snatched her hand away. Mike stared at her, frowning. His gaze flicked between her and now empty horizon.

Sally grimaced. 'I seem to have an electric personality today.'

She reached for his hand again and let him draw her up. She staggered, but Mike's hands on her shoulders steadied her. She flicked a glance at him and saw his cold eyes examining her. Cold, calculating, he could never have loved her. She felt her sliver of hope slide away like ice. Looking anywhere but his face, she noticed his fingerless leather gloves. No one of thirty should wear that sort of get up.

'Gosh,' Sally said. 'I thought Halloween was next Saturday, not today. What's your Trick or Treat costume? Darth Vader?'

'Not at all, the good guys wear at least one piece of white clothing.'

'Oh, right,' Sally said. She inspected him. 'I'm seeing all midnight here.'

A corner of his mouth twitched in a half-sneer, half-smile. 'I'm wearing white boxers.'

A smile tugged at her cheeks. He always could turn her anger to laughter.

He promised to write to you.

She turned away. No way would she let him see smiles, or tears on her face, again. As a distraction, she pounced on a ticket taker wearing a neon green tee shirt and blue jeans, both emblazoned with the orange Toowich Park logo. The beads hanging from the teenager's cat-ear ponytails clicked as she quivered under Sally's glare.

'If it wasn't Saturday, I'd be on my mobile to my boss,' Sally said, brushing moss and grit from her pink anorak. 'Your unsafe light fitting dropped on a health and safety inspector.'

A manager, his tee shirt logo subdued by a suit jacket, stepped between Sally and the ticket taker. Waving his teenage employee away, he held out a first aid kit. 'Do you need any help?'

Around them a security guard roped off the area with yellow and black hazard tape. Another took the number plates of cars in the closed-off zone.

Sally tucked her shaking arm around Timmy, staring blindly at the mess, suddenly realizing how close that lamp cover had come to landing on her head. *He saved me*—some of the warm feelings to Mike returned in a guilty thought. But her husband had saved her… and died… that had to mean more.

Gail stepped in and negotiated with the manager. She wangled an invitation to get Sally into the first aid room, until she had recovered.

'But I'll need to get my kids out of my car,' Gail added.

'Did you leave the car unlocked?' Sally turned to Timmy. Looking up, she saw the driver door of her car hanging open where he had climbed through to get out. Sally felt his shrug against her arm.

'Give me your keys,' Mike said. 'I'll lock up for you.'

Sally put her hand in her pocket, then looked at the car. 'I think I left them in the ignition.'

Gail pointed out Sally's red Ford. 'Get Dan and Sophie and meet us inside,' Gail ordered her brother. 'Come on Sally, you need a cuppa.'

'Where's my paper?' Sally said.

'Stop worrying about littering. You nearly died!'

'But…' Sally bit her lip. What could she say without getting Gail suspicious?

'Can you walk or will you wait until Mike gets back to carry you?'

Goaded, Sally set off towards the entrance on legs that shivered like jelly. 'I'd walk a million miles rather than have him carry me.'

Timmy hung on his mother's arm and Gail clumped along beside them; Sally almost had to wrench her neck to look up at her friend's face now that platform shoes were back in fashion.

'Shame, I was sort of hoping you two would make it up,' Gail said. 'He rescues you and you forget the reason you dumped him—you know the deal.'

'You can't dig for gossip from that long ago. Things happened.' Sally's lips thinned, holding back the complaint *it wasn't like that, he dumped me.* But she had worked hard to present the image of the jilt rather than the victim and for reasons of his own Mike didn't seem to have corrected her story to his sister.

Mike strode back. He pocketed Sally's keys. 'Walking this slowly will take forever,' he said and scooped her up.

'Let me down.' Sally struggled to be free even though the two hundred meters to the entrance, designed by the 1940s Concrete Bunker School of Architecture, stretched out like the Pennine Way to her unsteady legs.

Mike ignored her and kept on walking. 'Gail, go get your brats. I'll look after Sally.'

'Good idea.' Gail held out her hand. 'Timmy, come with Auntie Gail.'

Holding Gail's hand, but dragging his feet and looking to his mother to countermand the instruction, Timmy went.

'If you keep wriggling like that,' Mike said, 'I'm going to drop you.'

Sally lay still. Not that she believed he would drop her, his arms, resting against her back, had plenty of muscle—more than he used to have. She stuffed the memory of the last time he had held her into the black hole of the past.

The manager trotted to keep up with Mike and led them through an unused turnstile, ignoring the queues of people. The crowd craned to see the disaster victim, clearly expecting gore. Sally buried her burning cheeks in Mike's shoulder again.

'In here, please,' the manager said, opening a door labeled with a green cross. 'I'll see about some drinks for you.'

He closed the door, leaving Sally with Mike.

Inside, she struggled to be free.

Mike took two steps across the room and deposited her on the stretcher bed against the far wall. She dropped her legs over the side, sitting up.

'I'm not an invalid.'

He turned away with that half sneer on his lips again. A mirrored cabinet showed his hair falling around his face. He jerked the ponytail band from the nape of his neck.

'What did you do to the wind?' she asked.

He met her eyes in the mirror while he finger-combed his brown hair. 'How would I make wind go away?'

She had no answer to that, but angled for more information. 'There was a wind that pushed me under that lamp, and I saw you send it away.'

'Seeing the wind now, goodness.' He replaced the band. Along with the patronizing voice that ponytail was new. Neither was attractive.

'But there was—'

The door opened again and the manager entered, carrying a tray with an assortment of cups. Timmy pushed past him to reach his mother.

'You will be getting a phone call from my boss on Monday,' Sally said.

'Your report will arrive on his desk with mine,' said the manager. 'I hope you and your party will enjoy our hospitality free today, after your shock.' He set the tray down on a table.

Behind Timmy, Gail entered with Dan and Sophie. Sally couldn't help noticing that even in an emergency Gail's make-up looked just applied.

'Come on,' Gail said, leaning in to whisper, 'you'll do me a favor. I won't have to rely on Mike to pay for the kids and me.'

'I'm sorry, I can't; you know that.' She turned to the manager. 'We will pay, just like anyone else.'

'So proper,' Mike said.

'Oh, shut up,' Gail said. 'Nobody thinks your sarcasm is clever any more. Make yourself useful. Take the kids on the rides. Go on Timmy, with Dan and Sophie.'

Timmy wriggled, but Sally cuddled him closer.

'That's all right. Timmy and I'll be out on the rides soon. You go and enjoy yourselves.'

'Don't be silly,' Gail said, settling onto the only chair and crossing her legs comfortably. 'Why should Timmy be bored while we talk? We have Mike's help.'

'Babysitter general,' Mike said.

He folded his arms and leaned against the doorframe, his steel-gray eyes mocking her reluctance.

Sally glared at him. How could Gail think that Sally would send her only child off with a bastard like Mike?

'If you're sure,' Gail said. 'Mike, go get tickets for us all.'

Dismissed, Mike lounged away, Dan and Sophie at his heels.

Gail picked up two cups, she handed a large one with a straw to Timmy, and the tea to Sally, then got her own.

'Mum says we're going to have a great time this half term,' Timmy said, slurping his drink.

Sophie slammed open the door and dropped three tickets into her mother's lap. 'Uncle Mike used the accident to jump the queue.' She giggled and dashed away.

Sally fumbled through her anorak pockets for her purse. 'Can I give you the ticket money to pass on to Mike?'

Gail shrugged. 'It's not necessary. He's rolling in it.'

'I'm not his family.' Sally opened her purse and counted out the notes.

'Why are you here?' Gail reluctantly accepted the money. 'You said you weren't coming.'

'I'm meeting someone here, or at least I was,' Sally said, hoping a partial explanation would satisfy her friend. 'With this delay, he might think I've stood him up.'

Gail choked on her tea. 'He? You won't even go to the cinema with me!'

'It's no one you know,' Sally said.

'Did you meet him at work?' Gail settled back in her chair, ready for a long gossip.

'I think it's time to go on the rides,' Sally said, firmly closing the conversation.

'Are you sure you're ready to go out yet?'

'I'll be fine,' Sally said. Then seeing the doubt in her friend's eyes she added, 'Really. I'll be better off with something to distract me.'

The most important thing, Sally thought, *is to get Gail back to her family.*

She needed time to think. Something odd had happened out there and she wanted to know what. How on earth was she to find out? It was a shame that Mike seemed to know, and he was the one person she could never trust again.

Chapter Two

They emerged from under the covered entranceway into The Square, as Toowich Park grandly called it. Trees struggled to grow out of roughly tended beds. Around the base of the trunks the petals of the blood-red flowers had crinkled brown edges, hinting that the season for outdoor amusement parks was ending.

Either that, Sally thought, *or someone has poisoned those poor chrysanthemums with too much flat cola.*

'Look,' Sally said, pointing across The Square. 'There's your brother, with Dan and Sophie.'

Gail looked around. With his height, Mike stood out above the eager new arrivals, arguing about the best rides, as they parted around an employee, who made a half-hearted effort to pick up the litter.

Looking back over her shoulder Gail said, 'We are going to discuss the details later.'

Dan and Sophie each grabbed an arm. Sally could hear their excited gabble even over the other people in The Square. Mike hung back from the family group. The contented smile on his face faded as he saw Sally.

'Sally Cartwright?' a voice said from behind her.

She half-turned and saw a stringy man with salt and pepper hair standing with a hopeful smile on his face. He had a newspaper tucked under one arm, open at the personal ads. At her smile, he folded the paper and stuffed it into a pocket.

'I'm Pete Granger. I heard about the excitement, so I thought I'd wait and see if you still wanted to go on the rides?'

'Oh yes.' Sally smiled, more warmly than she might if Mike hadn't been watching. 'This is Timmy.'

Pete looked down at Timmy and put on a jolly smile. 'Hello Timmy.'

Timmy hung behind his mother, suddenly deciding to be shy. Sally gave Pete an apologetic smile.

Another squall line of odd clouds towered over the roller coasters, which arched to the sky then swooped down only to bend at the last minute.

A sideways look showed her nothing nearby that could fall on her.

Frowning, Mike strode towards Sally. His coat billowed, caught by the wind slicing around the corner of the entrance buildings.

The breeze brushing past Sally held the promise of winter. The strength of the gust had Sally glancing at the airplane chairs. The laughing people dangling legs above the ground swung around the Maypole with no hint of wind blowing them about. Puzzled, she glanced back at Mike.

And her vision blurred.

She saw two images of Mike. One strode in slow motion towards her. The other turned to face the threatening clouds, looming over the people screaming in delighted terror at the feigned danger of the roller coasters. This second image held up a hand, like a policeman stopping traffic. Like before, the clouds scattered and the afternoon sun brightened.

Sally blinked hard. Then all she could see was Mike striding towards her. She rubbed her eyes. *Did she need glasses?* But she thought double vision was different to that.

Pete glanced over his shoulder as the sunlight faded. Deliberately, Sally turned towards her host for the day.

'Are you fine now?' Mike asked, scrutinizing the man who stood with her. Despite her turning away, he had intruded.

Strands of Mike's hair had come free from his ponytail again. Her hands itched to tuck it neatly back into place. She hid them in her anorak pockets.

'Yes, thank you.' Sally turned back to Pete. 'Where do you think the rides for Children Timmy's age are?'

'Hold on.' Pete rummaged in his pocket, with a regretful look at the big roller coasters. 'I'm sure I've got a park map.'

Mike scowled and returned to the ice cream stand where Dan and Sophie wildly stabbed at the menu board.

Emerging from the map, Pete stared after Mike. 'Who was that?'

'He's the brother of a friend of mine. He's here with her and her kids,' Sally said. A spark of inspiration struck. 'You know on the dating site they tell us to always let people know where we are.'

'Wise,' he said. His eyes narrowed slightly, then he turned back to Sally. 'The cable car is over this way. It takes us straight to the rides for younger children, next to the zoo, so we can go there too. You'll like that won't you, Timmy?'

Timmy continued to stare at Pete from behind Sally.

An avenue of limp flags led to the cable car station. Sally eyed the flags. Were any more weird gusts of wind going come out of nowhere? Mike knew something about the wind, but she had no idea how to pry that information out of him.

No more banks of clouds appeared

To cover her nerves she said, 'We should get a great view of the whole park from up there. We can decide if there is anything in the main park we might want to go on.'

The cable car station stood on stilts. The metal steps rang under foot as they climbed. She could feel the stiff leather of her new shoes rubbing her heel. Maybe it wouldn't cause a blister.

At the top she looked back and saw Dan and Sophie pulling their Uncle Mike towards the cable cars. He laughed at them.

Pete pushed through the other potential passengers and grabbed three seats for them. 'Here Timmy, how about this window seat?'

Thankfully, the doors closed before Mike could join them in the car. He lifted a cupped hand and Sally saw that weird double vision again. Mike standing next to Dan, and Mike making a tossing gesture after the car she was in. The car jolted as it started up. Sally blinked and there was only one Mike, laughing at Dan.

'So Sally,' Pete said, turning so his knee rubbed against her jean-clad leg. Sally was grateful that he didn't try to put an arm along the seat behind her. 'What do you do when Timmy is at school? Do you garden?'

Suddenly, Sally wondered how Pete had known who she was? Without the newspaper, he had recognized her. And he had known who was in the accident.

'I… er.' Now she was just being silly, he must have been in the queue when she was brought in. 'I don't have time to do much gardening, beyond mowing the grass and remembering to put in some sunflower seeds for Timmy. I work part time with the Health and Safety Executive in York. You said you were a journalist?'

'A freelancer.' He fidgeted with his watch. 'I imagine that you aren't too happy about the accident earlier then?'

'It will go badly for them if our investigation finds that the faulty cover was reported and the report was not acted upon.' She paused a moment, then smiled at him. 'I'm not going to talk about my work. So what is your relaxation? Let me guess you're a keen gardener, right?'

Below them the park spread out. Toowich Hall, now a hotel but once home of a wealthy local mill owner, was visible. Careful landscaping made the park seem much bigger when you were walking around it. Ahead, Sally saw smaller rides suitable for children's Timmy's age.

'Mummy, I want to go on that ride,' Timmy interrupted. With his nose pressed against the glass, he pointed not to the carousel but to a river ride through the hippopotamus pen. A sign said Journey through the

Heart of Darkness. As they watched, a raft traveled up an artificial hill above the tree line. The river took it straight over a waterfall. The splash zone covered the entire raft.

'I don't know that I want to get soaked,' she said. 'I didn't bring changes of clothes for us.'

'It looks as if we could buy waterproof ponchos at the entrance to the ride,' Pete said, peering over her shoulder. 'It does look fun.'

'We'll see,' Sally said. She looked at the queue, calculating the waiting time.

At the next station Timmy jumped off; he had seen rides. When Sally and Pete caught up with him he was on a junior roller coaster set up like a Wild West mining train.

Laughing at his eagerness, Sally settled down to learn a bit more about her date, while waving as Timmy rode past.

'I have a fantastic allotment,' Pete said. 'I won prizes for my exotics. I grew Datara Stramonium last year for the allotment show. I have a secret ingredient.' He stared intently at her.

'That's nice.' Sally desperately searched for a change of topic. 'We went to Spain last year, to visit my mother. She retired out there. Do you take holidays abroad?'

'No, I'm afraid not,' Pete said. 'What made you join the Internet dating agency?'

'Pardon?' Sally stared at her hands, which she had to stop from fidgeting. 'I guess I wanted to get out more, make new friends, you know all the usual things.' She looked up and smiled.

'You don't think it's … dangerous?'

Sally blinked. 'How? I mean, the site tells us how to be careful.'

Timmy emerged from the ride and Sally grabbed his hand before he ran off again. Pleased for once he had interrupted she said, 'Do you think that's a petting zoo?'

'You'd never believe the trouble I have with rabbits,' Pete said. 'Do you have—'

'Rabbits are dull.' Timmy tugged on Sally's hand. 'Let's go there. Do you think they've got snakes that are poison?'

'Poisonous,' Sally corrected. She turned to Pete as he held open the door to the reptile house. The air smelled musty, warm after the nip in the air outside. 'You're being very kind about missing out on rides for yourself.'

He shrugged. 'I thought the idea is to give Timmy some fun. I'll stay after you've left and go on the other rides.'

'That's sensible. Thank you. Look Timmy, isn't that a grumpy looking crocodile?'

The couple in front of them gave the glass of the enclosure at last stroke and moved on to the next display.

Timmy gave her his special *stop embarrassing me* look and said, 'Mummy, it's an alligator.'

Checking the label, Sally saw that Timmy was right.

'Well at least one of our children is learning something at school,' Gail said.

Sally jumped. 'Are you following us?' she whispered.

Gail grinned as Pete went along with Timmy to a tank of fish, where Dan and Sophie tapped on the glass. One of the fish suddenly expanded. Sophie giggled as Timmy jumped back.

Sally gritted her teeth and was about to join Timmy when the alligator slapped its tail on the glass with a dull crack. Sally stopped and stared wide eyed as Mike stood between her and the alligator. The bright heat lights of the reptile house cast odd shadows as he ran a hand over the glass. 'Kinetic force transfer…' he muttered.

His head jerked up and he stared at fish tank.

'Is it breaking?' Sally said, her heart skipping as she scrutinized the alligator cage; the glass was smooth and unmarked.

Mike sprinted across to the tank and pulled the three children back. A panel in the tank cracked from top to bottom. Water spilled out over the granite floor. With the water came the fish. They flopped about. The puffer fish blew up with spikes over them unable to do anything.

Sophie burst into tears. Dan shook the water off his hands and glared at his soaking trousers.

'Stand back!' shouted a man, wearing the neon green uniform shirt pulled on over a black tee shirt and jeans. Accompanied by another employee they began scooping fish into a bucket.

'If you could leave by the nearest exist please,' the man said, ladling up a spiky fish.

Sally grabbed Timmy and hauled him out. 'This is turning out to be a very dangerous day.'

Mike scrubbed splash marks off his trench coat. 'If you're going to worry about health and safety all day, then you might as well go home.'

'Mummy.' Timmy tugged on her hand. 'Since we're wet anyway, can we go on the water ride?'

Sally sighed. 'Fine.'

Timmy shrieked in delight. 'Dan and Sophie too?'

Gail looked over at Mike who nodded.

As they left the building more employees in their uniform green shirt and blue jeans scrambled up to the door carrying buckets.

The water ride went well, and only a little extra water hit them by the end.

Pete had been a careful, but unexciting host. Sally was relieved to call an end to their day ostensibly so that Pete could at least enjoy some of the other rides before the park shut, but her feet hurt where the new leather was rubbing.

As he said goodbye at the entrance, Pete shook her hand. 'Let me walk you to your car?'

Sally could have groaned, she wanted to be allowed to hobble with her sore heel. 'That's all right, I wouldn't want you to miss your fun on the rides.'

'I could get back in, but that's fine.' With his eyes on the rides he asked, 'Can I call you again?'

'I'll e-mail you,' she blurted out, turning red.

'Let me know.' As he walked away he dropped his newspaper into the bin and made a beeline for the wildest roller coast.

Sally limped back to her car with Timmy. She patted all her pockets for her keys, then emptied them onto the car bonnet: purse, pen, receipt for some carrots, tissues...

No keys.

No! Why had she left her handbag at home? So maybe it was sensible not to take a bag when going to a place where you are likely to put it down and forget it, but still...

'Let me in the car, Mum, I'm tired,' Timmy whined.

Sally gritted her teeth and forced a jolly tone. 'I've lost the keys. Come on, let's go to the office and report it, in case they were handed in.'

'What if they weren't?' Timmy said

'Then we'll have to get a taxi home,' Sally said. She wanted nothing more than to get into her comfy shoes, sitting enticingly on the passenger seat.

Timmy leaned his back against the car and sagged to the ground. 'Go without me.'

'Stop it, Timmy. Get up, now.'

She reached to grab his hand to drag him if she had to when she saw the roped off area again. The broken glass had been swept up, but Sally could hear it shattering in her head.

She stared at hazard tape with her hands over her mouth.

'Here Timmy, open up the car and sit quietly. Your Mum will be better in a bit. Drink this, Sally.' As if from a distance she recognized Mike, she hadn't heard him arrive. He wrapped her hands around a flask and helped her bring it to her lips. Shaking, she did as she was told.

The brandy burnt her throat and she started coughing. As she focused on Mike's face, she could see him grinning at her reaction.

'Just a little more, hey Sal?' He lifted the flask to her lips. She turned her face away.

'I've got to drive,' she protested. 'My keys!' She looked around and saw Timmy sitting in the car.

'I forgot to return them to you earlier,' he said.

'Forgot, or was it mischief?'

'Genuinely forgot.' Mike raised his eyebrows. 'I sent Gail off without me. She and the kids are meeting our parents. I couldn't leave you stranded but I'll drive, okay?'

Sally held out her hand imperiously. 'I can drive my own car.'

He shook his head. 'Get your seat belt fastened back there, Timmy.'

Timmy scrambled into his car seat, eager to be rescued.

'Please?' Mike said.

The hand she held out was still shaking and there was a dreadful lump of ice in her stomach that the brandy had yet to melt. 'Drive then, it's all one to me.' She stomped to the passenger side.

'Have another sip of that brandy,' he said as she climbed in the passenger side. 'It'll help.'

As he got into the driving seat, she shoved her comfy shoes onto the floor, refusing to give in and wear them. She capped the flask and handed it back.

He accepted it with a shrug.

Putting the car into reverse, Mike pulled slowly out. He stopped halfway and stared at the dead bird.

'You had to park over that, didn't you?'

Sally shrugged. 'So what?' She could see now that the chalk marking around the dead bird were some sort of writing.

Mike shook his head and continued on.

Reprieved of the hike back to the ticket office, Timmy chattered away, more than making up for Sally's silence, until she felt like screaming at him to shut up.

Mike answered all of the little boy's questions with patronizing good humor, which encouraged Timmy to babble more. Maybe he did need a new dad, like her mother said. Look at the way he opened up.

As they approached York Ring Road Mike said, 'Where's your house? Is it close enough to Gail's so that I can walk?'

Sally opened her eyes. 'If you go to Gail's, I can drive from there.'

Mike shook his head. 'Just answer the question, Sally.'

'Why? You don't own the rights to any straight answer from me.'

'Pretty please with sugar on the top, can you answer my question?'

Sally rolled her eyes. 'Fine, Gail bought a house five minutes away from mine. So yes, if you want to walk you can.' Sally gave her address.

'There, that wasn't so hard.'

The pale October sun was setting, painting the clouds red, as Mike pulled up on Sally's drive. The 1920s red brick semi-detached stood back from the road behind a high privet hedge. On the four foot fence that separated the mirror image of her house and garden sat two crows. They angled their heads to observe the arrival.

Mike climbed out and dropped the keys into Sally's hand. He stared at the crows.

As Sally walked to the door they flew away, dragging their wings.

'Would you like some tea?' She almost bit her tongue to get the polite words out.

'I wouldn't strain your good manners so far,' he said, watching Timmy run into the house. 'He'll be a good kid, once he stops being such a mummy's boy.'

Sally bristled. 'He's not—'

Mike raised his hands, stepping back from her. 'Sorry no! Forget I said it.'

Mike gazed into her eyes. A frown creased his forehead. 'Will you be all right?'

Sally shrugged. 'I'll be fine.'

'Really?' His mouth flicked into a wry smile.

She shut the door on his inquisitiveness. Drawing the front room curtains, she noticed him straightening from the doorstep. He saw her and mouthed 'Just tying my shoelaces'.

Sally watched as he shut the gates over the drive entrance and walked away. She frowned. She'd forgotten to ask him about the wind. Now she would have to see him again to ask her questions.

Chapter Three

A howling dog briefly woke Sally; the bark was deep, not yappy like most of the dogs around here. Half asleep, she tugged the curtain over the gap that let in the bright moonlight. Shifting slightly, she dislodged the cat. Offended it jumped off the bed.

'Will it hurt?' she muttered and drifted back to sleep.

* * * *

'Is it going to hurt?' Sally asks, standing in front of the den they have been building all summer. The ground is like dirty powder; there's been so little rain this year.

'Don't be such a girl,' Mike says.

'Well, Duh!'

'Gail only plays with her dolls. You do the good stuff,' Mike says.

Sally flushes at the compliment. 'Let's get on with it, then. What d'we do?'

'We prick our fingers with this penknife and then hold them together.'

'That knife's dirty,' Sally objects. 'We could get… get blood poisoning or stuff.'

'Scaredy cat.' Mike sticks his tongue out at her.

'I'm not. Give it here.' She jabs at her ring finger. She squeezes out a perfect droplet of ruby blood. It hangs on her fingertip. 'Your turn.'

'You're as good as a boy.' Taking the penknife, he stabs his finger. His blood oozes out and they link fingers. The droplets of blood merge and a trickle runs down their hands. 'We're eternal best friends now.'

'My Mum says that married people have to be best friends.'

'Soppy girl,' Mike says. 'But I'll marry you, if I have to marry anyone.'

* * * *

A pounding on the front door woke Sally. Light around the edges of the curtains told her it was morning. Was it the postman? Had she slept that late? Why hadn't he rung the doorbell, like normal?

Groggily, she peered out of her bedroom curtains and saw Gail's car. A glance at the clock told her that it was 8.30. That was earlier than Gail normally dropped by. Sally smiled; Gail was a good friend to check on her after the shock yesterday.

20

She pulled her blue fleece dressing gown over her pajamas. Timmy had beaten her downstairs and was playing a shoot-em-up on his game console.

As she had seen Gail's car, Sally pulled open the front door without checking the spy hole.

The Sunday Paper crunched up, partially blocking the door's opening circle. The cat darted in and rubbed against her ankles.

'Gail, what are—' she said, and then the smile faded.

Mike Rider stood outside. Sally pushed the door to close it. Mike leaned his shoulder against her force and pushed back. The paper tore as the door pushed it aside

'We need to talk,' he announced. Grabbing her wrist, he pulled her into the kitchen-dining room.

The ever-hopeful cat ran ahead, looking for breakfast.

Gail trotted in behind him, shutting the door. 'Is this necessary?'

Sally tugged her wrist free. She rubbed her wrist and placed the table between her and Mike. 'What's this about?

Mike pulled a crumpled paper from his pocket and spread it out. It was folded open at the personal section.

Mike ran a finger down the ads and read out loud. '*Widow seeks: suitable role-model for young son.* Is this you?'

'What if it is?' Sally turned away to put the kettle on for coffee. Once on, she bent to stroke the twining cat.

'How could you be so stupid?' he shouted. 'If you want a man, can't you or Gail find one among your friends?'

Sally straightened. Reaching into a nearby cupboard she found a tin of cat food. 'This is none of your business.'

'Wouldn't you step in to stop someone from doing something dangerous like jumping off a cliff?'

'Dangerous?' Sally turned around. 'What's dangerous about a bit of dating?'

'Going off and meeting strangers,' Mike said. 'You didn't even let Gail know what you were doing.'

Sally opened her mouth to refute his comments when Gail pointed at the paper across from where her brother's finger had stabbed.

'Oh look,' she said. She lifted the paper for closer examination. 'Megachiroptera is playing the Whitby Goth Festival after all. I thought they were on a tour of Haiti. Oh it says they've been studying the voodoo rhythms for their new album. They're playing their set on Halloween! That's next Saturday.'

The combatants stopped arguing and stared at her.

'Since when did you follow the Goth scene?' Mike demanded.

'I picked up the habit from Dave, before the divorce. The music's not all bad and loud you know,' she said.

Argument interrupted, Sally and Mike stared helplessly at each other.

'What's the deal with the ad, then?' Gail asked, pulling out one of the dining chairs and sitting down.

'You know we didn't have a proper holiday this summer,' Sally said. 'I was short of funds. Timmy nagged me about how all his friends had a good time and he didn't. Well, this is a way to do fun things in the half-term break.'

'Huh?' Gail said.

Sally shrugged. 'In the web message, I've suggested that the men prove their suitability by arranging a day out at a local attraction for Timmy and me. That's what I was doing at Toowich Park yesterday, meeting one of the dates.'

'Wish I'd thought of that,' Gail said. 'And the man may insist on paying for both of you, you know as a way of impressing you. He might even turn out to be Mr. Right, or at least Mr. Right Amount.'

'So it's not a bad idea then?'

'It's the most idiotic plan I've ever heard,' Mike said.

Both Gail and Sally looked at him as if he was mad. Mike glared back at Sally.

'You can't seriously consider meeting men like that,' he said.

'What's wrong with it?' Sally asked.

'Don't listen to him Sally, the idea sounds great to me,' Gail said.

'What do you tell them?' Mike said, over Gail's comments. 'At the end of the day do you say *Actually, I've decided you aren't suitable*?'

'Is that really so bad?' Sally said. But she flushed, remembering how hard it had been yesterday telling Pete Granger—even though he made it clear the rides were more interesting than her.

'*Is that really so bad?*' Mike looked at Sally in disbelief. He ran a hand through his brown hair, loosening more strands from the ponytail.

Gail grinned at Sally and stage-whispered, 'Showing off the distinguished silvering at the temples, isn't he? He ought to use more dye.' She patted her hennaed head.

Sally sniggered; Gail was right, her brother had become a right poser.

Mike dropped his hand, flicking an irritated glance at his sister. 'You're teasing the men. That's what's wrong.'

'What do you know about it?' Gail demanded.

Suddenly Mike grinned. 'Know about what? Sally being a tease? Quite a lot actually.'

'You don't know anything about me,' Sally said. 'Not when we were eighteen, and certainly not now.'

'If you're still teasing men, then I'd say you haven't changed much in the last twelve years.'

'You've certainly changed,' Sally said. 'Are you so self-righteous that you can call other people on their moral behavior?'

'Well, I've never been promiscuous.'

'You'd never be able to accuse me of that.'

'You can't still be mad with me that we were both too drunk to do anything at Nige's party in the sixth form.'

'You can get out of this house, right now,' Sally said.

'You mean you two never…?' Gail said.

Mike shrugged, noncommittally.

Gail cackled. 'We all thought you'd broken up because you'd taken advantage of Sally when she was drunk. Do you mean to tell me that you broke up because you didn't?'

'You mean you never told your best mate?' Mike said. 'I thought you girls gossiped about everything.'

Sally's nails dug into her palms.

'Oh Sally!' Gail gasped with laughter. 'At least admit it's funny.'

'Uncle Mike,' Timmy said from the door. 'Do you know anything about these games?'

'Since when did Mike Rider become *Uncle*?' Sally asked.

Timmy shrugged. 'He's Auntie Gail's brother isn't he?'

'What're you playing?' Mike hooked an arm around Timmy's shoulder and led him back to the front room.

'Calm down, Sally. You're over reacting,' Gail said. 'Anyway, I think Mike's just jealous.'

'Jealous? Nonsense, we're nothing to each other anymore.'

'I don't think men ever really get over their first love.'

'I don't think he was ever in love with me,' Sally said. She was not going to admit that Gail was talking sense, for once. 'Did you want some coffee?'

Sally made a pot of coffee and sat with Gail in the kitchen diner, letting the boys play computer games. After a while Mike peered in through the hall door. He had picked up the paper from by the front door and straightened it out on the kitchen table. He glanced up at Sally, then back at the paper he was smoothing.

'Do you really let Timmy play that sort of game?'

'What's wrong with them? He said all his friends have it.' Sally forced herself not to flare up again at his criticism. Instead she lifted the pot. 'Coffee?'

'Black, please,' he said, frowning. As Sally put his mug down in front of him he said, 'I think Timmy might have been ly... I mean exaggerating a little. Gail doesn't even let Dan have those games.'

Gail glared at Mike, then turned back to her. 'I didn't like to say, but you do give in to Timmy more than I would, but I've got my mother and dad here to spoil them if I'm a strict single mum. Timmy's only got you. All the research does say...' Gail gave it up and shrugged. 'He's your son. This is your house. Just ignore Mike.'

Sally was quite prepared to do this. 'Best idea you've had all day.'

Mike kept his face down in the paper, sipping his coffee.

'There's been a break in at the Seaside Museum in Whitby,' he said.

Accepting the change of subject as a peace offering, Sally wrinkled her nose in mock disgust. 'What was taken? Old fish? I'll have to get a less provincial paper. I'm sure there's a war going on somewhere that would be more interesting.'

'Some Victorian jewelry.' Mike smiled at her. 'I'm in the antiquities trade myself, so this will be big news in our circles, in case some shows up at auction.'

'What happened to the engineering?'

Mike shrugged.

Gail said, 'I'm sure Sally doesn't really like intruders demanding that she explain her love life at 9 AM on a Sunday. And I don't like being dragged out without even being allowed to put on my makeup.'

'If you need some face cream,' Sally said 'I've got some in my samples drawer.'

Gail jumped up, shaking her head. 'You'd think it was a sin to throw things away in this house.' She opened a drawer in the kitchen and rummaged through it. She pulled out the cat's grooming brush. 'Is this supposed to be in here?'

Sally snatched it and returned it to the drawer. 'Yes, I know where it is if it's in there.'

Gail picked a spray can out next. The mixing ball inside rattled as she read the label. 'When did you go for Colloidal Silver Anti-microbial Sport Shoe Deodorizer?'

'They did a promotion at my Health Club,' Sally said. 'It had some pretty weird stuff. That was the least silly of the *alternative medicine* stuff.'

'It's not a crime to say you don't want any of their freebies,' Gail said. She bent down and dropped the shoe deodorizer into the bin. At Sally's half protest she added, 'It's not like you're ever going to use it.' She shoved a few more samples aside.

'Finally! Here's something useful.' Gail ripped open a sachet and smeared it over her face and neck.

Mike looked on, bemused.

'Don't you look so superior, you're to blame. I've got to get the kids ready for Church and Sunday school so, if you've finished your rant, may we go? I wonder if I can get Mum to babysit next Saturday. You're off to your conference aren't you, Mike?'

Mike nodded. Putting down the paper, he took two steps towards the door, and then turned back.

He caught Sally's left hand.

At his touch her stomach lurched.

Mike searched Sally's face as she tried to pull her hand away.

'Let me go!'

'Don't wreck dreams. Just take the ad out of the paper and say you've changed your mind. That's the safest, I mean best way.' His stroking thumb passed over her ring finger. He dropped her hand as if it burnt his palm. 'At least you had the courtesy to leave your wedding ring off yesterday.'

Sally shut the front door on him.

'I'm sure I need your permission to go out on dates,' Sally whispered, so that Timmy couldn't hear.

* * * *

Sally gathered up the last of the washing up into the bowl as a tap sounded at the back door. She looked out of the window. Gail stood there, still in her Sunday best church suit. She dumped the bowl and the rolling pin in the sink then unlocked the back door.

'I don't think the doorbell is working on the front,' Gail said, scrubbing her feet dry on the mat.

'Oh, that's why Mike knocked earlier,' Sally said. 'I wondered.'

'He didn't even try the doorbell,' Gail said. 'I think he just wanted to thump.'

Sally turned back to the sink and flicked the kettle on. 'Hope you don't mind, I just need to wash these up.'

'I don't know how you have the time to do home baking.' Gail sniffed the air. She got two mugs out of the cupboard and added teabags.

Sally put the scrubbed rolling pin on the drying rack. 'I was keeping Timmy busy.'

'You don't have a date for today, then?'

'We're going to the Water Park tomorrow,' Sally said. 'What's—'

A piteous mew sounded outside the back door and scrabbling on the cat flap, followed by yowling and hissing.

'Max! Firey! Not again!'

Sally bent and pushed open the cat flap.

Her ginger cat scrambled through. He turned and sat there, hissing at next-door's cat. Max batted at the cat flap. Firey batted back. The cat door clattered open then banged shut again.

Sally grabbed the rolling pin. She flung open the door and charged after the invader cat.

Max darted under the hedge, turned and sang a few swear words at her.

Sally walked back as her ginger tom lounged over to his bowl.

'Now why didn't he come in through the cat flap like...?' Sally said, half to herself as she stared down at an angular symbol drawn on the step. A drawing of a mountain with flags half way up it. Sally wrinkled her nose. The chalk was smudged by the catfight, but was still visible. Chalk markings—like the ones around the bird in the car park at the theme park.

'What's wrong?' Gail came to the door. She followed Sally's gaze. Her head jerked up and she stared around. Her hand touched her throat.

'What is it?' Sally asked.

'What?'

'That sign? Do you recognize it?'

'Me?' Gail forced a smile. 'No! Why would I know about mystic symbols? Let's have some tea.'

Sally frowned, but Gail had gone back inside. Sally followed her, and grabbed the boiling kettle. She lifted it off its base and poured the water over the back step.

'No!' Gail said. 'I mean why are you doing that?'

Sally retrieved the yard brush from the utility room, and scrubbed the chalk away. 'I don't want graffiti on my property.' She filled a jug from the hot tap and stalked away to the front door. Kicking the front door mat

26

out of the way, she revealed another symbol chalked on the red tiles of her porch.

Timmy emerged from the front room and stood beside Gail, who was watching Sally.

'What're you doing, Mum?'

'I'm cleaning the step.' Sally scrubbed away the symbol. Finished, she leaned the yard brush against the porch wall and turned back to Gail. 'Tell that brother of yours to stop drawing … those things on my doorsteps.'

'Why would Mike do that?'

'I don't know, but he can stop it.'

* * * *

After Timmy fell sleep that night, Sally pottered about, performing her nightly ritual of turning off all the switches in the house. She unplugged the TV and HiFi system, locked all the doors and left the keys in the lock for fire safety.

Finally, she put down some Meow Munchies for the cat rubbing against her legs.

Tonight, Sally decided, I'll have a long soak.

A quick rummage through her free sample drawer, in the kitchen, found a sachet of expensive bubble bath. Gail could mock Sally's habit of keeping the freebies that came in the post, but she always had a stand by.

She lowered herself into the hot water. If it wasn't Mike who had drawn the symbols—and why would he? —then who had? He couldn't have drawn the ones around the crow; he and Gail had just arrived. Even though she protested ignorance, Sally was sure that Gail knew more about the drawings than she let on.

What was going on? There was the rain of blood, the dead crow, those odd clouds, the wind that no one else felt and now mystical runes chalked on her doorstep.

But it was only the chalk drawings that anyone else had seen. She sat straight up. Was she going mad? Perhaps she had drawn the symbols herself. No! The smashed fish tank had to have been part of this as well. Everyone had seen that – Mike had been interested in it too. So she couldn't be going mad.

After all, what would happen to Timmy if she was sent to a secure hospital? Her Mum lived in Spain, and made it clear that she never intended to return to cold, dank England.

After ten minutes, she gave up on her bath. She wandered down to the kitchen to make a cup of tea, then back to her bedroom, turning out the light. She twitched her curtains aside. There was no point in trying to sleep even though the luminous hands on her bedside clock ticked on to midnight. Would Gail look after Timmy?

Even at this time on a Sunday night there were occasional cars and one pedestrian staggering and using the hedges as a prop; Mr. Wallis again, from three doors along.

At half past midnight, Sally's eyes drooped and she reached out to draw the curtains blocking out the bright moon.

A figure, wearing an ankle-length coat, detached itself from next door's hedge. Whoever it was looked around and seeing no one touched the streetlight. The light bulb at the top flared, and then flashed out. When her eyes had adjusted the figure had gone.

But Sally was sure that the person in the street was Mike.

Chapter Four

All she wanted was a lie in. A thud sounded on the roof, followed by skittering hops.

Now she had rats or something in the loft.

She flung back the covers and found her slippers. Perhaps last night had been another dream, Sally thought as she plodded downstairs.

Timmy had managed to find a classic Tom and Jerry cartoon. Tom had lost it, stuffing dynamite sticks in the mouse hole and everyone knew what that would lead to.

Today was marked on the calendar: she had a date with one David Grenill at the nearby water park this afternoon. That should be fun. She banished the nagging doubt, placed in her mind by Mike Rider, over the prudence of this course of action.

Sally shook her head. Last night must have been a dream. There was no way she had seen Mike blow out a streetlight with a touch. She was having such vivid dreams at the moment.

Turning on the kettle, Sally walked to the front door. She paused. What was she going to find outside?

Actually Sally, she thought, *what you are going to find is the milk for breakfast. There will be nothing sinister out there.*

Last night's image of Mike Rider was only a dream.

It took all her will to open the front door. There was a doormat. Nothing odd lurked on the front step or in her front garden. Taking a deep breath, she shoved the doormat onto the path below.

There Sally, nothing.

She tied her dressing gown more firmly and stepped out to pick up the milk from where the milkman leant over the gate and left it in the hidden spot under the hedge.

'Max! Max!' called her next-door neighbor. 'Oh Sally, have you seen Max? His supper last night was untouched. Where do think he could be?'

Sally straightened and looked around. 'I haven't seen him since yesterday afternoon. He and Firey had another fight. I'll check my garage and shed, maybe he's locked in again.'

'That'll be it. He'll be locked in someone's outbuildings.'

Sally picked up her milk.

Cawing sounded from above. Sally looked up. Three crows hop-skipped around her roof.

She bent and picked up a pebble. She lobbed it at the crows, but it hit the wall of the house and clattered against her windowpane.

The crows tilted their heads and regarded her.

'That's funny,' said her neighbor. 'They've only pooed on your half of the roof.'

Sally could see that the crows were ignoring her neighbor's house. Clutching her milk, she scampered to the front door. She was about to shut the door when a cat let out a long meowl.

Both Sally and her neighbor turned to start saying 'oh there's Max now' when Firey, with tail fluffed up, charged over the threshold and into the house. Sally followed him in. He hid under a chair and not even a tin of tuna could coax him out.

Why was the cat outside at all? His collar had a magnet that opened the cat flap. But he hadn't been able to get in yesterday either. Reaching under the chair, Sally tugged the collar over the head of the reluctant cat.

Returning to the kitchen, she held the magnet near the flap and listened for the tiny click. But she heard nothing. She pushed on the flap, which stayed firmly shut.

Well, perhaps that new battery Sally had put in last month was a dud. Sally found a new battery in her stores cupboard. After testing that the cat flap worked again, Sally dragged the cat out from under the chair and strapped the collar back around his neck. Once released, the cat scrambled for safety.

What had caused the cat to be so scared? The other cats in the area were fighters and Firey had been stuck out all night. That must be why.

Yesterday, Gail had said the doorbell wasn't working. Since she was in the mood, she changed the batteries on the inside unit. It made no difference when Sally tried the bell, so she took her screwdriver outside. Her battery tester showed the battery outside was the culprit.

The gate scraped over the concrete drive and Sally glanced up

It was that blasted Mike Rider again. Not only did he haunt her dreams, now he was turning up every second.

Sally plastered an intentionally false smile on her face and turned to him. 'Hello Mike, what do you need this time?'

'I've got the cheat sheet for the game that Timmy asked for. What's your problem here?'

'What is it about men that they hate to see a woman with a screwdriver in her hand?'

Through the open front door Timmy heard Mike's voice. He abandoned Tom and Jerry and ran through to the hall.

'Hiya, Uncle Mike,' he shouted.

'I spent ages on the Internet hunting this up for you.'

'I thought you didn't approve of the games I let Timmy play,' Sally said.

'He's your kid,' Mike said. 'I just asked to make sure you knew what he was playing. With no prejudice, what's wrong with the doorbell?'

'I need to add batteries to my shopping list. The one in the cat flap has gone too; the poor cat was stuck outside all night with all the other cats bullying him,' Sally said. 'I suppose you'd better come in, and show Timmy what you want to show him. I'd never hear the end of it if I sent you away.'

Sally stepped aside, trying to feel grateful that Mike was being carelessly kind to Timmy. She screwed the button unit back to the wall then returned the screwdriver to the kitchen. Mike closed the samples drawer as she entered and reached a hand for the cupboard above.

'You want some face cream?' she asked.

'Sorry, I was looking for a glass for some water, didn't want to bother you,' Mike said.

'In a drawer?'

He shrugged. 'You'd never believe where Gail keeps some of her stuff.'

Sally showed him the correct cupboard, wondering just how he'd acquired the sort of welcome where he could help himself to drinks in her house.

* * * *

Sally spotted her date even before she'd parked her car. He lounged at the top of the entrance steps, thumb sliding over his slick 3G phone. He looked more like the type favored by Gail, but Sally had chosen the men who had the most interesting ideas for filling the half-term break; she wasn't about to admit her own cravings for company.

'This is better than the boring summer holidays.' Timmy bounced in his seat. 'We did nothing for days.'

'It wasn't that bad.' Eyeing the smooth man, she wondered if the new swimming costume would be appropriate. She'd bought one with a skirt on it, as a sop to modesty, going swimming with a strange male. She hoped it would look all right, but now suspected it looked too staid and middle-aged.

Sally whisked Timmy up the steps. 'I hope you've not been waiting long, David.'

'Not at all,' David said. 'I'd wait a thousand times longer for you.' He slid his phone into the pocket of his slightly shiny jacket; his smiling eyes undressed her. He was a frog who had been kissed to make a man.

'Let's go inside,' David said. 'I know you'll enjoy the rides here, Timmy. The flumes are really fast.'

'Perhaps Timmy shouldn't go on them,' Sally said. 'There is a wave pool. That would be fun, wouldn't it Timmy?'

'They're perfectly safe, and I'm sure Timmy is the right height. What do you say, Timmy? I'll bet you're not a little girlie, too afraid to ride the flumes.'

That was the right note to take with Timmy, Sally noted sourly. It was a bit like the way Mike talked to him, a conspiracy amongst males against the over-protective women-folk. Timmy trotted alongside David eager to try out the fastest ride available. He walked straight through the entrance. Sally made for the ticket booth.

'I've got our tickets,' David said.

'Oh, thanks,' Sally said.

Sally had fully intended to pay her way on these excursions, despite Gail's jokes about Mr. Right Amount, but David had pre-empted her good intentions. He waved a piece of paper at the glassy-eyed attendant, who pressed the button three times to let them through, but otherwise ignored them. Sally pitied them; the attendants must have a boring time just passing people through all day. She followed after David and her son, who were now discussing video games.

This was a modern pool with a non-segregated changing area. Sally cornered her son and dragged him into one of the larger cubicles, before he could try and get changed with this new man.

Why was it that her son was attracted to the wrong sort? First he liked Mike Rider and now he was getting on with this David.

Sally bunged all their clothes into a locker and blew up the armbands for Timmy, while trying to stop him racing into the pools.

David waited by the showers for them. Meeting him at a pool seemed appropriate as his frog-prince smile surfaced again. He studied Sally's swimming dress, clearly admiring her figure. Sally smoothed down her skirt nervously.

He stripped off well. He had muscle, but no man boobs. She suppressed a desire to know how Mike Rider looked undressed. When he had carried her on Saturday, Sally had felt the muscle under his clothes.

Sally saw three pools under the glass roof, all decorated in a tropical theme. Tubes emerged at various places along the wall and people splashed out at a variety of speeds.

'Which is it first, Timmy?' David said. He turned to Sally. 'You were wise to choose a one-piece; sometimes the top of the two-piece can ride up. While most men here would like it, you wouldn't want to expose yourself.'

She crossed her arms over her chest. 'This is certainly more exciting than my health club pool.'

'Up here.' He gestured to steps.

'I want to go on the fastest one,' Timmy said.

Sally opened her mouth to say no, but David got in first. He bowed over in a conspiratorial fashion and stage-whispered in Timmy's ear, 'Why don't we work your mother up to the fast rides? A nice slow tube ride first, I think.'

Timmy nodded eagerly.

Helping Timmy with a huge ring, Sally climbed up to the top of the tower. Sally set Timmy going first then followed rapidly into her ring. They pushed off through a tunnel. This opened out into a pool then on into a river ride through artificially created white water. Timmy screamed with laughter. Even Sally lightened up, wondering why she had never come here before. It was so close.

David followed them, making his ring spin through the white water, encouraging Timmy to follow his lead.

As the ride emptied out into the main pool, Sally said, 'You really know how to pick a fun time.'

'Thank you. I love this sort of ride. Did you want me to take Timmy on the faster rides? You can just enjoy this tube river ride, if you like.'

'Oh no,' Sally said. 'I'm not going to miss a single one. They're such fun.'

'I'm glad you're enjoying it too.'

Timmy raced to the top of the tower.

'Stop running,' Sally said. 'They'll throw us out.'

He still reached the top before his mother. They joined the line for the bullet flume.

'If you want to go first to show Timmy the way,' David said.

But Timmy jumped in before his mother could stop him.

'I'd better go after him,' Sally said. Using the rail above the tube Sally launched herself feet first and hurtled down the thin tube. The racing water pushed her along. It spattered against her eyes so she had to keep them shut for most of the way down. The tube system flung her out into another part of the main pool. Rubbing her eyes clear she checked around for bright orange armbands. There seemed to be a plethora of them here. She splashed around looking for Timmy. She couldn't see him anywhere.

With a gnawing feeling in her stomach, Sally looked this way and that. She spotted David—he had Timmy. They were walking to the side.

Sally ploughed through the water towards them. She caught Timmy's armband.

'Don't you go getting lost like that again,' Sally said. 'You wait for me or I'll take you out.'

Timmy scrunched up his face in rebellion.

'You need to do as your mother says,' David said. 'If I hadn't found you and brought you to the side anything might have happened.'

Sally smiled at David, her first genuine one. 'Thank you. I'm always so scared of losing him. He's all I've got left.'

David nodded. 'I understand. Now, let's try a few more rides with Timmy being a good boy and being where his mother can find him.'

Sally agreed. 'I don't want to ruin this lovely afternoon by having to take you out of the pool and home, now do I?'

'Mu-u-um!' Timmy said.

'I mean it,' Sally said. 'You stay where I can find you. Is that clear?'

'Yes, mum.'

Despite his frogginess, David impressed Sally. He had everything planned for a well-coordinated afternoon. About an hour after they entered the park, and Timmy was beginning to flag, David led them over to the eating area that they could go in still wearing swimming costumes. Sally, not realizing that there was an eating area had left her money in the locker. David, with better planning, was wearing a waterproof purse.

'You must let me pay you back,' Sally said.

'As long as you're not feeling the pinch at the moment,' David said. 'After all one does hear of widows who can barely make ends meet.'

'Thankfully not me,' Sally said. 'My work has been very understanding about needing to take time off and things like that.'

Sally was not about to get into that sort of financial discussion with someone who, no matter how good at planning an afternoon's activity for a five-year-old, was still a stranger.

He accepted her reticence and went to the counter to buy a milk shake for Timmy and tea for Sally and himself.

David brought the drinks over to the table and placed the milk shake in front of Timmy. He lifted the teas off the tray. Smiling intently at Sally, he lifted a sachet of sugar.

'One or two sugars?'

Sally frowned at his certainty then shook her head. She lifted her tea away from him. 'I never take sugar in my tea, only in coffee.'

He blinked, as if something amazed him. 'Of course, you are wise. It must be how you kept your figure so perfect.'

No one could help but be pleased by a comment like that one.

After the break, they returned to riding the flumes. Timmy tried to drown himself in the wave pool more than once. Sally, for all her concern about safety, felt that this was the most fun she'd had for a long time. She had misjudged David, all because of his slick suit.

Once dried, Sally led Timmy out of the pool building. She felt it was odd that David hadn't waited to say good-bye. Then she saw him outside, talking on his mobile. Of course he would have had to go outside the building to answer his phone, out of good manners.

'...protected by something,' he said. Seeing her, he slipped the phone into his pocket.

'You didn't have to end your conversation,' Sally said. 'We would have waited.'

He shook his head. 'That's fine. It was just a secretary at work, who should have known better than to have called.'

Sally leaned on her car and got her purse ready.

'I can easily afford an afternoon of fun like this. Your company more than pays for the entrance fee,' David said, with his hands in his pockets.

'You never did say what your work was,' Sally said.

'I'm an appraiser for antique jewelry.'

Sally's mouth dropped open. 'That's two of you this week, though not dates,' she added hastily. 'What I mean is the brother of my best friend is also in the antiques trade. I expect you're interested in the Whitby Museum raid too.'

Sally pocketed her purse. David blinked at her. He cleared his throat.

'Of course we are all looking out for any samples that might turn up for sale on the black market,' he said. 'But I mustn't bore you with my work stories.'

He paused as she opened her car and sat in the driver's seat. She wound down the window.

'Thank you for a lovely afternoon, David.'

'I'm always happy to spend time with a beautiful woman,' he said. He pulled his right hand out of his pocket. 'Just a little something to remember this afternoon by.'

He leaned down. Sally thought he was going to try and kiss her, but he had a brooch in his hand. He rubbed a thumb over the back as if polishing it then pinned it on her sweater. With the black stone set in silver it looked like something from one of the historical shops.

'Gosh, that's too expensive for me to accept,' Sally said. 'It's only a first date.'

'First date,' he said, smiling broadly. 'That implies more. It's a reproduction. Don't worry about cost. You could get lots like it from the Argos catalogue for under a fiver, reproduction is in fashion this year. Though I shouldn't say that because you'd think I don't value you. Good bye, Timmy.'

He stepped away from the car and waved. As he lifted his hand, Sally saw a prick of red on his thumb like blood. Had he hurt his thumb on the brooch? She started the car, grateful that he didn't demand to know right now if she intended to see more of him, the way Pete Granger had.

As she pulled away Timmy said, 'Now he was good fun, almost as good as Uncle Mike.'

In her rear-view mirror she saw David Grenill gnaw at his thumbnail while watching the car drive away.

That afternoon had gone well, Sally congratulated herself. Mike's silliness about it being dangerous was something she could ignore.

'Mum, I'm hungry,' Timmy said. 'I want crisps.'

'Can't you wait until we get home?' Sally said. 'You'll ruin your appetite for your supper. It's only an hour and a bit.'

'I'm hungry now,' wailed Timmy.

'All right, I need some petrol anyway,' Sally said.

Smiling again, Timmy said, 'Can we have some music?'

Sally reached down and tapped on the radio. '…saw a black shadowy thing in the field across the Ring Road,' said a woman's voice from the speakers. 'And there you have it, that was the news at four thirty. The next summary of the news is at five thirty.'

'Aww Mum! Turn it over I want some music,' Timmy said.

Chapter Five

Just after midnight, squalls from outside woke Sally.

She jerked upright. Leaning out of bed, she twitched the curtains open a crack; she just knew Firey was fighting with Max again.

She jumped out of bed and stared.

The light from the nearly full moon cast a limelight on the play below. Stationed in the road, Mike Rider whacked at a shadowy cat-like creature. Well, it would have looked like a cat, if cats were Labrador sized.

It veered off; the spinning stick caught its rump.

Mike turned to follow the circling creature.

It paced, just out of range, lashing its long tail.

Mike waited, half crouched, and holding his hiking stick ready.

With a hiss the creature launched at Mike again.

He swung his stick and battered the cat on the side of the head as he dodged to the side.

The cat landed, missed its footing and fell onto its side.

Mike lunged in and bashed at the cat's ear.

It yowled in pain.

Sally clung to her curtains and peered out as Mike bludgeoned the cat.

It rolled, lashing out with hind claws that glinted in the moonlight. Mike flung himself away as the claws aimed for his stomach. One caught in the hem of his long coat.

It ripped as Mike tugged it free. Both combatants climbed to their feet.

Mike dashed in with a blow on the cat's rib cage that swept it out of its crouch. The cat twirled and batted at him with a front paw, but Mike was no longer there.

Sally stared but Mike had vanished.

The cat whirled this way and that, lashing out blindly with paws that caught nothing but air. The cat's rear jerked sideways. Mike reappeared, putting his foot down from booting the cat's backside.

Mike pointed his staff at the cat's rear paws.

Snarling, the cat pounced.

Its rear feet scrabbled on the tarmac as if on ice. Unable to find a grip, the cat sprawled on the ground, feet splayed.

Mike pointed down the road with his staff. It was a clear command.

The cat bared its teeth and tried to get its feet underneath for another pounce, but they skidded. It lashed out with its front paws. Mike danced out of reach.

Again he commanded the cat to leave with a point of his staff.

Ears down, the cat rolled over and bared its stomach.

Mike laid his staff over its neck. He lifted it and waved it over the ground. He pointed down the street for a third time. *Go!*

The black animal scrambled to its feet. Whatever had caused the slippery surface had vanished. Hissing murderous curses, it limped away.

Mike rubbed the back of his neck, watching as it vanished down the road. He checked the other way. Apparently satisfied, he twisted his hiking stick in his hands and pushed it against the ground. It shrank to baton sized and he hooked the loop over his wrist. This done, he paced back to her gate and tested the latch.

Peering through the gap in the curtains, Sally saw him use the baton-sized staff like a pen to trace that symbol that had been chalked on her front and back doorsteps. For a moment it glowed blue, but faded once the staff was removed.

Why use luminous paint for his graffiti if it was only going to fade immediately? Indeed, why had he used chalk before and not the fading paint? She twitched the curtain, debating whether to dash downstairs and demand some answers.

He took out his flask and swigged. It lifted his eyes and he saw her watching. He lifted his right hand still holding the extendible hiking stick and traced a symbol, different this time, in the air between them.

Sally drew back and her eyelids began to droop. She slid back into bed and pulled the duvet over her shoulders. Asking Mike what he was doing hanging round her house at midnight was relegated to the morning. She fell into a deep sleep.

* * * *

'Sorry, I haven't mended the doorbell yet,' Sally said opening the door for Gail. 'I thought you said you would phone?'

'I tried; your phone line must be down or something and your mobile isn't switched on.' Gail herded her children into the hall. 'Leave the door, Mike will be in soon. He had to park the car up the street.'

Leaving the door open, Sally picked up her telephone receiver. Holding it to her ear, she frowned. 'That's really odd. I'll add calling the phone company to my to do list for this morning.'

Both of them turned as the gate scraped over the concrete drive. A postman entered through the gate that Gail had closed.

'Morning,' he said, handing over her letters. His long black hair was slicked back into a ponytail down his back and his smile seemed straight from the jungle: something with stripes.

Sally returned it a little nervously, expecting a jaguar growl. 'You're new on this round.'

'I'm covering,' the man said. His eyes searched the hall behind her.

Sally replaced the telephone receiver and reached out for her post, holding the edge furthest from his black-painted fingernails.

'There's nothing odd about the phone line going down,' Gail said, quickly. 'It happens all the time. Is Timmy ready?'

Sally watched the man leave. He paused then stepped away. Glancing to the left, he scampered away to the right leaving the gate unlatched. Sally made a note to go out and shut it tonight. Mike walked through the gate. Sally motioned him inside.

Holding the post at arm's length, Sally eyed the pile.

'I said,' Gail said, 'is Timmy ready?'

'He took his portable game player back to bed after breakfast.' Checking to see there were no bills, Sally dumped the lot in the living room bin. 'I'll just get him. I need to get started on that ever-increasing to do list. Thanks for asking him over to play this morning.'

'It's not me who's going to be inconvenienced. My Mum and Dad are taking the lot of them out.'

When Sally trotted back downstairs, she found Gail's family had invaded her house. Dan and Sophie had turned on Timmy's game console and again Sally could see nothing bad about the game. It seemed to involve controlling a cartoon character that ran around collecting things. Why on Earth had Mike thought that Timmy's games were inappropriate for his age?

Gail had the kettle on and was chatting with Mike in the kitchen. Just the person she wanted to talk to this morning. What had gone on last night? It had to have been a dream. None of this weirdness could really be happening, could it? Well, she would ask Mike now.

In the front room, Dan and Sophie started shouting at each other – that was real. Gail rolled her eyes. She brushed past Sally and charged off to sort it out.

Mike remained leaning on the kitchen counter. 'I thought I'd come by and see if Timmy had got stuck with the game again.'

Sally frowned at Mike. 'I don't know where you get your energy from.'

Mike sipped his coffee and quirked an eyebrow.

Sally walked across the kitchen and poured herself a cup. 'I mean, you were hanging around in the street here until the early hours. There was this cat-thing. You fought, and ice on the street...' She tried to recapture what she had seen.

Mike shrugged. 'Are you sure you weren't having a dream?'

'Nightmare more like,' Sally said. 'Why are you following me around?'

Mike sipped his coffee.

Sally folded her arms. 'Well?'

'There are things I don't choose to tell you.' Then he grinned: it was like the sun coming out from behind a cloud. 'Glucose tablets.'

'I beg your pardon?' Sally gawped at him.

'I get my energy from glucose tablets.' He lifted a packet from his pocket and smiled at her in that superior way of his—that got right up her nose.

'You don't deny you've been stalking me?'

'Oh I deny that.'

'Then why did I see you outside my home at midnight last night?'

'I'd been out on the town with the lads, Nige and Sam, you'll remember them from school? I thought I'd come and serenade you—you know the odd ideas that happen when you've had a bit to drink. I changed my mind though, thought you might decide to throw a bucket of water over a cat fight.'

He tapped out a rhythm on the countertop with his index finger. Reflected sunlight flickered from a silver ring on his little finger; it caught and held her gaze.

'*They are even as sleep and fade away like the grass,*' Mike said. 'I'm sure what you think you saw was only a dream.'

She stood, watching the darting sunlight for a moment, then raised a hand to her temple; it throbbed with the flickering light.

'You weren't drunk,' Sally said. 'I saw you...' The words catfight had made her remember her fantasy of him fighting a cat as big as a dog. With sun coming through the window it all seemed a little silly now. Yes, it must have been a dream. But there was other stuff, wasn't there? A part of her was certain Mike was involved in something strange, but she couldn't quite put her finger on it.

'Well, what about Saturday night?' Sally said. 'I saw you then too.'

His smile turned into a sneer. 'Wishful dreaming on your part. I was tucked up in bed at Gail's house.'

'You never used to be this good at lying.'

'Will you two stop fighting?' Gail said. 'You're as bad as Dan and Sophie.'

Sally turned to see Gail standing in the doorway with her hands on her hips.

'I'd better hurry Timmy,' Sally said.

Once past Gail, she pressed a cool hand to her burning cheeks. A glance in the front room told her that Gail had sorted out the row between Dan and Sophie, who were now playing nicely again. She turned, about to go upstairs again to get Timmy, when she saw the empty bin. Hadn't she just dumped her junk mail in there? She must have put it in the kitchen bin and it had gone out of her head when arguing with Mike. How could he rouse her anger without even trying?

When half-term holiday was over, she was going to call David Grenill—he said flattering things. Sally tried to remember what he had said, but her mind kept returning to the way Mike sneered at her.

Timmy charged past her, thumping like a boulder pounding down the stairs. 'Uncle Mike, I'm here. Are you looking after us today?'

'Timmy, you need socks on,' Sally shouted. She continued on to his bedroom, knowing that once Timmy was downstairs nothing would get him back up to finish dressing.

While she was there she picked up Timmy's hairbrush as well. She lingered a few moments and twitched the covers straight on his bed and pulled back the curtains to let in the weak sunlight. Picking up his dirty clothes, she carried them to the laundry basket in the bathroom where a quick inspection showed that Timmy's toothbrush was dry. She sighed; now she would have to get into an argument with him over cleaning his teeth.

Timmy sat watching Mike show the three children how to pass an obstacle in the game.

She knelt down and pulled the socks over Timmy's feet. 'Now you need to brush your teeth, please Timmy.' She tried to say it firmly. 'You can't leave until you're done.'

Timmy shook his head, eyes glued to the screen.

Mike put down the game controller and switched off the television. 'That's right Tim, two shakes then we all have to go.'

Timmy sniffed and ran upstairs. Sally heard the tap running. Jealousy surged. How could Mike get Timmy to be obedient when she couldn't?

She stood at the window of her bedroom to watch them leave. Timmy had his hand in Mike's as he argued with Dan and Sophie over some little thing. Gail got them sorted into her car and pulled away.

The new postman walked back up the street on the other side. Across the road, her neighbor's little terrier yapped itself into a frenzy as he approached. With each tinny bark the dog launched itself at the chicken wire on the picket gate that kept him in the back garden while the neighbor was at work.

After the postman delivered the letters, he turned to the dog and did something Sally couldn't see. The dog tucked its tail between its legs and fled round the back.

The postman strutted to the next house.

With Timmy gone, Sally dashed down to hang the laundry out before she forgot. Firey jumped off the bed and followed her down. He waited in the kitchen, and then trotted out with her as she carried the basket down the garden.

There was a decent breeze along with the weak sunshine so Sally hoped the poly-cotton bed sheet would actually dry. Firey trotted along the path in front of her then stopped.

Sally swore. 'Firey do you want your tail trodden on?' She noticed the fence post. A black feather was tied onto each one with ginger colored thread.

Furious, Sally dropped the basket on the ground and reached for the totem. Firey hissed at her.

'Bad Firey!' She reached for the feather again.

Firey backed up against the post and batted at her hand. She snatched her hand away as she saw the ice-shimmer of his claws.

Announced by cawing, four crows dropped out of the trees behind her house. They back-winged as they reached the fence and circled away.

She stared at the retreating crows then looked down at Firey. He reached up and drew his claws down the post. Holding his tail in the air as a triumphant banner, he trotted on. Sally watched him make a circuit of the garden stopping at each fence post and sharpening his claws.

The top of every post wore a crow feather, tied to it with ginger thread. With her hands behind her back, Sally inspected the first feather more closely. She glanced up at the circling crows.

Something prevented them from flying over her garden.

After completing the full circuit, Firey trotted back to her. She bent and scratched his ears. 'Good cat.'

A Date with Darkness

Thoughtfully, she hung out the sheets on the line.

Chapter Six

Once she had argued the phone company into admitting it could send a repair technician around sooner than Friday fortnight, Sally dragged herself to the supermarket, bypassing the sale on Halloween costumes. She slipped her notepad from her pocket and, checking what she needed, headed straight for the fresh vegetables.

It was so good not to have to worry about watching out for a small boy while doing the shopping. Gail was such a good friend to take Timmy this morning. She was getting so much done today with not being at work and having Timmy watched by someone else.

On the end of the aisle two people with long black hair, and wearing all black, prodded a pumpkin with black-painted fingernails. One of them looked up as she passed and dug her elbow into her partner's ribs.

Sneaking glances, Sally saw they watched her until the next aisle hide them from her sight.

She darted towards the deli counter as the server handed some cheese over to rejected suitor Pete Granger. He dropped the packet into his basket and wrote something on his list. Sally backed into the aisle for butter and cheese before he could look around; she bumped into someone. She turned and saw a pale face highlighted with black lipstick.

'Sorry,' Sally muttered.

The black lips curved into a smile, a hint of pure white teeth gleamed. 'No problem.' The woman was dressed as a Bride of Dracula: neck dramatically made up in bruise colors that showed under her lace choker.

Peering round the end of the aisle at the deli counter Sally saw Pete had left. She darted up to order some cooked chicken. To her left a black clad arm took a ticket from the dispenser. Sally took a quick look around. Halloween was on Saturday: surely all the vampire costumes could wait until then for their airing?

She wondered if the supermarket was doing a Tuesday special, with a discount for people arriving in their Halloween costumes. If that were the case then she'd have dug out her black cat costume from Uni.

Diving past a man in a carnival cat mask, she found the freezer aisles were darker than the rest of the store. Above them the polystyrene tiles had been removed and the blackness of the wiring ducts swallowed the light from the fluorescent strips. Sally twitched, but she needed chips and frozen pies. A quick dash was needed. But unless they had rearranged the cabinet contents again, then she knew exactly where they were located.

From the corner of her eye something moved. She looked around, but there was no one near. Everyone avoided this aisle.

She took a deep breath. Dithering was getting her nowhere. She pushed the trolley into the darkened aisle, and realized all the cabinets were empty. One chugged away, making almost a purring sound.

Inky pools leaked out from under the refrigerators, forming a stinking puddle around the wheels of her shopping cart. Coughing at the acrid ammonia stench, Sally stepped back, tugging her trolley.

The wheels stuck.

She tugged again as the blackness oozed over the floor towards her.

She shoved, and then tugged harder to get the wheels loose. It was as if they were nailed to the floor. Her sweating palms slid off the plastic handle.

Stupid thing! She kicked at the trolley, trying to jerk it free.

At the jolt, the shadow pulled back, a little.

Sally kicked the trolley again.

It withdrew, like the tentacles on a sea urchin.

Encouraged, Sally stomped down hard on the inky liquid.

It spattered.

A spot of black liquid splashed onto her trainers. A drift of white smoke rose up from her toe. Sally lifted her foot to rub the shoe on her trousers…

'What are you doing?'

Sally jumped. She dropped her foot to the floor. An assistant walked towards her.

'I… needed chips…' She pulled the shopping cart, which glided smoothly towards her. The black puddle was gone.

'They've been moved to the next aisle,' said the assistant. 'This refrigeration unit had a coolant leak. If you'll come with me, this aisle isn't safe for customers.'

The employee escorted Sally back into the next aisle over where she loaded the chips and frozen pies into her trolley.

Turning back she saw a signboard she had walked straight past.

Aisle closed. Please ask for assistance.

The man in carnival mask must have been standing right in front of it, so she had missed reading the notice.

What had happened? That black shadowy puddle was not refrigerator coolant. It had tried to… Sally stopped her thought right there. The puddle had been coolant. A scorch mark on her trainer marked the place where the drop had landed. Nothing else was left.

Was coolant corrosive? It was a chemical, and chemicals were often corrosive: in her job she knew that.

With shaking hands, she checked her pad again and hastened to the cereal aisle. A Victorian-style widow inspected the sugar-frosted corn flakes. Sally grabbed the rice cereal and nearly ran. While she wasn't by any means the only normally dressed person, her pale blue anorak stood out.

Turning round to get to the aisle with tomato ketchup, she ran her trolley over Pete's foot.

Yelping, he dropped his basket and the contents spilled all over the floor

'Oh sorry!' Sally abandoned her trolley and grabbed for the cheese, while righting his basket.

'Hello, Sally,' Pete said. He flushed. 'It's okay. Let me get it.'

Between them they got Pete's shopping back together.

'It's nice to see someone else who isn't in a vampire costume,' Sally said handing him a packet of wild rice. Though he was wearing black jeans and shirt.

Pete looked at her with a puzzled look on his face. He touched his watch.

'You wouldn't say this was your normal shopping experience, then Sally?'

'No! Well—I suppose they're doing a promotion or something. Nothing really odd.'

'Nothing *really* odd?' he repeated.

Sally shrugged. 'I should have seen the notice about the closed aisle, but… anyway nice to see you again.'

Sally saw a notepad on the floor – she must have dropped her shopping list in the collision. She picked up the pad. Scrawled on it was a car registration number. She frowned. She knew that number, where from?

Sally saw her own notebook in her trolley. 'Is this yours?'

Pete turned. He glanced sharply at her as he reached for it. 'Yes it is, thanks.' He shoved it into his pocket. He walked towards the freezer compartments.

She snatched a bottle of ketchup and ran. Glad to have the last item on her list, Sally scarpered for the checkouts. At least all the staff wore the normal supermarket uniform.

While she loaded her bags into the car, she wondered about the car registration. Maybe he was going to buy a car and…

That was the number of Gail's car.

* * * *

Sally dumped the last of the shopping bags on the kitchen floor. Looking out of the kitchen window to check the sky; it was still clear. Her laundry fluttered on the line at the bottom of the garden as she tried to take advantage of the late October sunshine.

It flapped oddly in the heavy breeze. Frowning, Sally slipped out of her shoes and into some rubber boots for the walk over damp grass to the bottom of the garden.

As she opened the door the wind roared, caught in the trees beyond her hedge. Sullen clouds scudded over the washed-out blue sky. Staring at the trees, she watched five crows launch into the sky, singing raucous songs about the wind that had thrown them from their chosen perch.

Angry for getting superstitious, she stomped down the steps and onto the grass where, as if on cue, another gust blew the laundry. Through the bed sheets Sally could see the hedge. Something had slashed four parallel lines through each sheet. Mud edged each gaping hole.

Sally spun around looking for the source. The wheelie bin lay on its side. Identical parallel gouges, cutting through the thick plastic, left the contents of her bin spilling onto the drive.

A cloud drifted over the sun as the wind-roar died to a breathy whisper. The dense hedges, which she had grown for privacy, loomed over her. The privacy that had seemed so important took second place to the thought that the hedge blocked her path to safety in a neighbor's house.

Darting glances everywhere, Sally took one step backwards, then another. She turned and fled into the house, slamming the door shut behind her. She wrenched the door handle upwards and turned the key. She leaned her forehead against the door, panting heavily. She was safe.

But the door had been open for her entire time outside. And she had been turned away from the open door for most of the time she had been in the garden.

Almost unable to think, Sally grabbed for her mobile. She dare not go out again, nor did she dare stay in here. Her practiced thumb pressed the programmed memory of Gail's phone number.

Almost before it rang Mike answered. 'Sally?'

Grateful that it was Mike, Sally stammered out, 'There's something here. Something awful, it shredded the laundry and I don't know if it's in the house or in the garden.'

'Where are you?'

'I'm in the kitchen.' Sally was beginning to sob out her words.

'Can you see the door to the rest of the house? Is it open?' In the background, she could hear thudding footsteps.

'Yes.'

'Slam it shut and pull the table across. Then lock the kitchen door…'

'Already did that.' Sally crept across to the house door and slammed it shut. As quick as she could she pulled her kitchen table over the entryway.

'Good! Get a frying pan, cast iron if you've got it and stand where you can see both doors. Get out the other way if anything attempts to open either door. I'm nearly at your house.'

Trying to look over her shoulder and into the pan cupboard at the same time, Sally snatched up the rolling pin. She didn't have a cast iron skillet, but anything would do at a time like this.

A bang on the back door: Sally jumped round clutching the rolling pin. It was Mike. She dropped the phone and ran across to the door, flinging it open. Mike caught her in a tight hold, his eyes searching the house door.

Still holding her, he pushed her back into the kitchen and locked the door. He stood, catching his breath, while Sally clung to his chest.

He pushed her away. 'Sal, I'm going to leave you in here while I check out the house, OK?'

Sally nodded.

He twisted his baton and it became a hiking stick again. 'Right, you pull the table away, and then when I'm out the door, push it back. And Sal, be ready to pull it away if I need to get back through in a hurry.'

'Yes,' Sally said. Now that he was here, Sally could think clearly again. How had he known it was she when he answered the phone?

Gail must have caller ID enabled on her phone, Sally thought as she rammed the table back across the door. *Am I just trying to make a mystery of everything these days? I just want to go back to normal.*

Sally listened as she heard his footsteps go up the stairs and creak on the second from the top. He paused then, as if waiting for something. Then she heard him check out the bathroom and Timmy's bedroom.

As he came out of Timmy's room, Sally panicked. Had she left her dirty lingerie from yesterday out of the laundry basket? Wouldn't it be just her luck if she had forgotten last night and this morning?

He spent some time checking out her room. Then silence.

Suddenly Sally was ashamed of herself, flying into a panic like this. She stepped over to the kitchen counter and picked up the rolling pin; it was easier to carry and all of her pans were stainless steel, not cast iron. She shouldn't be relying on some near stranger to check out her house for invaders. This was her house.

Still it took all her courage to pull the table away from the door. She opened the door and out into the hall. Mike stood at the top of the stairs. He saw Sally and her rolling pin and smirked.

'Nothing here,' he said. His hiking stick was reduced to baton size again. He strolled down the stairs tossing something in his right hand. He held it up for her to see. 'What's this?'

It was the brooch that David Green had given to her yesterday. Sally wondered what she could say that would sound non-controversial.

'It's just a brooch I got recently,' Sally said. 'Reproduction jewelry is quite in fashion.'

Mike looked at her sharply but said nothing. Getting nothing more from her, he sauntered into the kitchen and over to the sink. Puzzled, Sally followed him. He ran the tap hot and looked around.

'Does that pot hold salt?'

'Yes.' She passed it to him as he put the plug in the sink. Tipping in about half the pot of salt, he handed it back. Sally returned it to its place, watching to see what odd thing Mike would do next.

He dunked the brooch into the hot salty water. Red stained the water briefly and then dissipated through the sink.

He grabbed the tea towel and tapped it dry carefully, then let the water drain out of the sink.

'Let's look at your laundry shall we?'

Sally stood in the kitchen, open mouthed at his cheek. How could he do something so weird and just expect her to accept it without question? He was halfway down the garden before she gathered her wits enough to follow him outside.

He had his hiking stick out again, which was something he seemed to do whenever he felt in danger.

Sally caught up with him as he studied the shredded sheets. As she opened her mouth to speak he waved his hand to silence her. After a moment or two of just staring, he downsized the hiking stick into a baton and hooked it onto his belt with a clip through the wrist loop of the stick.

He pulled a diary from the inner pocket of his flapping leather coat and flicked through the pages to the end of October.

'What are you doing?' demanded Sally.

'Checking the phases of the moon.'

There was a silence that Sally felt should be filled with explanations. Finally she said, 'Why?'

'I want to know when the nights of the full moon are.'

'Why?'

'You are beginning to sound like a toddler. There's no point in me telling you *why* anything, because you'd think my explanation was mad. Just accept that I know what I'm doing.'

'Oh For god's sake, try me!'

Mike shook his head.

'All right then,' Sally said. 'When are they?'

'Thursday, Friday and Saturday.'

'What is their relevance?'

Mike looked up from his diary. 'Brighter nights?' he suggested.

Sally gave up. 'So what caused that … that shredding? I saw you. You fought a … huge cat, is that what caused this?'

Mike snapped his diary shut and slid it away. 'Looks like a random maniac with a knife to me.'

'It looks like when Firey clawed my sofa to me. Scaled up a bit.'

Mike shrugged. 'Perhaps it was one of your *men friends* getting jealous of all the others.'

Sally huffed. 'Why do you say things like that? Can't you sustain niceness for longer than five minutes? You were wonderful running over here to help, and now you've reverted to the nasty London Mike.'

'If you're going to sign up for an Internet dating agency, then you're going to get a few weirdoes.'

'A few?' Sally said, staring at him. 'What's going on Mike? Ever since you showed up again, there's been blood in the rain, the crows are acting odd, the wind has been playing silly buggers and now this! What are you doing?'

'I don't know what you mean.'

'Please tell me?'

He shrugged. 'There's not much I can tell you. I don't know why you're the focus. Until I know why they've all decided you're so special I don't know what to do or say.'

'What do you mean *focus*? Who are *they*?' Sally almost screamed in her frustration.

Mike shook his head again. 'Look Sal, give it up. Say you've changed your mind. It's a real nuisance when I've got other things I should be doing.'

'Stop following me around, then,' shouted Sally. 'Perhaps I don't want all these weirdoes following me and that includes you. I don't need a jealous ex-boyfriend hanging around.'

Clenching his fists, Mike spun on his heel and stalked out of the garden. He stopped on the drive and righted her wheelie bin.

'Go!' she screamed. Close to tears, she stormed up the garden path and slammed the back door. Mike meant nothing to her.

Chapter Seven

Rather than face anymore slashed laundry, whatever had caused it, the rest of the wash was going in the tumble dryer, and hang the expense. Carrying a basket she caught herself tiptoeing to the back door and peering out.

This would never do. Was anything really happening or was she just going mad? A huge cat didn't slash your laundry just because you signed up to an Internet dating agency, whatever Mike said.

And what about Mike? He knew what was going on and kept it from her.

I've got to stop this silliness. If I get nervous then Mike has won. Sally flung the back door open and strode over to the garage.

She opened up the garage and stuffed the clothes into the dryer.

It didn't start.

Sally checked the switch was on at the wall, and slammed the dryer door again.

Still nothing.

Frowning, Sally walked back to the house. The drive was now clear of rubbish and the bin stood in its usual spot. She clenched her fists. He kept doing nice things and saying foul things. How was she supposed to take that? She locked the back door and went inspected the fuse box in the cupboard under the stairs.

The circuit breaker for the outside electricity had tripped.

Sally flipped it back into the on position. When she opened the back door again she could hear the tumble dryer turning.

Still thoughtful, Sally turned on the outside light. On checking, she realized that her guess was right; the bulb had blown. She went to the front door. The light for the front had done the same. Now that was odd.

So when had this blackout started? Sally thought for a moment. It had started on Sunday night, with the cat flap battery dying; today, everything on an exposed outside connection had blown.

Hold on, why was the television working? Timmy would have howled otherwise. Oh yes, the cable ran underground into her house, the same with the electricity. But both the electricity to the garage and the telephone wires were overhead cables that reached the house by running along the outside walls.

That was something to worry about.

She remembered Mike touching the streetlight, and the bulb blowing. Perhaps it was Mike setting up all these odd happenings, to make her give up Internet dating.

Sally jumped to her feet. She imaged what would happen if she went to the police and say my ex-boyfriend is making streetlights blow up with a touch. That was a one-way ticket to the funny farm.

She paced.

Gail knew something about it all. She had recognized the chalk drawings on the front and back steps. Sally needed to trick Gail into telling her what was going on.

She found she was in the front room, staring at the blank television screen. Games were strewn around the unit. Sally bent down and picked up one of the plastic cases. She started to put it away, but on impulse checked the rating. This was one of the games that Mike had been showing Timmy. The next one she picked up was the same. Both were rated age 3+; what on earth did Mike think was wrong with these games? She slid the boxes into the wooden storage rack she had bought for them—not that they ever went in unless she was tidying the front room.

There seemed to be more games than Sally remembered lying around the television. She picked up the next one, the cover showed a gangster firing his gun out of a car window, wrecking the car in front. There were six more that involved guns of some sort on the cover with lots of blood. Curious, Sally opened one of them and read the blurb. It left her horrified at the level of violence. When had she bought these? A vague memory surfaced of Timmy using his birthday money from his grandmother to buy games. No respectable shop would sell a child these games. She had better accept responsibility.

The edge of the leaflet caught her finger and stung as it cut her. Sally lifted the drop of blood into her mouth to stop dripping on the insert brochure.

David Grenill had lifted his thumb to his mouth as she drove away from the swimming pool. Mike had taken the brooch given her by David and washed off a blood-colored stain. She took her finger out of her mouth and the little prick of blood welled out again. Just like it had back when she and Mike had been ten, when they played the game of blood brothers: friends forever. Sally blinked away the tears.

As she stacked the games in the rack, she saw the age certificate on it: age 12 or above. All seven of the ones she had looked at were age twelve certification. Now she knew why Gail thought they were unsuitable.

It was going to cause a row, but some censorship was in order. Timmy had lied to her. Sally checked through all the games and hid them in her bedroom. Sally would just have to get some more, with particular regard to the certification.

Damn Mike for being right about the games.

A loud banging on the front door made Sally jump. She ran to the front window and saw Timmy, home for lunch.

As soon as the front door opened Timmy began nagging. 'Can we go to a burger bar for lunch mum? Dan and Sophie are going with their grandparents, why did you say I had to come home?'

'I don't like you to eat at fast food places too often.'

'Just going out with Dan and Sophie isn't too often.'

'You went to one last week with your friend.'

'But that wasn't burgers, that was chicken.'

'I've made a nice lunch for you, come on and eat it.'

'But I want to go to out. We could meet Dan and Sophie there.'

'Go and wash your hands for lunch, Timmy,' Sally said, trying to be firm like they said to do on all those TV programs that were put on to make non-perfect parents feel guilty.

That failed too. Eventually Timmy crawled to the bathroom and washed his hands, complaining that Mum never gave him any fun.

'But what about the days out I've arranged for you?' Sally asked.

'They're not for me,' Timmy said. 'They're for you. And if you think I'm going to let you marry any of the freaks we've seen so far, you're wrong.'

'But I thought you liked David Grenill.'

'Oh him, he's not as fun as Uncle Mike. I'll let you marry Uncle Mike if you like.'

'Well, I'm certainly not going to marry him,' Sally said.

'He's good with the games.'

'Hardly a reason for me to marry him. And anyway, I'm sure you've got more games than I remembered.'

Timmy smirked as his gaze slid away from hers.

'And I've taken away all the games that were unsuitable for your age group.'

Timmy frowned. 'All the other boys at school get games like that.'

54

'No they don't. Dan who is older than you doesn't get games like those shoot-em-ups.'

Timmy slid out of his chair

'Get back here and finish your lunch,' Sally shouted as he ran into the front room.

'I'd finished playing them anyway. You can get me some new games.'

'Come back and finish your lunch.'

'I'm full,' shouted Timmy. 'I'm going to play with my games.'

Sally opened her mouth to start an objection and send him outside. An image of the ripped sheets fluttered through her mind's eye and she shut her mouth.

Whatever had done that was still out there.

* * * *

Timmy refused to move from in front of the television. Eventually, after all her arguments, Sally still had to go to the postbox on her own. The bills had to go today.

'Well you must not open the door to anyone,' Sally said. 'And stay inside.'

'Right then, mum.'

She fought her reluctance—after all she was going five minutes down the road. Nothing could happen. Whatever had shredded the laundry had to be long gone.

She hovered at her front door like a mouse sure that the cat was still waiting. The privet hedge blocked her view of the street now that she was at ground level. It had seemed such a good selling point when they had bought the house, but now Sally could feel *things* hiding behind it, waiting to pounce on her.

This was ridiculous, she'd be checking under her bed for monsters tonight at this rate. She turned and locked the front door. Still she hesitated to step off the porch, then she shook herself and walked up the path and opened the garden gate. She carefully latched the gate closed and strode up the street.

The weak October sun cast feeble shadows on the faded tarmac of the footpath. Sally cast nervous glances around her. Her fingers clenched around her house keys as she crossed the road.

The bills posted, Sally checked the window of the post office. A picture of her neighbor's cat sat next to the picture of a small Jack Russell dog, missing since Saturday night.

Sally ran back over the road, and her shadow followed her. Sally glanced back. Had it looked liquid then? Nonsense.

Vanessa Knipe

Hedges cropped at head height lined her street, shutting out the view into people's houses, but again they cut off the safety of knowing that you were seen. Sally upped her pace. Nearly jogging now, she glanced back at her shadow; it stayed solidly behind her.

Another telegraph pole, another poster advertising a missing cat.

Something moved in the hedge next to her. A gate opened. Sally froze, staring—at two policemen who walked out. The owner of the house watched after them for a moment, then glancing around slammed her front door. Sally could hear bolts jerked home.

'Afternoon, ma'am.' They arrived at the next house and knocked on the door.

Cautiously Sally walked on, glancing this way and that at privet and leylandii that lined the street. It had seemed such a private street, but now the hedges were places danger could lurk. She flung open the iron gate on her drive and scampered to her front door.

Nothing had happened. There was nothing to happen.

Breathlessly, she fumbled her key into the lock.

'You live on this street, Ma'am?'

Sally caught her breath and turned with her keys held ready to punch into someone's face.

The two policemen stood at her gate.

She slipped her hand into her pocket and cleared her throat. 'Yes, can I help?'

'You had a postal delivery this morning?'

'Yes, the man said he was covering the round.'

The policemen looked at each other. 'You spoke with him?'

'Yes,' Sally said, darting her gaze between the two men. 'I had the door open as he arrived so we passed the time of day. You know.'

'So you can describe him?'

Sally blinked. 'What has he done? Did he rob some houses on this round? The dog over the road…' She realized she was babbling. 'Yes. He was about a head taller than me. His long, black hair was tied back in a ponytail. Dark complexion. I noticed that because you don't often see dark skinned people in York if they're not tourists.'

One of the policemen took notes. 'Did he have an accent?'

Sally shook her head. 'Not that I heard.'

The policeman smiled encouragingly. 'Go on please, Mrs…?'

'Cartwright, I'm Sally Cartwright. I own this house.' She patted the wall.

'So,' said the note-taking officer. 'A head taller than you, you're five six?'

'Yes.'

'Build? Was he fat, skinny?'

'He had one of those orange hi-vis jackets with the postal emblem on, they hide the figure.' She closed her eyes. 'He wasn't fat, but not skinny. I couldn't say if he lifted weights, sorry. His face wasn't fat.'

'Wearing postal uniform?'

'Dark trousers and shirt, it was the proper jacket and he did the whole street, because he came back down the other way. I was upstairs so I could see. The little dog across the road was yapping and yapping. Then it ran away frightened.'

'Thank you very much, Mrs. Cartwright.'

'What did he do?'

'Apparently, he mugged a postman so that he could do this round.'

'Is my regular man fine?' Sally asked.

'He's in hospital, stable. If you see this man again, do not approach him. Do not open the door. Call 999 immediately.'

Sally nodded.

They went on their way looking for more witnesses.

Opening the door, she found Timmy still sprawled on the front room carpet, playing games.

'When are we going on another daytrip? I'm bored,' Timmy said. 'Can you phone Uncle Mike and get him to bring another cheat sheet for me?'

There was no way she could phone him, just after she'd told him to go away. 'We have another trip tomorrow, to the half term fun fair at the Knavesmire.'

'Oh good,' Timmy said. 'Connor from school said that it was going to have all sorts of spooky rides this time, because half term has Halloween stuck on the end. Can I go trick or treating, mum?'

'I don't like you going out after dark Timmy,' Sally said. 'You know that.'

'Dan and Sophie are going out,' Timmy whined.

'You're a lot younger than them,' Sally said.

'I'm not younger than Sophie, she's in my class,' he said. 'You never let me have any fun.'

'What about the half term fun fair?'

Timmy shrugged. 'Are you going phone to Uncle Mike?'

'No I am not,' Sally said, as she fled the room.

Chapter Eight

Sally lay back in the bath, trying to will away the headache. Her fingers clenched as she remembered Timmy's nonsense.

Every five minutes he had called down after being put to bed. Then he'd stopped calling. Suspicious, Sally found him under the covers with his portable game player.

She'd grabbed it and the torch. 'That's the end of that toy. It's going straight in the bin.'

'You've just invented that rule,' Timmy screamed.

'If I didn't keep buying you these expensive computers games then we'd be able to go on better holidays. It's not like I enjoy relying on silly schemes to keep you happy.'

Sally had slammed the door on Timmy as she left. She heard him crying in the dark, but knew that if she went back in she'd just shout again. The tears hadn't lasted long—only fifteen minutes, then he had gone to sleep.

Of course, she hadn't put the expensive toy in the bin. It lay hidden in her drawer of free samples.

As she lay in the bath Sally thought Gail would be proud of her. She'd dumped some of the samples in the bin—the drawer was almost too full to stuff in the PSP.

And there was something else to think about. Where was Firey's grooming brush? As she pushed the samples over the game console, she'd noticed it was missing. Her mind drifted to the ginger colored thread wrapped around her fence posts and the pride Firey displayed as he'd patrolled the garden.

That was more nonsense, but everything that had happened recently was so improbable: the sheets; the cat thing—though she was sure that must be a dream; even those crows—more every time she looked. And why did Pete have Gail's car registration?

She would warn Gail, but there was nothing she could do about any of the rest of the bizarre goings-on, nothing at all. She breathed in the sweet herbal scent of the expensive bubble bath. She should have brought in a candle—a candle-lit bath was the most relaxation she knew. She closed her eyes and breathed.

A Date with Darkness

A crash and a thump echoed up the stairs. Sally nearly screamed. Just as she was beginning to feel happy, this had to happen.

She jumped out of the bath. The last time Firey had fought with another cat through the cat flap, the door had come off its hinges and ended up nearly in the dining room.

Wrapping a towel around her dripping body, Sally charged out of the bathroom and down the stairs. Firey was going to end up locked out of the house at night if this continued.

A loud meowl and Firey scrambled up the stairs, nearly knocking Sally over in his haste. Sally could hear his claws digging into the carpet. He disappeared into Sally's bedroom.

The thumping went on.

Sally continued down, determined to find out what was making the noise this time. As Sally entered the open plan dining room kitchen area, the thumping stopped.

A fur-covered arm reached in through the cat flap—aiming for the key that Sally always left in the lock for fire safety.

Sally slid open a drawer, grabbing the rolling pin. Two steps across the kitchen and she whacked down hard on the elbow.

A howl resounded outside the door. Clawed fingers scratched at the PVC door as the hand was yanked back outside. The cat flap slammed shut. Sally yanked the key from the lock and jabbed at the outside light switch.

No light. Damn, she'd failed to change the blown bulb.

A shadow loomed up into the light cast from the kitchen. The glass window of the door framed a dog-like head. The tongue lolled out on the side, but this wasn't your average Alsatian. Its clawed hands rested on the glass as it stared in.

Sally took an involuntary step back; she'd never seen a dog that big. The dog's mad eyes ogled her and it ran a dark tongue around its mouth, licking foam from the black lips. Such a human gesture that Sally looked down. The towel had fallen from around her. She stood naked to the humanlike dog. Water and bubbles dripped onto the floor and her hair dripped onto her bare shoulders.

Still clutching her rolling pin and never taking her eyes from the man-dog, Sally backed away from the door. She reached into the utility room and snagged her raincoat. She whipped it over her body, hugging it in place with her free hand—she dared not put down the rolling pin, her only defense. If there were going to be much more of this business she would have to buy a cast iron frying pan and hang the expense.

All the time those mad, red eyes watched her, eyeing the rolling pin like it wanted her to play fetch. It clawed at the glass and the glass squeaked, like a normal dog whining to get in. Sally clenched her teeth that threatened to chatter. She dared not leave.

She pointed to the dog. 'Home!' Her voice was shrill, like a mouse. She tried again. 'Home!'

The man-dog, and Sally had no doubt it was male, leaned back. He fell against the door like a battering ram.

It shuddered.

Again the man-dog battered against the door.

The frame wobbled and Sally felt the floor beneath her feet vibrate.

She clenched her hand around the rolling pin. Whatever it was, this creature wasn't getting into her house without a fight.

The creature lifted its head, like a dog hearing its master call. Then a stick whacked it around the head.

Had Mike come to her aid, again?

Sally raced to the window as the man-dog collected its feet and scrambled out of sight around the side of the house, scarpering towards the front street.

Freed from the gaze of the creature, Sally dropped the rolling pin and rammed her hands into sleeves of her coat. Zipping it up in one quick movement, Sally retrieved her weapon and ran to the front room. Flinging open her curtains, she looked for the creature. Out on the street she could hear a fight, but her high hedge blocked the view.

Furious with herself for not remembering a simple thing like that, Sally ran to her front door. Her hand stopped on the key. What was that dog creature? Its front legs had definitely been arms with clawed hands.

An image of the slashed laundry fluttered into her head.

Her hands were shaking so much that she couldn't turn the key. Hating herself, she crept upstairs to her bedroom.

When did I turn into the sort of woman who needs rescuing? Sally thought.

She stood at her bedroom room window with her hands holding onto the curtains, daring herself to open them. What the hell was going on? How could something like that be real?

She wrenched the curtain open.

A man faced off against the man-dog. He wore a long trench coat that flapped out behind him as he swung again with his stick.

It must be Mike again, despite being told not to be here. Sally sagged to the floor. Why, if he hated her so much, was he standing in front of her front gate holding it against something Sally would have sworn could never exist.

As the man-dog ducked away from the swing, Sally saw that it favored its front left leg. Despite her horror, Sally smiled. At least she'd done some damage in her own right.

It lunged at Mike. As it hit, a flash of lightening erupted from Mike's staff, flinging the man-dog across the road.

Slowly, it gathered its legs under it and scampered off into the night. Sally saw Mike sink into a crouch. Exhausted, he leaned heavily on his stick.

Still clutching her rolling pin, Sally skipped downstairs and opened her front door on the chain—though given that the creature had made the house shudder she doubted that would help at all.

'Has it gone?' Sally's whisper sounded shrill in her ears.

Mike jerked up, as if bitten. He pulled himself to his feet like it was a matter of pride that no one saw his exhausted state. He just nodded.

Sally unchained the door and set bare feet on the path. He took deep breaths.

'Why did you leave the gate open?' he asked as she walked over to him.

'I beg your pardon?' Sally eyed the high hedges down the street and held the rolling ready, eyes wide with fear.

'I made sure that with the iron gate shut you are safe, and you leave it open,' Mike said, though he nodded respectfully at the rolling pin. Sally looked down at it and smiled ruefully.

'It was reaching in through the cat flap so I gave it all I'd got.'

'Left arm was that? Thanks, I'd never have driven it off if you hadn't hurt it. God I need Nathan here.'

'Who's Nathan?'

'He was my tutor.' He lifted a hand to rub the sweat from his face. Blood glistened on his hand, where teeth had ripped into his flesh.

'You're hurt,' Sally said. 'Come in a get that cleaned up. You'd better go to hospital and get your rabies shots or something.'

She dragged at his coat. Pulling him into the light Sally saw that his face had gone ice pale.

Even his steely eyes had drained of their limited color as he looked at Sally. He pulled at her towards the kitchen.

'Silver,' he said. 'I need silver.' He slipped a hand into an inner pocket and slipped a ring over his right ring finger.'

'I don't know what you mean.'

61

'That silver spray,' Mike said. 'The one Gail was joshing you about.' He almost ran into the kitchen and yanked open her samples drawer. Frantically he shoved packets about, spilling them on the floor. Automatically, Sally crouched to pick them up.

'What silver spray?'

'The shoe deodorizer.'

'Gail threw it out, remember,' Sally said. 'Is it important?'

Mike turned and looked her straight in the eyes. 'Don't ask questions. Right now I need that silver spray.'

Sally nodded then opened the kitchen bin. It held a clean bag. She turned to the kitchen door. The dirty claw marks on the inner side reminded her of the man-dog. She turned back to Mike. He looked after her, desperation in his eyes. He was panting, almost like he was scared of something. He held his wounded hand away from his body, gripping at the wrist like a tourniquet.

'Is the man-dog going to come back?'

Mike blinked, then his eyes went blank. After a few moments he refocused on her and shook his head. Sally unlocked the back door.

The darkness called out to her. *Hide in me, you'll be safe. Nothing can see you here. Nothing can find you.*

She ignored the siren singing and lifted the bin lid. She lifted out the last two plastic shopping bags stuffed full of household rubbish as she couldn't remember when Gail had dropped the sample into the bin.

She dashed back into the kitchen and locked the door. Forgetting her usual cleanliness in Mike's urgency she ripped open the top bag onto the kitchen floor.

The metal cylinder rolled out over the wood laminate floor.

Mike pounced on it, like he was a cat after a mouse.

He ripped off the lid with his teeth and aimed it at the bites on his hand.

'I don't think that's for internal use.'

'Shut up, Sally.'

Since watching his intent spraying of his hand with a potential poison wasn't helping, Sally ran hot water into her washing up bowl and poured a good helping of disinfectant in to turn the water milky. She got the roll of paper towels and sat at the table opposite him and waited in silence, for an explanation or just the opportunity to help.

After spraying his wounds, he used his unhurt left wrist to unhook a necklace from around his neck. As he wrapped it around his wrist like a tourniquet, Sally realized it was a crucifix. Then resting his forehead on his left hand, he leaned over the injured hand resting on the local paper. His mouth moved, but Sally heard no sound.

His odd behavior all seemed part of this night. In fact it was just together with everything that had happened since Saturday.

Blood ran down his hand to stain the paper bright red. The rivulets down his wrist slowed to a trickle. Mike looked up. Color had returned to his cheeks, he no longer looked scared out of his skin.

'Where can I burn this paper?'

'Oh right, like I'm going to have open fires in the house with a child.' Mike just sighed.

'How about the barbecue? It's on the patio under its cover.'

He scrunched up the paper with his left hand, being careful not to let any of the red stain touch his skin. 'Matches?'

Sally stood. Walking over to the cupboard by the fridge, which held her outside cooking equipment, she tossed him a packet of matches.

He caught it awkwardly in his hurting right hand. Then seeing he still favored his right hand and his left was full she opened the back door for him and lifted up the cover on the barbecue.

'Gail and I had parties for the kids here last summer,' she said.

Mike still didn't speak. He dropped the stained paper into the pan of the barbecue. With difficulty he tried to light a match.

Sally shook her head. She took back the packet and held a lighted match to the paper, since he seemed to think it was essential.

Some of Mike's tension drained away as the paper crumbled into ashes. His breathing slowed and deepened.

'I'd better be getting back to Gail's,' he said finally. 'I'm spent for the night anyway.'

Sally grabbed for his right hand. 'Come back in and get this washed off. I've got the water ready. Hand in, this is going to sting.'

'Thanks for that.' He gritted his teeth against the sting of disinfectant. Sally unhooked the crucifix from around his wrist.

'I didn't know you were a Catholic,' Sally said. 'Gail isn't.'

'I'm not,' he said. 'But I am a Doctor of Theology. I got a bit carried away with studying. I've seen some odd things.'

'Things like that man-dog?' Sally asked. 'You know I'd understand a little better if you would just explain.'

Mike snorted. 'No you wouldn't. You have me locked up as insane. Besides, I've taken vows.'

'You're a priest?' Sally looked horrified.

'Not those sort of vows,' he said, laughing. 'Vows like … like signing the Official Secrets Act.'

They both looked at his hand as Sally lifted it out of the medicated water.

'That looks a bit better,' Sally said. 'It's even stopped bleeding. Do you want me to do something special with the bloody water?'

Mike sighed. 'It does need boiling, for 10 minutes, before you put it down the drain. That's why I was going home to Gail's house.'

Without speaking, but her body language clearly saying this is ridiculous, Sally poured the water into a pan and set it on the stovetop. She turned to see Mike slipping a glucose tablet into his mouth and washing it down with something from his flask.

'You could have asked for tea or coffee or something.'

Mike shook his head; he rubbed his eyes tiredly. 'I need the brandy.'

'Did you want me to make up the sofa bed? You don't look strong enough to walk back to Gail's.'

Mike frowned. 'Why are you wearing a raincoat in the house? That's not like you. You're so proper now.'

Sally's lips pursed at the criticism. 'I heard the noise when I was in the bath. This was the first thing to hand.'

Mike's eyes went wide. His mouth open to speak then shut again. Then after a few breaths he struggled to his feet. 'I think I had better leave, thanks all the same Sally.'

Leaning on the wall he walked to the front door. Sally dashed to the kitchen and picked up her car keys.

'Stop.'

Mike turned. Sally tossed him the keys. He fielded them.

'At least take my car.'

Mike nodded and dropped them in his pocket. On the way up the front path he bent and picked up his hiking staff. Leaning on that he wobbled down the drive to Sally's garage.

Sally shut the door and rested her forehead against it. She walked slowly back through to the kitchen. She heard him lift the garage door up and over. Watching from the window, she could see him moving slowly.

She wrenched the curtains across as she heard him slam the car door. So he still found her attractive, did he? Well she wasn't giving in to him this time: not when he had made it so clear he only wanted her body, not her.

The engine started and she heard him reverse up the drive. The pan came to the boil and hot disinfectant stung her nose and throat. As instructed Sally let the bubbles roil for 10 minutes. She imagined Mike boiling in the pan, not just his blood, then laughed at her own nonsense before pouring the milky, bloody mess down the drain.

Chapter Nine

He watches Sally open the door to the University room. It's a wrench. This is almost goodbye. How is he to keep someone as beautiful as Sally, when he's not there to chase other suitors away? Every man at the University would be after her.

Sally doesn't know how beautiful she is. She wraps her arms around his neck and he feels his despair rise. This is goodbye. He sinks into her kiss. Again there's a hint of more on offer. This time he isn't too drunk to take it.

'Lock the door, Sally.' He feels his voice grow rough.

She seems to hang back a little, just like her usual teases. 'What? Here?'

'Yes, here and now.'

Sally locks the door and smiles at him, that lovely shy smile, which hides the fire burning in her. Her face lifts for another kiss, surrendering totally to him. Sally is his loyal friend. He knows that once this is done she will believe herself as good as married to him. And he needs that promise, that unconditional love. Pressing his need against Sally's round stomach he loses all his thoughts, burning in the forest fire of Sally's kisses.

* * * *

Sally sprang up, her hand pressed against her mouth. She could feel his mouth burning against hers. If she closed her eyes again she could feel Mike's hands pushing up her sweater and caressing her breasts.

But her dream had been from Mike's point of view. Was her subconscious trying to find a reason for his desertion, now he had inexplicably returned and was protecting her from… she didn't know what?

In an effort to scrub the lingering sensation of Mike's hot lips against hers, she rubbed her mouth with the back of her hand. But nothing could erase the memory of that night in her college room, like she would have burnt up from the fire inside if Mike hadn't taken her. Nothing. Not even the years with her husband.

She knew now that she had always held that back from Timothy, never wanting to be betrayed by giving all herself again. Sally muffled her tears in her duvet. She had loved Timothy, she had. She just had never given him everything he was worth.

The moon glared at her through the crack in the curtains as she tried to recall the love she had shared with Timothy but it was Mike's kisses that she remembered, Mike's touch upon her eager body. Exhausted by the tears she had shed and the battle of guilt raging within her she turned her face into the pillow hoping to find a cool spot, hoping to alleviate the aching need burning through her body.

Eventually, she slept.

* * * *

'Mummy!' Timmy shouted in her ear.

Sally blinked. 'Let me sleep Timmy. Mummy's tired.'

'Uncle Mike's at the door. He wants to talk to you. And you never asked him to get the cheat sheet, even though he came round last night.'

That woke Sally. 'How do you know he came round last night?'

'Duh! He had the car keys.'

'Tell him I'll be down in a minute. Show him where the coffee is, please.'

'You mean a *Mummy minute* that takes half an hour, I bet.' He scampered out of the room.

'Don't be cheeky,' Sally shouted after him.

After a quick shower and dragging some clothes on, Sally went down the stairs.

Mike, looking well rested despite last night, was helping Timmy with a game. He had a coffee mug in his hand. He sipped at the mug and smiled at Sally as she came down the stairs. With scalding cheeks, Sally thrust the memory the dream away.

'Can we talk?' she asked from the door.

Mike looked down at Tim. 'See how to do that now, Tim?'

'Yeah, thanks Uncle Mike.'

He followed Sally through into the kitchen and returned her car keys. 'Are you going to have screaming hysterics, demanding answers I can't give?'

She lifted a hand to slap him but he caught her wrist.

She glared. 'Oh, I'm tempted.'

With his free hand Mike reached out and stroked her cheek with his thumb. 'Oh, so am I.'

Sally snapped her mouth shut.

He stared into her face. 'Are you all right? You don't look well this morning.'

'Maybe fights like that are normal for you, but I think I'm entitled to nightmares when… when *things* start crawling through my cat flap and the person who knows what's going on won't tell me.'

Mike opened his mouth to answer then he shut it. He leaned into his wrist. Almost like he was going against his own will, he bent to touch her lips with his.

'Stop it!' She brought her hand between them and tried to push at his chest. The hand that had held her wrist slid around her back and pulled her into the kiss. It was light but lingering, an electrostatic charge held them together. Sally's heart was racing when he broke contact. He stared into her eyes, visibly trying to get his breathing back to normal. He scrubbed his mouth with the back of his hand.

'Oh God! I can't,' he whispered. 'I can't.'

Sally opened her mouth to speak, but he rested his thumb across her lips and shook his head.

'Thanks for dressing before you came down,' he said finally.

He left her standing in the kitchen. Her hand slid down to the worktop to support her. A thin tear dripped down her cheek. He stepped into the front room to talk in a low voice to Timmy.

'See ya, Tim,' he said, leaving the house.

I won't cry, Sally thought. She bit into her knuckles to hold back the tears.

He had betrayed her once: a one-night stand. It was true despite the spin her dreams were trying to put on it. But the man who had just been here didn't fit the image of a vile seducer.

Determined not to give in to tears, she put the kettle on. Mechanically she put bread in the toaster and set out two bowls of cereal. After a bit, her daily routine took over; there was no room for tears in that.

'Mummy, when are we going to the fun fair?' Timmy shouted through from the front room.

'After lunch.'

Sally did the usual after breakfast things, and then went to find Timmy. He was slouched in a chair—the one Mike had been sitting in, playing on his game console. There were now three games boxes in the rack.

Sally frowned. 'Have you taken back one of the games I put away yesterday?' She flicked through the games on the rack but none of them had the 12+ certificate.

Timmy looked up sharply, then at his game rack.

'No, mummy,' he said. 'Remember, I went out yesterday with Dan's Grannie. I took some of my birthday money with me and got a game Dan said was good fun.'

'If you've got that much birthday money left, perhaps we should put some in the bank,' she said.

'But I've got to get new games now that you've taken my old ones away.'

'You got these games before you knew I would be censoring your collection.'

Timmy shrugged. 'Yeah, well.'

Nothing that had gone on since she started this dating business had made very much sense. Even Mike's behavior was reasonable when taken in context with the rest of the madness.

She returned to the kitchen and sorted out the recycling, for something to do. Behind all the cardboard boxes, which needed flattening before placing in the recycling bag, Sally found a scrunched up tea towel. She grabbed it to ram it in the washing machine when something clattered out on to the floor. It was David Grenill's brooch. Sally picked it up. She put the tea towel in the wash and stood looking at the brooch. Now she thought about it, both David's behavior and Mike's had been peculiar over this piece of jewelry.

Today's paper still carried the Whitby Museum Raid on the front page, even though it was lower down, hidden under the agricultural subsidies row and the latest War on Crime initiative announced by the government.

She weighed the brooch in her hand as she read the article (cont. on page 9). On page nine, Sally found a website address that would show pictures of all the articles allegedly stolen. Picking up the paper, Sally drifted to the computer in a daze. David had reacted oddly to her mention of the burglary.

She turned on the computer and while she was waiting she continued to read the article. A pop-up box appeared when she started her browser.

Unexpected closedown of browser. Do you want to restore previous session?

Sally managed to prevent automatic pilot from clicking on cancel. When had her browser stopped suddenly? No time that she could remember. Had someone else used her computer? She clicked on OK.

The Grange

Appeared across her screen. An hourglass turned over. As the page loaded a tag appeared.

They are hiding it from you.

Finally the rest of the page emerged as a mist drifted away from view, revealing the black web page. Down the left hand side was a list of options written in scarlet italics.

Werewolves, Vampires, Church of England, Herbalism, Witches (white and black), Current Investigation…

Hold on a minute, thought Sally, Church of England in this list?
She clicked on the CofE listing. Mist swamped the screen again, then cleared onto a new page.

Church of England
For thousands of years the officers of the church have been covering up the very existence of these Creatures of the Night.

For one moment the website had interested Sally, the words *cover up* told her all she needed to know. A crank wrote those words. Sniggering, she returned to Home and clicked on Vampires. She skimmed through text until her eye caught on a name.

It has come to the attention of this reporter, that five years ago, an Officer under instruction, one Mike Rider, uncovered a nest of the Creatures, masquerading as a modeling agency. The Vile Creatures lured young women to their doom by promising them eternal slenderness

Mike? Oh honestly! Sally thought, although it could explain some of the models who hit the magazine covers. Returning again to the root menu, she randomly chose Herbalism.

Someone has been stealing seeds from my prize winning Datura Stromonium. Either my fellows on the allotments have decided to try and win the exotics prize at this

70

year's show—or consider this, the other name for Datura is Zombie Cucumber. You can depend on this reporter to find out. There will be no more cover-ups.

Sally giggled. She ought to email this page to Gail; it was hilarious. Clicking on Werewolves brought her to a similar page of stories, this time about people, mostly men, who turned into ... Oh!

She remembered the clawed arm reaching through her cat flap. But it couldn't be true. Sally sat back and stared at the screen. Werewolves belonged in the movies, not breaking into a house.

This was a crank website, it had to be.

Clicking on *How to tell if THEY are after you?* Sally studied the new menu this brought up. The first item that caught her attention was *Strange Bird Reactions*. With a glance out of the window she clicked.

...Crows especially can sense bad magic. Their senses are particularly keen when it comes to spells that start with one of their number being slain.

Sally thought about the dead bird in the car park at the theme park.

She chose Current Investigation. Skim-reading the article gave her the information that the reporter was looking at dating agencies as a possible source of victims for the Creatures of the Night. He had located someone who practically had a target painted on her heart and was following her closely.

This was all nonsense. Who had been using her computer to call up this rubbish?

'Timmy!' she shouted. 'Have you had my computer on?'

'No!' he shouted back.

She frowned, the only other person it could have been was Mike. But surely he would have taken more care to erase the history. It was a mystery, and she hated mysteries. Angrily, she clicked on the little house symbol. It took her back to the search page of her browser.

Just about to get out of her computing chair, she remembered why she had turned on the computer in the first place. She typed in the reference from the newspaper.

This website showed a brooch very similar to the one that lay on Sally's desk.

A comment box under the picture declared that piece to be the most valuable. It had a story of a European Count giving it to his mistress attached to it.

She wondered what to do next. Would she get sent to prison for receiving stolen goods? Probably not and anyway David had said it was reproduction. Reproductions had to copy something and a storied brooch in a museum would be a very good piece to copy.

And she was no longer surprised that Mike failed to recognize the piece, she was convinced he had nothing to do with antiques. She would keep it safe and when Mike was gone, she would ask Gail what she thought. She supposed that Mike had to keep up his pretense; it gave him a few likely answers to cover his uncanny lifestyle.

Chapter Ten

After breakfast, Timmy scrambled upstairs. Sally heard running water and ran up after him. He gave her a broad grin as he cleaned his teeth.

Sally placed a hand on his forehead. His temperature was normal.

'What was that for?' Timmy demanded after rinsing.

'You have never cleaned your teeth without being asked,' she said.

Timmy shrugged. He remained subdued and well behaved for the rest of the morning.

They had a light lunch and Timmy was sitting in the car waiting for her when she was ready.

'Gosh! You really are keen to get to the fun fair,' she said.

'Dan thinks it's going to have spooky rides. I want to go on them all.' His eyes glowed, a little like last night's huge man-dog—and she refused to call it a wer… anything else.

'I'm sure we can manage that,' Sally said, turning a shudder into sitting in the driver's seat.

The date with David had been so much fun, so Sally set out feeling optimistic that her plan was working. Maybe she could meet a really nice man on her date today, who would… would what? She tried to ignore the little voice that said, trying to arrange a distraction from Mike?

Parking near the Knavesmire was terrible.

'Muu-um!' Timmy said. 'We could walk from home quicker.'

'That's not true.' Sally grasped Timmy firmly by the hand and hauled him along.

Timmy shut up and smiled what he obviously thought was a saintly smile.

Now what's he up to? she thought.

Sally had almost greeted his whining with relief. At least he'd stopped being eerily good.

Her copy of the newspaper was tucked under her arm so that she could be recognized. Relieved, she came up on the ticket booths before meeting her quarry; it had felt irksome when David Grenill paid for their trip to the Water Park.

Sally bought two tickets and hung around looking for a man with a matching newspaper.

Crowding round the ticket booth, a group of University students dressed up for Halloween chattered and giggled. Timmy hugged closer to her trousers. She had seen too much black clothing this week. What was it about a certain type of person who thought that black hair dye and leather collars were cool?

A man bounced up to her like an eager puppy. 'Sally? Please let it be Sally Cartwright and Timmy.'

She wanted to throw her rolled up newspaper for a game of fetch. 'You must be Jack Harper?'

'That's right,' Jack said. 'Is it all the Halloween rides we're going on then, Timmy?'

Timmy smiled and emerged from behind Sally.

'Yes.'

Jack bent low and whispered, 'I heard a secret that a famous cartoon dog might be putting in an appearance today.'

Timmy broke into huge grin. 'Where?'

Sally felt ashamed for her first impression of Jack. He had accurately judged Timmy's interest. She smiled as Jack waved a hand out in a direction, then suddenly a pamphlet appeared in his hand.

Timmy's eyes were wide with excitement. 'Oh cool you're a magician!'

'I have a little skill,' Jack said lowering his eyes. 'Are you interested in magic, Timmy?'

Timmy nodded eagerly.

'I thought you said you worked for Leeds City Council?' Sally asked.

'I do,' Jack said, grinning. 'Everyone's got to have a hobby.'

With his left hand he produced a 10p coin from behind Timmy's ear and handed it to the boy with a slight bow.

'You've hurt your arm,' Sally said, noticing his wrist wrapped in an elastic bandage.

'It's nothing,' Jack said. He tugged down the cuff on his left sleeve over the dressing. He unfolded the pamphlet—it was a site map of the fun fair, along with the times when the characters would parade.

'Look they're out now: let's go and find him.' Timmy raced into the crowd of black overcoats.

Sally and Jack charged after him.

'I'm sorry he's not usually like this,' Sally said.

'That's all right, I'm glad he's excited,' Jack said. 'It would have been a bit disappointing to have suggested the half term fun fair, only to find Timmy didn't enjoy fun fairs.'

'Stop right now, young man,' Sally shouted.

A number of boys turned, looked, and then turned away again. Timmy stood still, like someone had tied his leash to a pole.

'Mum we'll miss the parade if you don't hurry,' he said.

'You will stay at my side or I'll hold your hand for the entire time you're here.'

Timmy screwed up his face, and then he seemed to remember something. He walked with bouncy impatient steps at Sally's side. Sally had no idea what had made him so obedient, but for the moment she was grateful.

Sally looked around. 'Is it my imagination or aren't there an awful lot of Goth types here?' she whispered to Jack.

He looked around and frowned. He tucked a hand through her arm. Sally almost heard a low growl.

In other circumstances she might have objected to the possessiveness, but here she felt disturbed by the proliferation of black hair and clothes. The Goths faded into the crowd.

'I expect it's something to do with Halloween,' he said.

Timmy grabbed Sally's hand and pointed. 'Mum, look they're all here!'

Sally hastily disengaged her other arm from Jack's.

'Mum, they're signing autographs,' Timmy said. 'Do you have some paper or something?' He sounded so urgent that Sally scrabbled through her bag and got out her shopping list notebook with her pen.

'Here you go Timmy.'

Jack stood at her side, watching as Timmy stood in the queue for autographs.

'It's nice that he like dogs,' Jack said.

'Do you have dogs?' Sally asked, more for something to say.

'I breed dogs, yes.'

'Oh I hope not big dogs! I had a little fright with a big dog recently,' Sally said.

'That's a shame. The owner should keep the dog on a leash if they are near people.'

Timmy came back holding Sally's book triumphantly. 'Keep this safe, Mum. Dan'll be green with envy when he sees these in my book. Can we go on the ghost train now?'

Jack produced the pamphlet again, working out where they were as Sally tucked the shopping book away in her handbag. She smiled at the neat line of kids worshipping the cartoon characters, waiting for the men folk to decide a direction.

'Is that your boy going off with that man?' said a voice from the crowd.

Sally looked up and saw Timmy trotting beside Jack. She tried to see who had spoken, but there were only Goth folk nearby.

They should have waited. Perhaps they thought she had realized.

'Thanks. He's with me,' she said to the general area.

Sally power-walked, trying not to break into a run, to catch up with Jack and Timmy. She managed to slip into line just before they got on the replica steam train Ghost Ride. She squeezed in on the seat next to Timmy. He had never been on a spooky ride before so she grabbed his hand. Jack slid into the seat opposite.

The carriage speakers announced, 'Would parents please ensure that hands, feet and heads remain in the carriage at all times.'

Jack sniggered. 'I don't know. They could get extra exhibits if they left the odd severed hand lying around.'

Sally cast him a disapproving glance, then turned back to Timmy. 'Hold on tight, darling.'

'Mum, I'm not a baby. I don't need to hold hands.'

But Sally kept hold. The train ran into a dark tunnel and eerie noises started playing from the carriage speakers.

Jack stretched out his feet and put his hands behind his head, watching Timmy's reaction as the train chugged past backlit tombstones that lifted and skeletons rose up, groaning. The odd lighting effects in here made Jack's eyes seem luminous. Like a fox caught in car headlights. He rubbed his injured left wrist with his right hand and smiled at her.

Timmy snuggled close to Sally, with his eyes open wide. He watched the ghost models fly out of painted mansion backdrops and heard the clip clop as the haunted ghost rider came close to the train.

As he got out of the train he said, 'Mum, I want to be a ghost rider for my trick or treat costume on Saturday.'

'I said you're not going out after dark, Timmy.'

'But Dan and Sophie are going.'

'I doubt it very much,' Sally said. 'Dan and Sophie are going to stay at their grandparents for the night.'

'I'll be the only kid in class whose mother won't let him go out. How am I supposed to get all the sweets everyone else gets?'

'I'll buy you some sweets,' Sally hissed. 'Now shut up and enjoy the funfair.'

Timmy looked about to argue, then he lowered his eyes and screwed up his mouth.

'How about we try the boat ride? It's right here,' Jack said into the breach. 'Then we can try the Helter Skelter and the Ferris wheel.'

Sally smiled her thanks at Jack for his obvious attempts to distract Timmy.

What had caused Timmy's usual behavior? He obviously wanted to argue but was stopping himself on some thought. She needed to get him home and squeeze it out of him, but she was committed to this afternoon. She joined the queue for the boat ride.

A sign showed people screaming as they dropped into a dark abyss, which they called The Dead Man's Drop. A darkened tunnel swallowed the logs, through the open mouth of a demonic face.

'Do you really want to get soaked?' Sally said.

'They had fun.' Timmy pointed at the laughing people climbing out of the logs, their coats speckled with water.

She shook her head and zipped her anorak as far as it would go and did the same for Timmy just before they reached the head of the queue.

The operator lifted Timmy down into the front seat and strapped him in. 'You sit right there, hey boy. Mummy next and then Daddy.'

Sally flushed as she eased into the seat. Her feet splashed in the bilges, but the seat was dry. Behind her Jack's legs stretched out to touch her thighs. Sally tried not to twitch away from sitting between a man's legs like that.

A scuffle sounded behind them, as their log was setting off. Sally glanced back. The operator stared blankly as two of the University students dressed as Dracula and Bride had shoved to the front of the queue and climbed into the log behind. One of them traced a pattern in the air that looked similar to the symbol that Mike had chalked on her doorstep. Her finger left a green trail in the air, for a moment.

'What's that? How did that happen?' Sally said.

Jack had turned to look as well. He smirked, barring his pointed canines.

'Why didn't the operators stop them?' Sally asked. 'I'm getting a bit sick of being followed around.'

'Someone as beautiful as you is always going to attract attention.' He rubbed his left hand over his mouth. Those canines looked very sharp.

'I think I want to get off,' Sally said. 'Isn't there an emergency stop?' She hunted in the seat. The mouth of the tunnel loomed over them and she struggled with the clasp on the seat belt.

'Mum, what's wrong?' Timmy asked.

'I don't know, but something is really out of order here,' she said.

The log slid into the demon's mouth, and the darkness reached out for them. She needed to get Timmy and herself out onto the side before it became too dark to see. She turned in her seat to look at the entrance.

'Nothing's wrong,' Jack said. His voice came out low and growly. 'I'm just looking for a cure for a … certain condition and Timmy can provide it.'

In the dim light, Sally saw that Jack had his harness free. His lips were pulled back away from his mouth exposing his unnaturally sharp teeth in a snarl.

By now she had unfastened her own harness. Sally twisted to keep Timmy behind her.

'Stop this,' shouted Sally. 'I don't know what you mean.'

'And I'm going to believe that?' he snarled. 'When you have one of *them* coming at your every call.'

An emergency exit sign glowed and she saw Jack crouch to lunge past her to get at Timmy.

Sally batted at him. 'Stop that!'

'I'm going to get my cure,' he snarled. 'Out of my way, bitch.'

'Mum!' Timmy struggled with his harness fastening.

Sally could barely see Jack as they moved away from the brief light of the exit sign. She clenched her fists, and squinted into the gloom. Seeing him move again, she swung her handbag around at his head. 'Get off my son!'

The water sounded more intense here.

Jack launched at Timmy again, pushing her aside.

The edge of the log boat slammed against her rib cage. The log rocked, splashing cold water over her knees.

Suddenly there was grinding noise and the boat jerked forward. Jack's leap went too far. He fell on hands and knees in the flume of water—it barely covered his ankles. The water bubbled around the log boat and rushed past him. Her eyes adapted slightly to the dark and she saw one of his back feet was over the edge of drop in the dark.

'Damn!' said a voice down the line. 'My handbag fell into the mechanism.'

More splashing noises and Sally saw two people dressed in dark clothes wading through the log run, their pale faces phosphorescent.

Jack growled deep in his chest. He got his feet under him, his attention all on the newcomers.

'Back off, wolf,' said another voice, this time male. 'You're not getting them. They're ours.'

'I need the boy,' Jack said. 'Take the woman.'

'No fucking way. We're taking both.'

'And this way,' said the woman. 'We get to keep the fee of that shithead broker.'

Sally remembered the most important thing taught by her woman's self-defense course at University: she screamed.

Chapter Eleven

Light flared through the tunnel. Mike waded through ankle deep water towards them, prodding the water with his hiking stick before setting down his foot. No longer the angsty man from this morning, he exuded confidence. A glowing aura surrounded him, coming from no obvious source.

Sally felt a blush running up her cheeks. What was he doing here? She kept her place between Timmy and Jack as the Goths stepped aside for Mike.

From his crouch, Jack tensed. He launched at Mike and Sally saw claws growing out of his finger ends.

Mike whacked at Jack with his stick.

The wolfman crashed against the tunnel wall and slid down until he sat beside the flume.

'I thought you'd had enough last night,' Mike said. 'But if you want more, I can give it.'

Last Night? Horrified, Sally glanced at Jack's left wrist—the one with the elastic bandage.

'By what right do you protect her?' Jack snarled. He licked his bandaged wrist. He glanced between Sally and Mike, lifting his nose like a dog. Sally edged away in the log boat.

'My blood sister requested my aid,' Mike said.

'That's not the only blood involved here.' Jack sniffed the air. 'I can smell *ordes ad fratres faciendum* between you. She said she was a widow. She said the boy was true innocent, protected from harm with his father's life. The Liar!'

Jack sprang down into the darkness of Dead Man's drop—about ten feet—and vanished into the darkness.

'Uncle Mike,' Timmy wailed.

'Shut up for now, Tim,' Mike said. He turned to face the other contenders for Sally. 'Anyone else want to take me?'

Sally wrapped her arms around Timmy and stared as the Bride of Dracula stepped forward; dark streaks ran down the whiteface make up, as if her mascara had run, but intentionally. She lifted her right hand. Darkness gathered, forming a black hole in her open palm. 'Fuck you.'

A Date with Darkness

A hatch opened in the roof flooding the tunnel in light. 'What's going on here?'

To Sally's relief, a site security man lowered himself down and straddled the water track. Another one peered in through the roof.

Mike's luminescence dimmed.

The woman smiled sweetly at the new arrivals. 'I dropped my handbag in the mechanism, look it's right there, all chewed up. I'm very sorry.' She bent to pick up a mangled leather bag. As she looked at Mike, her lips curled back in a pure snarl.

The man dressed as Dracula leaned towards Mike. As he moved closer Sally could see the lines under the whiteface – he was older than he looked. Mike brought his staff between them. 'Really? A blood marriage? I thought you Nature Haters were against a good screw,' the man whispered to Mike. 'Remember we saved her for you. You owe us.'

'You saved them for yourselves, Mike said, flushing. 'I owe you nothing. Sally let's get you out of here. You'll have to wade.' He compressed his hiking stick into a baton again then he reached over and picked up Timmy, who snuggled in, hugging Mike's neck.

Sally stepped gingerly out of the log into the greasy water. It came up to her ankles and began a capillary action up her socks and trouser legs. Along the line of the log ride, the security guards helped stranded log riders out of escape hatches along the route. Sally followed after Mike. She glanced at the Goths and shrank into his side as they past. The woman flung back her head and shrieked with laughter.

'Do you mean you haven't told her?' the man whispered to Mike.

Mike ignored him.

With soaking feet, Sally was helped onto the embarkation platform. A colleague of Sally's from her Health and Safety Office stood there.

'Sally, that's two incidents you've been in this week,' said the officer. 'I'll have to let the boss know, and we can send you out the next time the government suggests cutting our department's budget. What has happened?'

Sally licked her lips. She wanted to scream at Mike, to get him to tell her what was going on, but instead she said. 'I think someone dropped a handbag into the mechanism. Look, you've certainly got my address, I need to get home and dry Timmy.'

'Go on then, Sally. The boss'll be looking for your report on Monday.'

'Of course.' Sally turned, looking for Mike.

He had walked to the edge of the platform and was stepping down into the crowd. Sally hastened after him. As she caught up with him he nodded to a woman standing in the queue. Her heavy eye make-up and black hair marked her out.

'Thanks for tip off, Selina.' Mike smiled at her.

'That's okay, Mike. Any time.'

Sally stared at her. From the voice, this was the same woman who had warned her that Jack had gone off with Timmy.

Scarlet lips curved into a smile. 'I tagged Mike as soon as I saw one of the Wolf fraternity making off with a little boy.'

Sally forced a smile. Glancing at Mike, she saw that while she had been talking, Mike had wrapped Timmy up in his leather coat.

'Coming? I'll carry Tim to your car,' Mike said. 'He's shaking.'

Sally looked back at the woman and stammered some thanks. A boy ran up to the woman, waving a magazine. 'Look Mum! I got his autograph!'

The Goth woman tucked an arm around the boy and inspected the magazine. Sally followed Mike as he carried her own son.

'My car's quite a way away,' Sally said. 'Are you with Gail?'

'Not today,' Mike said. 'They're visiting a castle. Their trip to the funfair is on Friday. You should have gone with them.'

'So what are you doing here?'

Mike didn't answer.

'You're following me again, aren't you?' Her voice was rising in anger.

'Can we have this argument when we get you home?' Mike hissed at her. 'I'd rather not attract any more attention than I've already done.'

Sally stalked along the road. Every step squelched in the long walk back to her car. Her feet were frozen and her trouser legs flapped damply around her ankles. She wanted to break down and cry, but from inside Mike's coat Timmy was chatting happily with the man he saw as his rescuer.

Sally was going to get an explanation from Mike if it killed her. Producing her keys she opened the car. Mike bent in and fastened Timmy into his booster seat, while Sally got into the driver's side. She was so used to Mike giving her orders that she was surprised when he just climbed in the passenger side with no comment.

'I thought you wanted to get home in a hurry to have a row with me, so let's get on with it,' Mike said.

'Why are you cross with Uncle Mike?' Timmy asked

Sally started the engine. Unable to come up with an answer for Timmy, she ignored his question and pulled out into the traffic.

Timmy warbled away in the background. 'And I've been really good today, haven't I Mummy? I've done everything you said without arguing.'

Sally frowned. 'Yes I don't know why, but you have.'

'Uncle Mike said I was to be good.'

'Timmy now's not a good time to talk about this,' Mike said. 'Your Mum's busy driving.'

'No, I want to hear about this.'

Timmy shut his mouth, hearing the edge to his mother's voice.

In the rear view mirror Sally saw him looking very wide-eyed as his face swung to look between the two furious adults.

Sally pulled into her drive and let Mike and Timmy out of the car. With tightly compressed lips, she handed a house key over to Mike and drove the car into the garage.

When Sally opened her front door she heard the shower going. She kicked off her damp shoes and sat on the bottom step to peel off the soaking socks. She stood and lifted her hands to her waist to unbutton her trousers then remembered Mike was still in the house. Fighting against her tears she stumbled up the stairs to her bedroom.

Mike came out of the bathroom: he had bare feet too.

'I put Timmy in a warm shower,' he said. 'I hope that will cancel out some of the shock.'

Sally made to push by.

Mike stopped her and lifted her face to look in her eyes.

She refused to look at him. If she did she would burst into tears and she needed her anger, she needed to fight to learn what he knew.

'So you're telling Timmy to behave now,' Sally said. 'Undermining my authority with him.

'I could see you were feeling stressed, so I asked him if he could show me how well he could behave.'

'Did Timmy know you were following? Is that why I've seen him rein in his naughtiness? What have you promised him?'

'It's not like Timmy is the best behaved child in the world,' Mike said. 'He's spoilt by only having a mother, not rotten yet, but if something isn't done soon he'll be bad. Gail tells me what he's like at school.'

'It's just a boy's wild spirits.'

Mike shook his head. 'Go and get into something dry Sal, I'll put the kettle on.'

'I need to know what is happening here.'

Mike skipped downstairs. Timmy started singing in the shower. Sally flounced into her bedroom. She hated being ordered around so casually by Mike. And hated the fact that he was right, she needed to be dry.

With her feet encased in dry socks and fluffy warm slippers and wearing dry trousers, Sally walked downstairs trying to think what she was going to say.

Mike had brewed a pot of tea. He saw her and poured out.

'I can't tell you,' he said. 'It doesn't matter what you scream at me, I can't tell you what's going on.'

'Can't or won't?' Sally said.

'I can't,' Mike said.

'Then I'm calling the police. I'm not having these madmen, and that includes you, chasing me around the place.'

'The police can't do anything for you,' Mike said. 'They'd refer you to my department. Ironic isn't it? The only person who can help you is the man you dumped twelve years ago.'

'Me dump you?' Sally screamed. 'I was seduced by someone I trusted and then he left me with not another word until I got this snatch letter congratulating me on my marriage. What happened to you Mike? Bright lights of the city blind you to the beauties of countrified Sally? How many pretty girls got their claws in you before you forgot me? Me dump you? I wrote to that address you gave me every evening for three weeks, and then once a week for over a year. It took me eighteen months before I finally believed my friends when they said you were a shit for leaving like that. I heard nothing from you.'

'Right! I'm sure you did. And as for hearing from me, I wrote letters to your college once a week for six months and I…' Mike stopped. A look of blinding comprehension fell onto Mike's face. It dropped quickly into fury. 'Did you say eighteen months? Nathan.' He swore. He turned on his heel preparing to walk out. Overhead the shower stopped.

'Where do you think you're going? Do you think you can just walk out again with no explanations?'

'I need to talk to someone,' Mike said. 'And it might be a good idea to stay away from people like that recent date, Lycanthropy is a sexually transmitted disease you know.'

Sally stood at the table trembling as she held back her anger.

'You bastard!' she shouted.

She picked up her untouched mug of tea, hurling it at his retreating back. The mug smashed on the wall, staining the white paint with tea. Mike did not look back.

'Uncle Mike, where are you going? I've been good. You promised.'

Mike turned with his hand on the front door and looked up. He nodded, then slid a game box out of his pocket. He set it on the stairs.

'There Sally, that's what I promised him if he was good.' Mike was angry enough to forget caution.

'Is that why Timmy has more games?'

'I've been slipping him games as bribes and to make sure he had games suitable for his age. Which you don't even seem to care about.'

Timmy slid down the steps on his bottom, wrapped in his dressing gown. He grabbed the game as if he knew his mother was going to throw it back at Mike.

'Will you stop telling me how to look after my own son?'

'Someone needs to. If it weren't for the danger you've put yourself and Timmy in, I'd say that this plan of yours for finding a new dad for him was a good one. He certainly needs a firmer hand than yours on his reins. You've just chosen the most dangerous way you could think of going about it.'

Timmy sat on the stairs, tears running down his cheeks. 'Mummy, Uncle Mike,' he said. 'Don't shout.'

Mike turned back to the front door. Both Sally and Mike were too far gone in their own anger and misery to help Timmy.

'If you walk out of here now, this time, without telling me why, without telling me what is happening, you walk out for good. And. Stop. Following. Me!'

Mike opened the front door. He slammed the door shut behind him. Sally ran to the door and locked it behind him.

'Mummy, why did you throw Uncle Mike out,' Timmy wept. 'He's the good guy. He's the one I want for my new dad.'

'Give me that game.'

'It's mine,' Timmy said. 'I was good like Uncle Mike said me to be. I earned it. You're not having it just because you've decided not to like Uncle Mike.'

Timmy scrambled back up the stairs and slammed his bedroom door. He turned the lock.

Sally banged on the door. 'Let me in.'

'It's mine,' Timmy repeated.

Suddenly even the air seemed to weigh her down. What was the point of this argument? Her heavy footsteps plodded downstairs and she dropped in front of the television preparing to drown in the flickering images. The cartoon channels were not what she needed so she hopped to the news channel.

'And these are the scenes where the sheep farmers are protesting against the imminent release of wolves into the Scottish Highlands.' The picture showed scenes of angry farmers waving their (hopefully empty) shotguns at images of timber wolves.

Sally flicked to a new channel at random. It was one of the documentary channels. It had a serious looking person on talking about how the White Witches of England put up their spells in the war to protect England from Nazi invasion.

Another flick and it was a promotion for a new series based on the book by Sir Nathaniel Trewithick, The Superstitions and Customs of Great Britain. The first episode was The Beast of Bodmin. A huge shadowy cat-like creature drifted across the screen. Sally could do without any more cranks with the current madness in her life. She blanked the screen.

Very soon now she was going to have to get up and start making dinner, because that was what she had to do.

Chapter Twelve

'**Come** in Michael Rider.' A blond man sitting behind an antique desk greets him. The paneled study is weighted with history but the green leather on the writing pad looks like spring.

The man smiles and rises from behind the desk. He's built like he's cast from the same mold as angels – appropriate considering Mike has accepted an invitation from one of the Theology Professors.

Mike stares him in the eye; it's odd—Mike is used to looking down on people.

He walks across the room and shakes Mike warmly by the hand. 'I'm Nathaniel Trewithick. Come, I've got tea set up here.'

He gestures at a table set for two at the tall, leaded window that overlooks an oasis of peace in frantic London. For a moment, Mike almost breathes the fresh air from the village he grew up in.

Mike sits and accepts his tea; daylight shines through the china cup when he lifts it to his lips. 'What I don't understand is why you are asking an engineering student to take a tutorial in, what did you call it? Practical Theology?'

Trewithick brushes a strand of hair behind his ear in an embarrassed gesture and Mike wonders if the blond hair, tied back in a ponytail, would brush his shoulders.

'Because,' says Trewithick, 'we believe that you are one of the people who are uniquely qualified for our department.'

'But what is *Practical Theology*?'

A tap sounds on the study door and they both look up. A man, younger than Trewithick, opens the door and walks in. Trewithick stands to meet his friend. He's shorter than Mike with dark brown hair and a close-cropped beard.

'Dunkley, this is Mike Rider.' Trewithick introduces them. 'I believe you would like to meet him too.'

Mr. Dunkley nods a greeting. 'You were asking about Practical Theology, Mr. Rider? Let me show you.' He lifts a fisted hand. '*He holds lightning in his hand.*' Dunkley speaks with a slight Scottish accent.

When he unclenches his fingers, he holds a ball of lightning, glowing like a plasma ball.

Mike boggles. 'Magic?'

Dunkley shakes his head. A long plait of brown hair flicks around his waist. 'Magic is smoke and mirrors, Mr. Rider, illusion such as you see on any stage. This is Practical Theology.'

Mr. Trewithick joins in with his easy, public smile. 'Basically, we'd like to teach you this. It is rare to find this Inherent Cræft outside of certain families, so we wanted to test you in a weekly tutorial…'

'It's not as rare as you and the Council would like to believe' Mr. Dunkley closes his hand and the lightning vanishes. He stuffs his hands in his pockets as if embarrassed by the display of power.

Trewithick smiles. 'But you'd be my apprentice, that's what we call students in this department. Dunkley already has one. You'll meet Dave Green later.'

'Are you interested?' Dunkley asks.

Mike nods, then realizes he has left his mouth open; he shuts it and coughs to clear his throat. 'I'd like to try.'

Trewithick's smile broadens. 'We have a little a contract for you to sign. And because we are … magicians, we have our own little rituals.'

Dunkley winces. 'We are not magicians.'

Trewithick smirks at his friend; Mike sees the mischief dancing in his eyes.

Dunkley sighs.

Trewithick picks up an old-fashioned stylus pen from his desk.

Mr. Dunkley twists the lid from a new pot of ink, and picks off the foil seal.

Mike is awed. He is being let into secrets from day one.

Mr. Trewithick pricks his finger and allows a drop of blood to fall into the inkpot. Mr. Dunkley does the same with his own stylus, and then Mr. Trewithick pushes the pot towards Mike with a fresh stylus sealed in polythene.

'That will be your pen, for the rest of your life. Guard it. However well you think you have washed it, it will have your blood on the nib.'

Mike fumbles open the stylus and pricks his finger allowing a drop of blood to fall into the pot.

Dipping their pen nibs into the pot, Mr. Trewithick and Mr. Dunkley sign a paper, and turn the sheet to face Mike. He skims over the document, hurrying because of his awe; it's a confidentiality document—nothing discussed in this department can be talked about outside.

He dips his stylus in the inkpot and signs his name.

'And now,' Dunkley says. 'We must show you what to do with the bloody ink.'

* * * *

Sally woke up with moon shining in her face.

Last evening had been foul. Timmy had refused to come out, and when Sally had finally found the key he had fallen asleep. The tear tracks on his face told Sally too much. She had covered him as lightly as she could and left a kiss on the tearstains.

Then she had gone to bed herself. With the result that she had been dreaming that she was Mike, again. Now she was wide-awake at midnight and the bright, full moon shone into her face. She walked across the room and started to pull the curtain closed.

Mike was at his self-appointed post outside her house. He sat, slumped on the brick gatepost. His hiking stick was extended at full length, but he hunched over it. His mobile phone lay on his knee.

Fury threatened to explode. She found she was panting, her hands clenched around the curtains as if she was going to rip them down. She wanted to run out into the road to scream at him some more, to shriek at him to leave her alone.

He shifted and twisted his neck as if to relieve a crick. He rubbed a hand over his face and his hair had rattails hanging free of the ponytail band.

When she forced her hands from the curtains, the fabric was crumpled where she had gripped so hard. She couldn't take or give any more misery. A tear trickled down her cheek.

She let it.

The phone rang. Mike picked it up, checked who was calling. He lifted his arm, as if he intended to smash it against the road but he halted his action and dropped the phone back on his knee. It rang few more times then fell silent.

Otherwise, he sat motionless.

At one, he pocketed his phone, pushed himself standing and crept away. He walked like an old man, leaning heavily on the staff.

He didn't look back.

Sally pulled her curtains across and lay back on her bed. She must have slept again, because the next time she checked her clock it was half past four. Thirst drove her from her bed. Sleeping again would be impossible, she knew, so she went down to the kitchen for a cup of tea.

Mike had raised a point in their fight last night that she had been trying to avoid thinking about. Timmy's behavior was not going to correct itself. He had responded so well to both David Grenill and Mike. He did need a dad. And Sally, despite her avowed purpose of trying to fill the half-term break with fun days, had hoped she might meet a new man. But all that had turned up was a whole lot of trouble, and her old boyfriend.

They had both written and, despite the problems with the Royal Mail, there was no way Sally could believe all those letters were simply in a dead letter office. Someone must have stopped them arriving. Mike seemed to think it was someone called *Nathan*.

Sally poured the hot water over her teabag and mashed it with a spoon to get the tea to brew quicker.

In the dark before dawn, Sally knew she didn't want to be alone anymore. But Mike was right about one thing: there were wrong ways to go about this search. She turned on the computer.

The paper came at 7 o'clock and Sally settled down to read it. Before Timmy woke up she had read it end to end. She would have to call Gail. There were apparently only a few remaining tickets to see the band Megachiroptera perform a world premiere of their new single, Innocent's Sacrifice.

Timmy was subdued when he got up. He cuddled his new game to his chest defiantly.

'It's all right Timmy, you did earn it,' Sally said. 'You were very good. How would you like to go to see a castle?'

'Who are we going with today?'

'No one Timmy,' Sally said. 'It's just the two of us. We'll go and be knights at Helmsley Castle; how about it?'

Timmy smiled. 'It sounds like fun. Can we have a burger for lunch?'

'I don't know if there is a burger bar at Helmsley. We'll have lunch in a café.'

'Are we going out with any other men?'

'No, I've cancelled the other two.'

'Good. Now you've got to make friends with Uncle Mike again.'

'No Timmy,' Sally said. 'Just us two.'

'But…'

'Timmy, no.'

'Can we have wooden swords at the castle? And fight battles?'

'Now that sounds just like what I had in mind.'

For once Sally loved the drive with Timmy. She spent her time pointing out the Anglo-Saxon field systems, and Timmy retaliated by pointing out every tractor winter-plowing those same fields.

They reached Helmsley just before lunch and Sally insisted on finding a café rather than a Macdonald's. Timmy was still subdued and well behaved, but did manage to order a cheeseburger; it came with a salad side dish, but Sally relented and didn't force him to eat more than the tomatoes and cucumber slices.

Pennants flew about the entrance as they walked up the back lane to the castle. Men in armor and their ladies in long dresses walked about welcoming everyone into the Visitor's Center. It turned out that Sally had chosen a day to visit when English Heritage were staging mock battles inside the castle walls.

Timmy danced around his mother as she paid for their tickets.

'Mummy, Mummy, you promised me a sword.'

Laughing at him, Sally nodded at him to pick up a sword and shield, which Sally added to her bill.

Hacking at imaginary foes, Timmy charged out of the center. Sally cast an apologetic smile at the ticket taker, who just laughed.

'Here's schedule of events. I expect you'll need it.'

Sally murmured her thanks and chased after her son through the high banks of the drained moat that was now the walkway to the castle entrance.

He had vanished.

'Timmy!' she called. Stopping a re-enactor she asked, 'Did you see a little boy running this way? He had a sword and a shield.'

The man in medieval clothes grinned. 'Then I expect he was rounded up. We're running a Squires' Training Camp for all the little boys with swords. If you continue on you'll see a pavilion erected in front of the statues of the three warriors.'

Sally caught her breath, and thanked him. She ran up the path. *Oh please let him be there*, she begged the infinite. *Let this be normal, not more weirdness.*

A circle of mothers gathered near a marquee. Panting, Sally joined the ring. And there was Timmy staring open mouthed as the instructors showed the boys how to hold their swords correctly. He saw his mother and waggled his sword.

The instructor rapped his shield. 'Pay attention, boy. No flirting with the ladies.'

Timmy giggled but returned his attention to the demonstration.

Checking her schedule of events, Sally learned that today the group was to re-enact the lives of people who had lived in the castle through the ages. She smiled wryly, it sounded like the sort of fun that she should have arranged all holiday, without any strange men involved.

Sally pulled her camera out of her pocket and lifted it to take a photograph of his training for Timmy, when he had show and tell at school on Monday. On the subject of *what I did this holiday,* "I learnt how to fight with swords" seemed a better memory than "Mummy dragged me around trying to find a new husband, and failed."

The picture in the viewfinder halted Sally's chain of thought. The way Timmy was being shown to handle the sword was the image of the way Mike had batted away at those Night Creatures with his hiking stick.

Startled, Sally lowered the camera, shot untaken. Looking at the boys and men in the *Squires' Training Camp* she saw they were all practicing the moves Mike made. Timmy looked over her to make sure she was paying attention to him, and she quickly lifted the camera again with a smile. He made a good pose and Sally took the picture.

Timmy was released from the camp, as the next lot of trainee squires got shanghaied from their mothers.

They entered the castle proper through the cannon and age-shattered gates. Here and there among the ruins, tents with displays had been put up. Among the foundations of the kitchens, the re-enactors were cooking a meal over a fire.

Timmy sheathed his sword through his belt and handed the shield to his mother. 'That sword training was fun. Are we going to see the matches where the knights fight each other? And I want to do archery.'

'When does that happen?'

'Look at your leaflet, mum.'

Sally checked the times, and the place. The archery was set up in the chapel ruins. She planned the afternoon around the events and Timmy's desire to learn archery.

Watching the knights fighting, Sally got the impression that these very practiced men were on par with the level of skill that Mike had displayed on her street at midnight.

At the arming tent, Sally was startled to see the athletic, muscular bodies under the chain mail armor. She remembered the muscle in Mike's arms as he had carried her last Saturday.

They reached the Archery practice range, and Timmy got shown how to use a bow – 'Mummy, I need a bow and arrow set.' Then Sally walked Timmy around the other events. Sally enjoyed the fencing matches; she liked seeing the men wearing lace. To Timmy they were girlie, not like the proper sword training he had received.

After the shows, Sally avoided buying the extra toy and followed Timmy as he strutted back to the car. With his sword and shield, he clearly felt like a big man. He objected to going in his booster seat until Sally refused to drive unless he was strapped in, with the sword in the boot.

On the journey back to York they sang along to songs from the radio. Driving up their street, Sally was surprised to see Gail's car and a police van sitting outside her house.

Chapter Thirteen

Sally pulled up into her drive as Gail walked out of the front door. She was sure she had locked the door when they left, but then she remembered that Gail kept the spare house key.

Leaving Timmy strapped in, Sally climbed out of the car. 'What's happened, Gail?'

'I came around because I got the feeling that you and Mike had another big row yesterday. He's been moping about the house all day instead of following you around like some lost puppy. You didn't answer the door, so I went round the back to see if your car was in the garage. Your back door has been forced open. I called the police for you.'

Sally's heart sank. She had quit the Internet dating site: the horror should be over, her details banished to the ether. In tears, she ran around to the back door.

'Forced' wasn't the word Sally would have used. She expected to see crowbar damage, but black soot curled up her back wall with a jagged branching pattern. Her patio pots were shattered. These uPVC security doors took a lot of damage—the plastic covering to the metal frame had melted. It looked like someone had put a bomb to it.

Two policemen measured the damage.

Sally shrank back against the garage wall. 'Oh Gail, what am I going to do now?'

'You get someone out to board it up tonight and get the double glazing people out to measure up for a new door, and yes you can call the insurance company. But you and Timmy are staying over at my house tonight.'

'Mrs. Cartwright?' said a police officer. 'We've got people knocking on doors to find out if anyone heard the explosion. Is there anyone you know of who might do this to your house? An ex-husband? That sort of thing.'

Gail tutted. 'I told you Sally was a widow.'

The policeman twitched a smile. 'Have you been feeling threatened by anyone?'

'I … er …' She glanced at Gail, who gave her a tight smile.

And how was she going to explain the dog-man coming in through the catflap without ending up under hospital sedation?

Sally saw the policeman look between the two women during the silent exchange. He jotted something down in his notebook. 'Can you tell us any more about the new postman from two days ago? You were the only person he talked to.'

A weight fell off Sally's shoulders. Of course the man who had mugged the real postman must have done so to check out the road. It had nothing to do with the weirdness. 'I gave the only description I had.'

The policeman nodded. 'And I'll need you to tell me if anything is missing from your house.'

'Oh! Yes!' That was something she could deal with. For a moment she pressed her face into her hands, then she leaned her head back. 'Gail, do me a favor and take Timmy round to your house now.'

'Good idea,' Gail said. 'I'll leave him with my mum and be right back.'

By the time Gail returned, Sally had discovered that some jewelry was missing, including the piece given her by David Grenill, and filled the police in on the Internet dating as a by the way.

She was on the phone to an insurance call center when Gail walked in the front door.

'Of course it was a forced entry,' Sally said, screwing the telephone wire into a knot in place of the call center employee's neck. 'There is evidence that it was a bomb.'

Sally covered the mouthpiece with her hand and hissed to Gail, 'They're checking to see if I'm covered for that!'

Gail mimed putting on the kettle. Sally shook her head and pointed to the bags she had managed to pack for herself and Timmy.

Gail picked up the bags as a manager came on the line to speak with Sally.

The double glazing people chose that moment to arrive. Gail took them to the back door while Sally explained, yet again about the bomb on the back door.

Finally reaching a consensus with the insurance company, Sally cradled the phone and rested her head against the frosted glass of the front door. Like this was getting things done! She sighed and walked to the kitchen, finding the two double glazing men had finished the measuring.

'We'll just board this up for you,' said the older of the two men. 'Then we'll let you know. Thankfully the brickwork wasn't damaged or there'd be trouble fitting the new door.'

Sally gave them her mobile phone number: she wasn't keen to stay in a house without a back door. Perhaps she could get a hotel room for herself and Timmy tomorrow.

Gail inspected the boarding then said, 'Come on, let's get over to my house. My mum has a pot of tea waiting for you. You know what we're going to do? Mum said she'll stay over as well, so Mike has got the sofa tonight, and us girls are going to have a night out.'

'Oh no Gail, I couldn't.'

'You can and you will.'

* * * *

Unfortunately for Sally, Gail was very persuasive and Sally found herself leaving Timmy in the care of Gail's mum and heading into York for a girl's night out.

'I tried phone for tickets to the concert on Saturday, but they'd all sold out,' Gail said as she jumped out of the taxi in the center of York.

Sally followed her more slowly. 'I'm sorry,' she said. 'I saw a mention of the limited numbers in the paper this morning, but I forgot to call you.'

Gail shrugged. 'I'm the one who should have got round to it sooner. Let's go get some food, hey?'

Gail strode along, looking at home on the stilts she wore for shoes.

Sally grimaced. She had never been fond of high heels.

Gail had always loved her teen-dolls whose feet were shaped for heels only. An image drifted through Sally's head of Gail walking around barefooted on tiptoe, her feet deformed by years of stilettos like those of her plastic dolls.

'Good to see you smile,' Gail said. She wore a pencil skirt in her favorite lime green, which together with the hennaed hair, shouted 'look at me.' 'You've been a right misery these last few days. And Mike too. Why can't you two get together and have a good screw. See if you've been missing anything, instead of moping around after each other. Timmy told Dan that Mike's been following you around.'

'He has a bit.' Sally was unsure what to say to her friend. She was still reeling from the understanding that someone had deliberately forced them apart. Still, she could have put that behind her if Mike had explained what was going on?

The two women entered Gail's favorite restaurant.

Immediately, Sally felt out of place in her comfortable clothes. Though most people were looking at Gail, Sally still felt that her slacks and trainers were wrong for this setting. Everyone here was dressed in the

96

height of fashion. She shrank away, as even the waiter seemed to turn his nose up at serving someone so poorly dressed.

He led them to a back corner away from the door.

'Perhaps this wasn't a good idea,' she whispered as they sat.

'Don't be silly,' Gail said. 'You need to get away from the nastiness that has happened this week.'

The white linen tablecloth let restaurant get away with dim lights. Tucked away in the darkened corner, Sally felt less obvious. Their table was in a snug alcove so no one could see her lack of fashion sense.

She stroked a hand over the nearest wooden beam to see if it was real or a reproduction. She thought it might be real: a lot of the shops and cafés in York retained uneven floors and walls from their mediaeval origins—it created ambience for the tourist trade.

'You need to get out more anyway,' Gail continued. 'Timmy is fine with my parents. Mind you, you should have let me put some makeup on you.'

'I've never worn makeup.'

'Yeah I know, but if you're not going to go for Mike and you want a new guy, then you'd better start making the most of those blonde curls and sweet face, while they're still here. A bit of makeup and maybe freshen up the gold a bit, would do wonders for your love life.'

Sally just studied Gail's appearance critically.

Gail grinned. 'Okay, I'm not the best advert for my advice, but then you didn't marry a con artist.'

Their waiter took their order. Gail insisted on wine, since they had come into York city center in a taxi.

'I'm not going to miss out on the chance of some decent wine,' she said.

Sally agreed with her choice but returned to a previous thought.

'I do wish I'd met this Dave Green of yours before the divorce,' she said. 'I'm sure he can't be half as bad as you make out.'

'He was much worse, honey. Even the judge felt that once he was let out of prison, he should only have short supervised visits to the kids. He doesn't take me up on it, thank God.'

'Timothy was a great person,' Sally said. 'It won't be betraying him to get involved with another man, will it?'

'Since he was such a great man, he would hate you to be unhappy.' Gail suddenly looked thoughtful. 'Why did you let everyone think that you and Mike broke up because of what we thought happened at Nige's party?'

Sally shrugged. 'I can't talk about it right now.'

'Mike is still in love with you. I'm his sister, I know these things.'

'Please Gail, I don't want to talk about it.'

'I think you're in love with him. That's why you row so much.' Gail held up her hand to stop Sally. 'I'm only bringing it up because Dan says Timmy's upset by you two arguing.'

'Why don't you just tell Mike to go back to where ever he appeared from?'

'I can't because he's going to a conference up here. He felt like he ought to see his family for a bit. He's not even been home for Christmas forever. Did you know he's gone all religious? I mean more than just church on Sunday. He has Ph.D. in it.'

'Yes, I ... he told me,' Sally said. 'So what are you going to do about your concert?'

Gail shook her head. 'Okay, if you don't want to talk I'll have to lump it. If I'd got myself organized then I would be going to see that world premiere on Saturday night but I'm not. I'll see Megachiroptera the next time they tour.'

The waiter came and put the food on the table. He looked around, leaned closer and said, 'I heard that some tout has Megachiroptera tickets going at the Hours of Darkness Club.'

Gail's eyes widened in avarice.

'But Gail,' Sally teased, picking up her fork and spearing a meatball. 'I thought that you'd just talked yourself out of going.'

Gail took in Sally's teasing tone then giggled. 'You're right. I couldn't pay a tout's money anyway. Thanks for the info, though.'

He nodded and walked away.

'Now look at that waiter,' Gail said. 'Isn't he just the goods? Brown hair and eyes, rich coffee skin.'

Under Gail's instruction Sally looked up from her dinner, just as the waiter went through the swing door. Behind the door was a person dressed in black. The waiter shook his head and passed through. Sally tried to see more clearly, but the door swung shut. It was probably just the manager questioning the waiter on whether he was chatting up a guest.

I'm just imagining attackers lurking everywhere, Sally thought. It was all finished now. She deleted everything on the dating site and cancelled the other two appointments.

Except that it hadn't. What about the break in?

'Not my type really,' Sally said, as Gail awaited her verdict.

'I know your type,' Gail said. 'I think it has steel-gray eyes and light brown hair.'

'I told you, I'm not interested in your brother.' Sally grew annoyed at Gail's persistence. 'I hope he's not going to turn up tonight.'

'He's off working somewhere,' Gail said. 'I know you are—'

'How did you find out about this restaurant?' Sally said.

Gail captured another pasta penne on her fork. 'We came here for the work's Christmas do last year.'

Ignoring Gail, Sally concentrated on her food; even she had to admit it was worth coming out for. Her friend tried to bring up Mike again, but Sally changed the subject and kept them chatting about little things.

Gail insisted on paying for this treat.

'And you'll pay for our next night out together.'

'Gail, I can't...'

'You can and you will,' Gail said. 'Timmy's fine with my mum, and I can see that you're ready to get back into life, or why did you think up this scheme to fill the holiday? We'll find you someone, even if it's not my little bro.'

They walked down the steps and into the street.

'So,' Gail said. 'The night's still young. Now what should we do?'

'We're going home aren't we?' Sally stared at Gail, who grinned.

'I thought we could go clubbing.'

Sally's mouth dropped open. 'I've never been clubbing in my life and I—'

'Then now's the time to start.' Gail walked down the street while Sally stared after her. 'Are you coming?'

Sally sighed, and then followed her friend.

Chapter Fourteen

Sally trailed after Gail, wishing that she'd brought her coat. The evening had turned cold while they were inside, or else the restaurant had been too warm. When she caught up with Gail she said, 'I doubt we'll find anyone for me in one of those sorts of places.'

Gail smiled, wryly. 'Actually Sally, I'm following up that lead on Megachiroptera tickets. So this is for me.'

Sally relaxed. 'That's fine, why didn't you just say? Are we going to this Hours of Darkness club? I'm not really dressed to go into a Goth haunt.'

Gail glanced at her clothes. 'Those gray slacks are dark enough to pass for black, and the purple in your sweater is great. You're dressed conservatively enough so you won't get hit on for some S&M action.'

Sally snorted, but now she knew Gail had put a hold on the idea of hunting for a new man for her, she was curious. She followed her friend into the Shambles where the mediaeval houses almost touched at the top stories, and on into Petergate. In a side street off Petergate, Sally saw two huge black shapes leaning against a wall. She halted.

Gail looked back. 'Come on, it's just there, by the bouncers.'

Sally sagged in relief. 'Bouncers! Of course, sorry Gail.'

Between the bouncers, stairs led down into the basement. A board on one side of the door announced that Batmobile were playing tonight. On the other side a board advertised Black Lagoon at £2.00 and Half-Price Zombies. Sally assumed they were drinks.

The bouncers looked them over. The one on the left glanced over at his mate, who nodded and said, 'Have a nice evening, ladies.'

Gail paid the admission, though how she managed to have money in that evening bag, which looked just big enough for a slim-line mobile phone, Sally couldn't guess.

'Batmobile? Who are they?' Sally asked.

Gail turned her head, to speak over the music that was getting louder as they went down. 'It'll be a cover name for one of the big groups attempting something new before putting their name to it. We've gotta try those Zombies.'

'We've to function in the morning.'

'Don't be a spoil sport.'

Colors on the dark spectrum rotated round the room. From the smell in here, Sally thought that some people must be taking advantage of the fog machines and flouting the smoking ban.

Shadows lurched and spun following the weaving light display, untamed by the music. Every shade of black was present in the clothing on the dance floor.

Gail stood on the edge staring at the group on the small stage. 'I can't figure out who they are.'

'While you're doing that,' Sally said. 'I'll get us some drinks.'

'I'll have a pint of snakebite and black,' Gail said.

Dubiously, Sally studied the bar list and tried to work out if she knew what was in any of them.

A youngish man lurched over to the bar and pushed ahead of her. 'Two more Zombies.'

He looked like he'd had enough to Sally, but the bar tender called his assistant over to make the Zombies and looked at her for her order. She ordered Gail's snakebite, picking something at random from the list for herself and hoped when she got it, it would be drinkable.

'Not Zombies?' the bartender asked. 'They're half-price.'

'Maybe later,' Sally said.

A strong smell of pineapples drifted over from where the assistant mixed the Zombies. Sally turned away carrying her drinks, but heard the assistant say, 'Drinks are too slow. They're going to have to find another way.'

Gail was in a conversation with a Goth woman when Sally arrived with the drinks.

'My cousin phoned me, he works as a waiter and said you were looking for tickets, so I was coming here anyway.'

'I'm not sure I can afford a tout's prices,' Gail said. Sally could see the avaricious gleam in her friend's eyes as she let her eyes rest on the black lace top the Goth woman was wearing.

'Really, it's not a bad deal,' the woman said. 'I'm not a tout. I bought the extra tickets for my brother and his girlfriend and they can't make the festival this year, after all. I was hoping to get my money back on the deal, nothing more.'

Relaxing at hearing the educated voice, Sally handed Gail her drink and turned to watch the band.

She took a sip of something that looked like road tar, but tasted sweet. She found she was enjoying the strong Caribbean rhythm, almost like a heartbeat. Sally felt her feet tapping in time but the dance looked robotic, almost anti-time, and involved a lot of shuffling.

Behind her, Gail negotiated for her tickets—with any luck they'd be out of here and along to a cash machine before too long. She took another sip at her glass of road tar, then a bigger one. It was quite good, actually.

As she watched, she began to see patterns in the way the dancers moved, as if this were an orchestrated ballet. Perhaps that's how it was in clubs. It wasn't like she would know.

One of the dancers tripped. He collapsed to the floor and lay still. No one helped him up. Then another dancer fell over him.

Sally dumped her glass on the nearest surface. It seemed like the Zombies were working.

She ran between the oblivious people and hauled the second fallen man off the first. Once upright, he returned to the shuffling dance. His face flushed with the exertion, even though the dance was slow.

Turning to the remaining downed man, she saw he remained still. She peered at him in the shifting light. His chest was still. She touched his throat.

'That's all right, miss.' The bar assistant arrived at her side. 'I'll get him up. You go and enjoy your evening.'

'But he's not breathing,' Sally said.

The bartender joined them. 'He'll be fine.'

Sally back away. His pulse had stuttered under her fingers and stopped.

The bartender and his assistant hauled the man to the side. The circling lights made it difficult to see what happened next, but she was sure they had slipped something into his mouth and tugged a stud from his nose.

Sally returned to where she had last seen Gail she watched. To her amazement, the bartender set the drunk on his feet and let him continue dancing.

She must have moved her hand when she was feeling for a pulse, but she thought that bar staff ought to be more responsible and help people into a taxi when they got that wasted.

The assistant returned to the bar and slipped a bottle under the counter while the bartender watched the drunk for another moment. He rejoined his assistant.

Gail waited for her with her new best friend—as long as the other woman had Megachiroptera tickets. 'Always jumping in to help people, that's my Sally. Look I hope you don't mind, but I want to get to a cash machine to pay for my tickets. Did you want to wait here?'

'I'll walk with you,' Sally said.

The Goth woman led the way up the stairs.

When the volume had died enough for real conversation Sally said, 'Who are you planning on taking with you?'

Gail tilted her head. 'You want to come?'

'Thanks, but I'll give it a miss.'

Gail grinned. 'There's this guy at work…'

They were outside the club now. The bouncers stood gazing into the distance on either side of the door. The Goth Woman turned to Gail. 'That was Megachiroptera, you know. Trying out their new Haitian sound.'

Gail stopped, and then shrugged. 'I'll hear them at the concert anyway.'

'I thought it sounded a bit Caribbean,' Sally said.

'My bank's this way.' Gail took the lead toward Parliament Street, the Goth woman stepping up beside her.

As Sally set to follow, a hand covered in a leather half glove slipped over her mouth.

With another arm around her waist, her captor dragged her along the road.

She kicked back, but her trainers impacted on knee-high boots.

Reflected a shop window, she could see Gail talking cheerfully to the Goth woman and herself being pulled backward. The reflection showed no sign of the attacker.

She tried screaming but the hand got in the way. She wriggled her head about. The studded leather covered the palm but not the fingers. She got her mouth open and bit down hard on the white flesh.

Behind her, somebody swore. The hand shifted to get her mouth back on leather. It gave her enough room.

'Gai…' Her shout was muffled instantly.

Gail looked up. Horror crossed her face. 'Sally!' She dug into her evening bag for her mobile.

The Goth woman shoved Gail to the ground and stamped down hard on Gail's evening bag with her Doc Martins.

Even from a distance Sally heard the crunch of broken technology. *No!* She wouldn't be able to call Mike for help this time.

Gail rolled out of the way, and then Sally was hauled out of viewing range.

She tried to wriggle and drop her mobile for Gail.

Still kicking, Sally was hugged tightly to the man's chest and whisked across the road into a side passage. It was as if he didn't notice her weight. The man dropped her and shoved her against a wall. A second man punched Sally in the stomach.

'That's right,' her kidnapper hissed. 'The fear and pain give such a savor to the meal.'

Sally's scream came out as a whimper. When she opened her mouth, they stuffed a rag between her teeth.

She tried to spit out the dusty-tasting cloth. Through pain-squinted eyelids Sally saw the man who had captured her untie a bandanna with a skull and rose motif from around his neck. He wrapped the scarf around Sally's face and tied it tight behind her head, with no regard for blonde curls.

Tears leaked out of her eyes with the pain of the pulled hair.

The man stood back.

Sally dropped into a heap on the ground.

The man lifted her face with his toe.

She looked in eyes of deepest black. It was a yet another man dressed in black trying to kidnap her. She had expected the man who had tried to fight Jack Harper for her at the Fun Fair.

'I was most upset, most, when you cancelled our … dinner date, Sally.'

I deleted the profile, her mind screamed. The weirdness was supposed to be over.

The man made a sharp gesture with his left hand. 'Pick her up,' he said. 'Carry her. And get the van nearer.'

'Yes sir.' Sally recognized the bouncer from the club. The Goth woman who had lured Gail, joined them in the alley.

'I'll get the van, sir.' The woman rubbed against his arm like a cat looking for attention.

He brushed her off. 'Go then.'

She sprinted away.

The club bouncer picked Sally up and flung her over his shoulder in a fireman's lift. All Sally saw now was the back of a black shirt. It had a pattern printed on it in red and gray.

With her free hands, she thumped on the man's back.

He dropped her on the ground. Before she could get her feet under her to run, he grabbed her feet and wrists. 'I need to tie her hands,' the bouncer said. His pale face almost glowed in the dark alley. 'I'm getting bruises.'

'Here use this.'

The kidnapper emerged from the shadows and slipped a belt from his skintight jeans. The belt had to be ornament—those jeans were glued onto his body. Sally struggled and writhed, trying to get free of the man's hold on her wrists. Not all her self-defense lessons at University could help her escape.

As the belt went around her wrists the man crouched. He held her legs down, almost absently, but he looked so skinny. 'I was so looking forward to meeting your delicious sounding son. The innocent preserved by his father's sacrifice.'

Sally struggled as the bouncer pulled the belt from her trousers and tied her ankles.

'Remember, we arranged to meet at a restaurant, there was a ball pool for Timmy to play in, while we would chat.'

The bouncer wrenched the studded leather belt as tight as he could.

'Hurry up.' The man turned away from Sally. 'Cath will have the van on double yellows. We don't need another parking fine.'

The bouncer hoisted Sally over his shoulder again.

Hog-tied she tried to be a dead weight. From the muscle under the bouncer's shirt, Sally could tell this would cause him no trouble.

'We'll find your son sooner or later,' the man said. 'From wherever you and the Church have him hidden.'

The words sent a shiver through Sally. She could see people around in the streets, but no one took any notice of the two men carrying a bound woman. She tried to catch an eye, but no one looked their way.

They passed a café advertising free Wi-Fi. People sat in the window oblivious to the kidnappers walking past them. Sally could see herself carried like a sack of potatoes over the bouncer's shoulder, but though she knew he walked next to her, there was no reflection of the leader. What on Earth?

Then she saw Mike. He sat focused on his netbook, drinking coffee.

She struggled and bounced. Surely Mike could see her. He lifted the coffee cup to his lips, intent on his screen.

They walked past.

She thought they were heading towards the minister, but only the pounding of their boots on the stone pavements gave her any indication of distance passing. The walls closed over them as they entered one of the snickleways.

'You must be damned stupid or just careless to walk past one of us with a bound woman,' a familiar voice said, from the shadows.

The kidnapper swore and turned to face the challenger.

Chapter Fifteen

'**Bloody** Hell, you lot never give up do you.' Mike stood prepared to rescue her, yet again.

Mike's actions made no sense. One minute he was slagging her off, the next he was rescuing her. At the moment it didn't matter—with the rag in her mouth cheering was impossible, but Sally wished she could.

'I really thought there were rules about this. She advertised. She's ours.'

'Can't help you there. If you drag a bound woman openly through the streets, I have to take notice,' Mike said. 'You'd better be good. Who wants a fight? I'm right in the mood for it.'

The bouncer hefted Sally off his shoulder and dropped her on the ground.

Unable to break her fall she landed with jarring pain on her hip. She twisted in her bindings and saw Mike pushing up his sleeves with a very nasty look on his face. His hiking stick was full length.

The kidnapper gestured the bouncer to his side. 'Your turn to worry, nature killer.'

Mike sneered and pointed with his hiking stick. *Fire and brimstone, storm and tempest; this shall be their portion to drink.*'

The bouncer's eyes widened. He lifted his hands and backed as far as he could before hitting a wall. He slid down into a fetal ball, rocking and moaning, covering his face with his hands.

'So you can summon visions into minds, can you Nature Hater?' The kidnapper shrugged. 'A party trick.'

The bouncer scrambled to his feet and tried to run. 'No! NO! I didn't do that! It wasn't me!' He stumbled over Sally, crushing her legs under his muscle-bound body. He squirmed, rolling off her and back up against the wall as he screamed, 'No!'

The kidnapper frowned.

'You might want to worry now, demon spawn,' Mike said. 'My tutor was Nathaniel Trewithick.'

Now where had Sally heard that name recently? She tried to caterpillar away from where the two men now faced each other. It was a small yard, open to the sky, unlike the two snickleways that led here. The electric lights fixed to the walls crackled and flickered.

Sally saw shadows creeping out of the alleys, tentacles of darkness crawling over the cracked paving slabs.

She wriggled and tried to catch Mike's attention, but he was focused totally on his opponent.

'Nathan Trewithick's replacement, how nice to meet you.' The kidnapper raised up a hand holding a twig. With a flick, it turned into a twisted Gandalf-type staff.

Before he could do any more, Mike raised his staff again shouting, '*He cast forth lightnings and destroyed them.*'

Blue lightning burst from the tip. He used the lightning to whip at the other man, driving him back towards the shadows.

The streetlights flashed out.

The kidnapper raised his oaken staff and spoke in a language unfamiliar to Sally. Water curled up from every crack in the pavement and fell in a deluge from the clear, star-ridden sky around Mike.

Mike laughed. 'No, not water. Don't your masters teach you anything? This is what happens when water meets electricity.' His lightning crackled along the water path back to the kidnapper.

The man convulsed as the electricity hit him. Weakly, he gestured with his staff.

Under her back Sally felt the slab heat; steam seared her lungs as she breathed. Sweat clung to her skin. The sweltering air proved too much for the bouncer. His hands fell slack from his face as his eyes rolled up in his head.

'*He came flying on the wings of the wind.*' The mist cleared, and Sally saw Mike finishing a gesture. With the mist, the water had cleared, and the slab again chilled Sally's back as she lay helpless, hoping Mike knew what he was doing.

'Earth,' Mike said in a teaching sort of voice. 'If you go against one of us, you must always use Earth. Use the opponent's strength against him.'

Twirling his great oaken staff around his head and shouting instructions in the unknown language, the kidnapper swirled the air around him in a vortex.

Sally choked again as the summoning sucked all the air from the little alleyway they were in. It was worse than the howling gales at Toowich Park that had stolen her breath. From deep within the twisting mass of air, Sally was sure she could see eyes—which had to be a hallucination from lack of oxygen.

A Date with Darkness

Pointing the gnarled end of the staff at Mike, the kidnapper barked out more words. The Vortex thrummed against the pavement; she felt the vibrations in the stone as it twisted towards Mike.

Again, Mike barked out the quote about lightning. Again, an electrical flash chopped through the twirling air to hit his opponent. Mike smiled in that same horrible, patronizing way that he used to depress her female aspirations.

The vortex shattered.

Sally gasped for breath as best she could with her mouth tied shut.

'Earth,' Mike suggested. He leant casually on his hiking stick. Even to Sally it felt very offensive, and he was her rescuer.

In a fit of anger the kidnapper spoke in his strange tongue, pulling dust into another Vortex.

This Vortex sank into the ground around his feet pushing up the ground lifting him into the air. He stood on a growing mound of writhing, churning earth that drove its way through the cracks in the paving slabs and wriggled like living creatures towards the main mass. It pushed up the slabs and the leading edge crept closer to Sally.

She tried to shuffle back away from that dreadful crushing noise that sounded in the ground as it swallowed the paving slabs nearest the fight. Slabs cracked and sent dust flying into the air to fill the Earth Vortex the kidnapper called to subdue Mike's lightning.

'Better,' Mike said, still taunting his opponent. *'All things are safe home.'* He lifted his stick and nothing seemed to happen.

Above them, the kidnapper laughed. Sally got her heels on the ground and caterpillared away from the sucking vortex. She wanted to scream at Mike to do something, but the rag in her mouth stopped any noise.

The paving under her feet buckled.

With a hideous crack, the slab shattered and the earth underneath began to join the vortex.

Her right shoe sank into the shifting mud. Sally yanked her foot out and the shoe crawled along with the earth, and then sank slowly into the mound.

Sally backed up against the wall near the bouncer. She tried to sit up, to pull away from the monstrosity that was building, but the bindings held her prone. Under her back the next slab lifted.

Then the buckle on the belt that tied her feet pulled towards Mike. With a clang, a discarded metal bottle top flew along the alleyway and hit the glass window behind. A rattling, clanking noise sounded down the snickleway. Sally saw the summoned tin cans that had been called by the magnetic attraction just before they slammed into the back of the kidnapper. The pull was strong enough to drag Sally closer to the mud Vortex underneath the kidnapper.

'Mmmm!' she screamed.

Mike ignored her protests.

The dust storm formed itself into lines like those seen around the magnets in the school experiments with iron filings.

'Of course,' mocked Mike. 'If you do use Earth, I'll change from using lightning to using magnetism.'

The sucking vortex on the street stopped as the kidnapper redirected his power use. The mound sank slowly back to ground level until it was a small heap of dust with Sally's dirty shoe sitting on the top.

The kidnapper made a hurling motion with his staff—from the intonation Sally guessed the accompanying words were foul—and fire flung from the tip towards Mike.

'*The springs of the water were seen.*' With a clockwise motion of his staff, Mike gathered the firestorm into a fire devil. The fire devil shrank into his staff as he absorbed the power.

'No, no,' Mike said in his lecturing voice. 'No fire in a built up area. That is definitely in those rules you tried to invoke earlier. Don't try and convince me to follow the same rules that you are ignoring. However, I think your victim is uncomfortable; let's end this game.'

The end of Mike's staff crackled and whip of lightning crashed down towards the kidnapper.

In an attempt to deflect the lightning lash, the kidnapper raised his staff.

The lash impacted on the wood, left it smoldering and smelling of fire.

The kidnapper hurriedly brought the foot of his staff down to where his earthen vortex had eaten up the York stone paving slabs. Blue light crackled down the length of wood, and it shattered in a shower of splinters.

Sally ducked her head, screwing her eyes shut, expecting every second the sting of splinters on her bare face. Nothing landed, the lightning must have burnt up the wood.

Sally opened her eyes in time to see the kidnapper scamper away. The shadowy tentacles that had crept into the courtyard slid away in the bright light that Mike summoned.

'If his student can do this, Nathan needs no replacement against Creatures as weak as you.'

Lash followed lash. In the blue light Sally finally saw they were in the little square courtyard in front of the Barley Hall. Mike's lightning reflected off the glass viewing panels. It left branching jagged lines of soot where it struck the uneven paving slabs. Each time the lightning struck a slab settled back into place. Where the Vortex had been her shoe now sat, as if it had never been buried.

The kidnapper ran down the passage, leaving his follower hunched against the wall like a passed out drunk.

Still watching the way the kidnapper had taken, Mike put a hand on the belts holding Sally and they dropped away.

She brought up her numb hands to pull away the bandanna over her mouth and she spat out the rag that stopped her from calling out for help.

With no regard for her lack of circulation, Mike dragged her to her feet.

'Come on, Sal,' Mike said. 'I can't hold them off for long, despite my boasts.' He got her to her feet. 'Thank God you're not wearing the silly spikes that Gail likes to wear. Now run, towards the Minster. They won't touch us there—we all respect sanctuary.'

Sally pulled her hand free and stuffed her foot into the newly emerged trainer.

Mike grabbed her and tugged her towards the alley opposite.

She hesitated at the edge of the dark. She remembered this was once called Grope lane—appropriate at the moment, whatever Mike had been doing had blown all the electric lights.

He dragged her again and she staggered along after him. 'Was that some sort of Taser?'

'God Sally, you're the hardest nut I've ever faced. You see a werewolf in your house and you still think that it's odd that I can call lightning by magic. Fine we'll call it a Taser if it makes you feel happier.'

'Werewolf?' Sally stopped dead. 'Nonsense! They're just stories. It… it must have been a mutant Alsatian escaped from a research laboratory.'

Mike shook his head. 'Fine. Mutant Alsatian, and I wasn't calling lightning from my magical wizard's staff. I'll let you in on a secret Sally: those people back there weren't kidnapping you to take you to a health spa. We're running for your life here.' He grabbed her hand and set off again.

'But what about Gail?' Sally dragged against his towing hand.

'She fine! Get a move on!'

Running to keep up with the hand he held firmly, Sally found enough breath to say, 'He talked about eating me and Timmy.'

'Well he was a vampire,' Mike said. 'It's my job to fight creatures like that when they get out of hand. But he was mostly sticking to the rules, I'm breaking them here.'

'How did you get involved?'

'I signed up for the wrong course at college,' Mike said. 'We'll talk when we get you home.'

Their feet slapped the concrete slabs of Stonegate. None of the late night window shoppers paid attention to two people charging down the street towards them. They just stepped aside without comment.

As she and Mike charged down Low Petergate towards the Minster, Sally hung back.

'I've got to stop,' she panted. 'Surely they won't touch us with *magic* among all these witnesses?'

Mike dragged at her hand. Sally staggered on.

'In case you hadn't noticed no one can see us at the moment. You don't think I'd risk throwing lightning about if I hadn't put up an aversion field.'

'How the hell would I know?' She didn't have the breath to scream at him, but she tried.

Mike dragged Sally onto the Minster steps and sank down. He rested his head on his knees blowing out his breath. His hand drifted to his pocket. He slid a glucose tablet into his mouth.

'Touch the door handle will you, Sal?'

Sally gave him a look, but took the remaining two steps and put a hand on the cast iron doorknob.

'Now what?' she said, standing there.

'One touch is OK, Sal, you don't need to stand like a stuffed goose. We're under sanctuary now, until we get off the steps.'

He visibly regained color and got to his feet. Joining Sally in the shadow of the portico, he wrapped an arm around her shoulders. His touch warmed her, chasing away the fear and shadows.

'You do get into some messes,' he said, his mouth against her hair. 'It's a full time job keep you safe. I've fought enough Creatures of the Night this past week to fill an average five horror flicks—just for you.'

Sally leaned against his chest. 'Look, thanks for the rescue and all that. But if you're going start talking cryptic nonsense again and refuse to tell me what's going on, just don't say any more will you.'

Mike nodded, his chin brushing her hair.

Sally looked up at him, a little surprised that he was so close.

He smiled down at her. Very slowly he leaned down. There was no reluctance in his face this time, just wonder.

Still breathless from the dash through the streets of York, Sally lifted her face to meet his lips. Her arms went up around his neck to bring his height down to match hers, just like she had always done.

She wanted to melt into him.

Mike's arms tightened around her. Loose ends of his long hair tickled her cheek.

She pulled out of his kiss long enough to catch a breath and tucked a strand of hair behind his ear.

'Where did that come from?' Sally asked.

Mike's smile was wry. 'Call it my reward for rescuing you.'

He leaned forward again, suggesting he wanted more.

Sally lifted her head again. His kiss was real magic—it sent her floating higher than the Minster and locked out the world.

'Well, I never! And in the church doorway too,' a voice said. Footsteps clattered on the stone flags.

Mike swung around grabbing for his cane, but the elderly couple had moved on, taking their disdain with them. He let out a heavy sigh and pulled her close again.

'Oh Mike, what happened to us?' she said, resting her head on his chest.

'I'll get you home and I'll tell you what I can.' His breath tickled as it fanned wisps of her hair. 'There really are things I can't tell you, despite the fact I was tricked into taking the vows.'

He pulled out of her arms, and reached into his coat pocket for his mobile. 'You didn't happen to bring your car in did you?'

'I've been drinking,' Sally said. 'We came into town in a taxi.'

He nodded and used his thumb to dial a number. He got through to a taxi firm and ordered a cab to pick them up at the Minster taxi rank.

'Come on, it's safe for us to move off here now,' Mike said. He linked his fingers through hers and led her to wait by the South African War Memorial.

'You said Gail was okay?' Sally said, suddenly remembering her friend.

'She's fine. I told her to get home. She'll be waiting for us,' he said. He put a relaxed arm around her shoulders and pulled her close, as if he couldn't bear to have her separate from him. 'But if you don't mind, we'll go to your house first and have a chat. Gail doesn't want to know about my real career.'

'Your family don't know you're a... a ... well what are you?'

'I'm an Investigator for the Church Office of misuse of Cræft. Witch finder is easier to say. Here's our taxi.'

He opened the door and gave the driver Sally's address.

In the darkness of the taxicab, she felt him draw away from her.

Chapter Sixteen

Mike paid off the taxi and waited until she opened the front door. He hesitated on the doorstep a moment, sighed then entered.

Sally locked the door and turned, lifting her face to him, trying to reclaim the closeness they'd shared in the shadow of the Minster.

Mike tried to push her away, but she clung on until he sank into the embrace. Still kissing her, he pushed Sally against the wall, his hands hunting for skin under her blouse.

Sally dug her fingers into Mike's hair, pulling him closer. The ponytail band fell onto the floor and his hair brushed her cheek with its own type of kiss. Sally dropped her hands to his shoulders and under his coat to slip it off.

Mike pulled away, just far enough so that his coat stayed on. He looked into her eyes and shook his head. 'Sally, I've missed you every minute.' He rested his lips on her hair, and then let them slide to touch her lips again. He let the kiss linger, until it ended in a sigh.

Sally tightened her grip around his neck. 'Mike, please.'

'I've got to tell you a lot of things.' With a sort of shrug he freed himself and turned on the hall light. 'Right now, I hate Nathan.'

'Mike, I don't understand.' She lifted her face for another kiss.

'We're not teenagers any more to be carried away by the heat of the moment.' He paused. 'Sally forgive me, but when I thought you'd gone off with another man without even telling me I signed a contract for the full training. Part of that contract insists that we place our responsibility to the Church Office before all other desires and relationships.'

'What!'

Mike removed his coat hanging it on the coat rack. 'Nathan admitted that he'd been ordered to intercept our letters.'

Sally pulled a face.

Mike shrugged. 'It's the tangle of emotional relationships. He says he hates having to deal with broken-hearted young men. He doesn't have much respect for woman, even if he is one of the best demon hunters around. On no account would he ever put any person before his duty. One of my other tutors told me he couldn't have a relationship and not put that person before his duty.'

'That's silly!'

'Any relationship with you, given how I feel about you, would have to come before my other commitments.'

Sally bit back the 'damn your silly council', that she wanted to say and replaced it with, 'How much are you going to tell me?'

'I can't quantify information. I need some coffee.'

'I need a cold shower, but fine, we'll do coffee.' She led the way into the open plan kitchen dining room and set the kettle going. The smell of burnt plastic hung around. Looking at the blank board that covered the gap where her door should be, made her shudder. Outside the moonlight would be illuminating the jagged soot marks up the wall. Sally stared at the board.

She darted a glance at him. 'You didn't do that did you?'

Mike looked at the door then back at her. 'Why would I need to bust in? All I do is knock.'

'The lightning you … called in Grope Lane,' she whispered. 'It made marks on the pavement like the soot marks on my wall.'

'Really?' Mike leaned over the sink to try and see the wall by the window. 'If you wanted to be melodramatic, I suppose you could use lightning to open a door. It's easier to use a lock-opening spell. I'll check it out in daylight. The fingerprint might still be read.'

'None of this makes sense,' she said. 'Have I walked into a fairy tale while I wasn't looking?'

Mike came away from the window and stood before her. 'You want a fairy tale, okay. A long time ago, before the Romans, Britain was turned into a sort of prison. Nature Spirits that had been annoying humans were driven over the salty water and bound to stay. Stone circles, monoliths, the howes, they're all part of it. The Druids were there to placate them, and the Wizard Smiths to bind them with iron and stone.'

Mike sank into a chair at the dining room table and rubbed a hand over his mouth, like he was trying scrub off her kisses.

'Then the Romans slaughtered the Druids,' continued Mike. 'God knows why. Perhaps they thought that rampaging Nature Spirits would weaken the population for the invasion. They left the Smiths because they needed the weaponry—Romans were crap at working iron. In the end, the Smiths had to ally with the Roman Catholic Church to keep the spirits bound. When Rome was chucked out, the Witch Finders remained. We keep them from infecting too many people.' Mike looked up and sighed. 'Vowing to keep the people of Great Britain safe.'

'If that contract was signed because they tricked you, it can't be valid,' Sally said.

'I wish that were the case. I signed it in blood.'

'Oh! I dreamt that.'

Mike looked up sharply. 'I beg your pardon?'

'I've been having the oddest dreams recently. They started with me remembering before you left, then I started to dream about your life after you'd gone and I dreamt that you signed a contract with drops of blood in the ink.'

Mike looked at her in horror. He lifted his left hand and took hers. Then he stroked her ring finger with his.

'Oh hell! That's what the wolf meant. This is just one more complication we could do without.'

'Go on, tell me the worst.' Sally sat down next to him.

'That game we played as kids, you know pricked fingers vowed to marry and all that stuff. Because I became a Witch Finder, it became a proper contract. One we consummated. I wish I were talking to Nathan right now.' He kept stroking her hand in a way that made Sally want to scream or jump him.

Instead she removed her hand. 'Can you tell me what has been going on, please? Without the additional complications.'

Mike stared bleakly at the table. 'I was sent here to discover why the Creatures of the Night were converging on York. It was your dating profile. Why the hell didn't you just write Sacrificial Victim Altar Ready in the advert? It would have had the same effect.'

Sally huffed. Mike smiled, ruefully.

'It's true. Timmy is a very special sort of person, magically speaking. His father gave up his life to save you and Timmy on the day he was born, and then you called the boy Timothy, after his father. There is a belief among the Werewolf community that infecting an innocent like Timmy will cure them.'

'You mean Jack Harper is a pedophile?' Sally demanded.

'What? How would I know that?'

'You said that Lycanthropy was a sexually transmitted disease,' Sally said.

'Oh! Sorry, I was cross when I said that. It's just the transfer of saliva, biting or kissing, will infect a person with a demon. I don't know what the necromancers—that's Vampires to you—want with Timmy, but it's not going to be pleasant. He has a powerful life force and that will feed into any magic they perform. You're too trusting to be in this game. Several times this week I've been able to divert your question with very simple spells.'

'You did what!'

'Why else would you ignore a rain of blood? Sally, I've been trying to protect you. As long as you didn't understand it all, while you were still ignorant you were safer, believe me. Their magic grows with belief and Halloween is a powerful belief focus, especially as this Halloween falls on the full moon.'

'And that's the reason I'm being chased around by all these strange people?' Sally knew she'd asked for an explanation, but she couldn't believe this. 'Well the first one, Pete Granger, at least he was normal wasn't he?'

'I can only tell if someone is part of our community when they are actually using magic, but there were at least three sets of magic used at Toowich Park—only two were directed at you, mind.'

'What!'

Mike shrugged. 'Someone had an Identification set on you—that was your electric personality—anyone who knew your name would recognize you. And there was the rain, that was designed to leach into your skin and make you more, umm amenable. The crack in the alligator tank had nothing to do with you.'

Sally shut her eyes. 'Why doesn't everyone know? We could protect ourselves.'

Mike shook his head. 'The last time everyone knew, innocent people were lynched. The mob doesn't think. It's safer this way.'

'Oh come on!' Her eyes snapped open again.

'Oh! Come on!' Mike repeated. 'And the tabloids didn't whip the mob into such a frenzy that it lynched a pediatrician rather than a pedophile?'

Sally bit her lip and stared at the table.

Mike sighed. 'I just wish you'd listened to me last Sunday.'

'It's not my fault,' Sally whispered. She dropped her face into her hands.

Mike stayed silent.

Sally looked up at him, demanding reassurance. 'But I didn't know.'

'Now that I know about the blood tie between us, I can protect you, legally, like I've been doing. I even took out your land phone line, because it's a direct path into the house for certain types of spirit. But God, it's eating me, being around you.'

Sally frowned. 'What was that about rules?'

Mike winced. 'There aren't enough of us to enforce a blanket ban on all their activities. So we have guidelines that if one of *them* crosses, we take *them* out.'

Sally saw what that meant immediately. 'You mean that these creatures can just pick someone from a dating site and eat them? That's in these rules?'

Mike clenched his fists. 'We can't save everyone from themselves.'

'That is so Dark Ages. The woman is to blame for being raped because she wore a short skirt or got drunk, is that it?'

Mike grimaced. 'It's not just women: men are taken too. Equal opportunity stupidity.'

'And no one notices people going missing?'

'You'd be surprised at how much people don't want to see. Think about all the people who vanish in one year, who are never found. As long as *they* stay within limits and don't draw attention to *themselves* we leave *them*. That said,' Mike tried to graft a smile on his sober face, 'most of the Nature Spirits are totally harmless and eager to have any sort of worshipper.'

Mike was talking about letting people get murdered. She shook the thought off and concentrated on the main point: she had nearly been killed and eaten. 'Can you teach me? I'm getting so sick of this damsel in distress malarkey.'

'*You're* sick of it?' Mike glowered.

She slammed her hand on the table. 'I don't believe any of this. You are just insane. This is all insane.'

Mike lifted his hand together in a prayer-like gesture then pulled them slowly apart. Lightning crackled between his fingers, like a plasma globe.

'Is it like those witches in the war?' Sally said, fascinated despite her anger. 'They cast their spells to try and keep England safe from the Nazi's. I saw a TV program.'

Mike sneered. 'Nothing like that. Witches don't work the way we do. Their skills are gifted not internal.'

'Aren't witches just female wizards?'

'There are no female wizards. Women can't do real magic. Their hormones get in the way.'

'What?'

Belatedly recognizing shaky ground, Mike made a pacifying gesture. 'It's what I've been told.'

'Oh! I remember, wizards are in all the stories from the Dark Ages. That's got to be the real reason why you're spouting that bull.' Sally rolled her eyes in disbelief. 'How did you get involved?'

'I told you,' he said wryly. 'I signed up to the wrong course at college. I accidentally signed on for a seven-year apprenticeship to Nathaniel Trewithick. That's why no one heard from me.'

'What's so special about eighteen months?'

'I beg your pardon?'

'It was my saying eighteen months that made you realize that we'd been tricked.'

'Oh that!' Mike smile was genuine this time. 'I demanded to know why I hadn't been taught scrying like all the other apprentices had. It was eighteen months after my course began. And Nathan taught me just so I could see you kiss that Timothy Cartwright. I signed up for the full course right there.'

Sally dropped her face back into her hands. She bit her lip trying not to cry. 'There has to be a proper explanation, even for the crows,' she muttered. Lifting her head she added, 'You know, the website said they're hanging around waiting for me to die.'

Mike sniggered. 'Crows are pretty intelligent. They're not going to hang around on the off chance of a meal. They're hanging around hoping you will lead them to the one who sacrificed their brother. I've got Firey holding them off for you here; he thinks he's tiger-sized anyway so it wasn't difficult.'

Sally giggled.

'I think I'd better make that coffee,' Mike said. He got up and set the kettle to boil again. He picked out two mugs from the draining board. 'Do you still have sugar in your coffee?'

'Oh? Yes two spoons. And milk, it's in the fridge.'

Mike brought the coffee across. Sally looked up miserably. She had got Mike back, their separation hadn't been either of their faults, and it turned out to be worse than before.

Mike checked his watch, and then stirred two sugars into Sally's cup. He handed it over to her.

'What time is it?' Sally asked.

'Huh?' Mike stiffened.

'You just checked your watch.'

'Oh that!' He checked his watch again. 'It's a bit after midnight.'

Cupping her mug in both hands, she sipped.

Mike relaxed his tension and drank his own black.

'You didn't used to drink coffee like that,' Sally said.

He looked down at his cup. 'Working with the sort of forces I do, you learn to be careful about what people put in your drinks.' He dropped his cup on the table and looked out the window at the full moon. 'I need to walk you to Gail's house.'

Sally thought the moon was beautiful. *Romantic,* she thought dreamily. She smiled at him and shifted from her chair onto his knee. She cuddled her arms around his neck. She could feel Mike stroking her hair. She nuzzled into his hand.

'Forget your silly vows,' Sally said. 'We could go upstairs. After all, with you being all religious now, we're practically married anyway.'

'Now what do you mean?'

'We promised to marry and we…' Sally giggled, in vague way. She shook her head to try and clear the fog that seemed to be crawling into her head. She was so tired. 'We consummated it, so we're married.'

'Oh that! We've both had lovers since then.'

Sally leaned in to nibble his ear. 'I've only had one,' she whispered.

Mike clenched his lips and shook his head. He stood abruptly. Sally staggered to her feet. Her head felt like a straw sack. She shook her head to try and clear her ears.

'Stop it, Sally, please.'

'This has all got to be a bad dream,' Sally said.

'It will be when you wake up in the morning.'

'What do you mean?' Sally looked at him: he had gone fuzzy around the edges.

'Damn,' Mike said, looking into her eyes. 'I forgot you'd had something to drink as well.'

Sally held herself upright by the table. 'What have you done?' She looked at his half-drunk cup of black coffee. 'What did you put in my coffee? Barbiturates?'

'Nothing so crude, darling Sally.' With very little effort he bent and lifted her into his arms. 'I work in Cræft, after all. I put an anti-coffee spell on your drink. Coffee makes you sharp and awake. Anti-coffee makes you sleepy and … and it makes you forget. I'm sorry Sally but that's the only way I could get them to agree to let me tell you.'

'If I forgot it again immediately, what's the point in that?'

'Don't worry, I'll leave you feeling reassured. When you wake up tomorrow you'll feel a lot better about this whole situation.'

'You bastard,' whispered Sally against his shoulder. 'Maybe you didn't choose to betray me last time, but you did this time. Tell them to go to Hell.'

Distantly she could feel her tears soaking into his shirt. She heard Mike snicker.

'I said that to Nathan, and he told me that he'd destroyed too many demons that even a visit there would be a social faux pas.'

Chapter Seventeen

'**You** mean you've been baiting a bear!' Mike turns and sees a man breaking free of some iron chains as he sprouts fur on muscular arms. Sally runs... runs into...

A room lighted by banks of computer screens. 'Kill or be killed little fifth year,' a man spits in Mike's face. Blood runs everywhere... Sally cringes away...

Green, Green everywhere... Mike stands with a red-haired young man. The man turns stricken eyes to Mike. 'What have I done?'

Sally looks around to see what he's talking about and sees the young man—his red hair now in long plait down his back—standing over a wolf. Mike kneels by the creature as it slowly turns back into a man. 'Unorthodox,' Mike says. 'But thanks.'

The young man grins, polishing a set of iron knuckle-dusters. 'I'm not a gentleman. I don't have to give them a sporting chance.'

He pounds the knuckle-dusters into his palm. Pain...

* * * *

The headache woke Sally next morning. Her neck was stiff, and the crick throbbed in time with the pulse in her temple. She groaned and lay back down.

It was still darkish, so no need to worry about getting up yet. She looked around and saw a cold cup of tea on an unfamiliar bedside table. She looked around in the gloom and remembered that she was staying at Gail's house, because of the break-in. She had no idea how she got here, though.

She sat up. Pain lanced through her forehead, but she endured and shifted back to rest on the padded headboard. Knowing Gail, it was going to be covered in pink velvet.

Thinking over last night she vaguely recalled being rescued by Mike, yet again. But from what? She rubbed her eyes. Her arms ached and she saw bruises on her wrists.

She flung back the duvet and swung her feet out of bed. Similar bruises marked her ankles. What had happened last night?

The door opened a crack, and Gail peeped in. 'Thought I heard you move; you've slept forever. These curtains are blackout. It's nearly 11 o'clock.'

'Timmy!' She pushed up onto her feet. Her ears buzzed and the room swayed. She almost fell, before she sat.

Gail pressed her against the pillows. 'And stay there, while I fetch you a fresh cup of tea.' She relented enough to add, 'Timmy's fine. Sophie's cross because and I quote "she's a girlie and can't play with guns". They're playing with Dan's shooting gallery.'

'I don't like Timmy to play war games.'

'From the woman who lets her son play the shoot-em-ups on his game console,' Gail said, picking up the mug of cold tea.

Sally lay there feeling really off. With light from the hall, she saw her guess had been correct, this was Gail's bed from when she was a teenager. It was all pink and velvety and soft. From before life had hit them all hard.

Now she was conscious, she could hear Timmy and Dan's muffled shouts.

'How much did I drink last night?' she asked when Gail got back.

'Not much,' Gail said. 'But if you're not used to it... And you had another bad shock. Do you know what happened?'

Sally frowned, but the effort was too much. 'Not much. I...'

Gail waited for a moment then said, 'You were well out of it when Mike brought you home last night. He drove you round in your car, because he'd forgotten you were staying here and had the taxi take you to your house. I would have waited in town for you, but he got all masterful and told me to go home where I'd be safe. You know how he's become.'

That got a smile out of Sally. 'He's insufferable these days.'

Gail returned the smile. 'Anyway, he went back to sleep over at your house, as an added measure of security he says.'

Sally nodded, vaguely. She had the impression of being with Gail in the restaurant, but nothing much after that. She tried to force images over the gap in her memory, but nothing fitted a hole that contained bruises on her wrists and ankles.

After drinking her tea, Sally crawled out of bed and into the shower. She was determined to get back home and start sorting out the mess left by the burglars and the police.

Gail cornered her and tried to get some breakfast into her, but she felt a little sick.

'Do you know what's going on?' Sally asked.

Gail fussed with the washing up. 'It's like Mike says—that sort of ad can attract the weirdoes. That must be what's happened here.'

'It's more than that.' Sally pressed her hand to her forehead. 'I can't remember anything. It's like someone's built Hadrian's Wall in my head.'

Gail splashed water about. 'It'll be okay, Sally. No one can find you here.'

Sally wondered about the firmness of Gail's reply.

'I thought Timmy and I could move to a hotel today.'

Gail spun around. Water pattered from her yellow washing-up gloves onto the linoleum. 'You're staying here, and that's final.'

The terror in Gail's voice silenced Sally.

Timmy was content to stay playing with Dan, so Sally took the five-minute walk home alone.

The day was a dull 2D monochrome, hedges painted as scenery to a tedious play. Even the minimal sunlight had her frowning, wishing for the sunglasses that she kept in her car. That and the something that nagged at the back of her mind and refuse to work lose, like it was stuck behind the wall and there was no gate on this side.

As she stood in her porch rubbing her temples, the front door opened.

'Did you forget your keys?' Mike asked.

He held a cup of coffee—there was something about coffee. She rubbed at her temples, but the slight recollection slid away.

'No, they're right here,' Sally said. 'Gail told me you'd stayed here over night, but I'd forgotten.'

'It's good you're here,' he said. 'I just called Gail, the police are on their way. They've found some things on those allotments by the railway tracks. They seem to correlate with what you lost.'

Sally rubbed her eyes and nodded. She walked into the kitchen and went to her medicine cupboard.

Mike followed her looking concerned. 'Are you okay?'

Sally shook her head, and regretted when the pain flared up again. 'I've got a headache as big as Yorkshire. It's not like I even had very much to drink last night, according to Gail.' She massaged the knot in her neck. 'I wonder if I'm coming down with something. My brain feels like I've got a feather pillow stuffed into my skull instead of the gray matter.' She drew out the packet of painkillers and promptly dropped it on the floor.

Mike crouched to retrieve the packet. 'Maybe you should lie down instead of taking medicine.'

'My head's got to be clear with the police coming around.' Sally took the packet out of his hands and got a glass of water. 'I swear I'll never go out with Gail again.' She swallowed two tablets.

A knock sounded through the house.

'Didn't you get the doorbell fixed yet?' Mike asked.

'Like I've had the time,' Sally said, going to answer the door.

'Would you like me to do it for you?'

'Male DIY instincts kick in, even when it's not his own home.'

'Actually, I meant answer the door.' He walked close behind her in a protective sort of way.

She swung around on him. 'Will you just quit that? I'm so sick of your creeping around after me. Leave me alone.'

Mike nearly turned on his heel in anger then he said, 'Sally, I've been your friend forever, haven't I? I'm going to be a little protective. Just humor my silly male prejudices, please.'

'Gah! Go into the front room and let me deal with the police alone. Last I looked I'm a grown up.'

As they could both see the uniforms through the frosted glass, Mike did a hand shrug and left her to it.

Still Sally checked through the spy hole, just to make sure. She recognized one of the officers from the previous day, so she opened the door.

'Come on in, please,' she said after inspecting the two officers' ID. One of the men carried a briefcase. Sally led them into her dining area and gestured that they should sit around the table.

'Can I get you something to drink?' she asked.

'Not for me,' said one, he looked at the man with the briefcase who shook his head. 'No, thank you.'

'We have a statement from you about the property you have had taken,' said the officer with the case. 'Pieces similar to your descriptions have been found.'

He opened his case and took out some photographs.

Sally took the first picture and smiled. 'That's the necklace my mother gave me when I was sixteen.'

She spent the next 30 minutes identifying the jewelry. 'The only piece you haven't found is the one that I thought might be related to the Whitby break-in.'

'That is correct,' said the officer. 'We have brought some additional photographs for you to look at. Could you tell me please if your missing piece is shown in one of these.'

He laid a series of five photographs of similar pieces of jewelry on the table. Sally studied them then pointed to the fourth one.

'That's the broach I was given. Or,' she added cautiously, 'that piece is the duplicate of the one I had. He told me it was a reproduction, which was why it took me so long to get suspicious. Even after I had looked at the pictures on the website, I thought, well reproductions have to copy something don't they? So was this an attempt to recover a stolen item?'

'I'm afraid we cannot comment on our investigation at present. We have your description of the suspect on record, and must reiterate, it you see him again do not approach him, call the police immediately.' He studied her for a moment. 'Are you sure that this David Grinell and the postman were not the same man?'

'Unless David had plastic surgery between Monday and Wednesday, then I'm absolutely sure. He'd also have to have his feet cut off to be the same height as the postman.'

The officer noted that down.

The other officer gathered the photographs back into his briefcase. 'Thank you for your time, Mrs. Cartwright. We will arrange to return your property at the earliest convenience.'

Sally showed the men out then went to the front room to find Mike. He dropped the magazine he had been flicking through onto the coffee table and stood, scowling.

'Gosh has your male ego been twomped on?' lisped Sally, trying for the same patronizing tone he used. 'Didn't your whittle Sally let you deal wiv the nasty policemen for her?'

She hated herself for saying the words. Last night, at some point, she was sure she had been friendly with Mike again, positive they had kissed and made up. It was as if she was forced to spit out the hateful words. Almost as if she were trying to hide how much she wanted him, as much from herself as from him.

Mike clenched his fists.

'You know you won't hit me,' Sally said, folding her arms. 'So why not say what you want to say and then get home to Gail.'

He released his fists and closed his eyes. Sally could see a look of despair in his eyes before the lids dropped shut.

'I'm sorry Mike,' Sally said. 'I don't know what's going on, but this weirdness started when I saw you again. I need... I need my life to be normal again. I've done what you said to do. In fact, I'll even admit for the sake of your ego, that I shouldn't have done it to begin with. I've deleted my profile on the website and cancelled all the dates. Even though you've been very protective, I would prefer you to continue with your own plans and just get out of my life again. All the arguments are upsetting Timmy.'

She rubbed her head again. Why was she saying this? The words felt like they had been written on her brain in an odd sort of teleprompter, overwriting the part where she pleaded with him to stay.

He nodded, and looked up at her. 'We are both grown-ups, the arguing has been a bit silly over something that happened 12 years ago. I don't have any more to say. My conference is tomorrow. I'll be gone by morning.'

His words sounded as stilted and rehearsed as hers, but she said, 'Thank you.'

She should feel relieved, he was doing what she asked, but she felt like she should stop him from going. Sally wanted to kiss the sadness from his eyes. Half of her brain rebelled and thought Mike was a heel for abandoning her, the other half, which was wrapped up in the feather quilt, knew she had made up with Mike last night when he had rescued her.

Instead she showed him to the front door. Her aching eyelids drooped and she leaned her forehead on the cool plastic, trying to figure out what was happening in her own head.

Was this what it was like to be insane?

Chapter Eighteen

After Mike left, Sally pottered around, but until the insurance forms arrived on Monday then there was nothing she could do. She just didn't want to return to Gail's house and face Mike again. Eventually, though, she had to.

Her ankles ached too much to walk back, so she justified getting out the car by deciding to take Timmy to a burger bar for lunch. She drove around to Gail's house and parked at the curbside.

Looking over Gail's garden wall, Sally saw there was a committee on the lawn. Mike stood, looking frustrated, beside two bags. Gail and her mum were trying to start Gail's car, and all three kids were trying to get Uncle Mike to join them in a kick about with a football.

'What's the trouble?' Sally asked as she got out of her car and joined the committee.

'My car won't start,' Gail said. 'And Mike's got to catch his train. It'll have to be a taxi and a later train, I'm sorry Mike.'

'Does it need a jump,' asked Sally. She started towards the boot of her car to fetch her jump leads.

'No,' Gail said, stopping her friend.

Gail's mother turned the key again. The noise from Gail's car made it clear that the battery was fine.

'Can you get the bonnet release lever, mum?'

Mrs. Rider reached down and pulled the lever. Gail lifted the bonnet and peered inside. Sally drifted over to join her.

'Give it another go, mum.'

The battery turned the engine over, but nothing caught.

'I don't suppose you're out of petrol, are you?' Sally asked.

A look of enlightenment and hope spread across Gail's face as she looked at Sally. Then Gail leaned over her mother to check the petrol gauge. 'Damn, I hoped it was going to be that simple. It's probably the fuel injector clogged or something. Sorry, Mike.'

Mike leaned on the car and absently traced a figure in the dust. 'I'll phone for a taxi and hope it gets here.' He lifted his mobile out of his pocket.

'I thought you were leaving tomorrow?' Sally said.

Mike grimaced. 'I got a call from the conference committee querying my presentation, so I need to be there early to sort out the differences.'

'Wait dear,' Mrs. Rider said. She heaved her comfortable body out of the car. 'I'll just run over and get my car.'

'It'd take too long,' Mike said. 'But thanks for the thought, mum.'

Sally sighed. Life was conspiring against her. 'Get in,' she said.

Walking back to her car, she lifted the boot on the hatch back. 'I'll run you over to the station now.'

'Can I come?' Timmy demanded.

Sally shook her head. 'No Timmy, you stay here. When I get back we'll go out for fast food for lunch.'

'Yippee!' Timmy said. He danced around Gail's front garden. 'We're going to get a burger, we're going to get a burger.'

'Mum?' Sophie said. 'If your car doesn't work how are we going to see the sailing ship tomorrow? Uncle Mike told us we can't miss it and we go back to school on Monday.'

Gail said something soothing as Sally unlocked her boot to let Mike dump his bags inside. He still used the same backpack and suitcase, well-worn now, not spanking new like last time, which he'd put in the boot of her borrowed family car for his journey to the London train twelve years ago.

Sally frowned. There was something about that journey or his time in London that she needed to remember.

Shaking her head to try and clear the stuffiness from her brain, she got into the driver's side.

Mike awkwardly sat in the passenger seat. He fastened his seat belt and sat with his hiking stick at baton size, looking at his hands. He had his leather coat wrapped round him, like he was trying to avoid contamination from anything that belonged to Sally.

She rubbed at her forehead then started the engine. The headache was coming back.

Mike looked at her oddly. 'Are you sure you're well enough to drive?'

'I'm fine,' Sally said. 'The headache went for a bit but it's coming back. I'll dig out the extra strength pain-killers when I get home.' She pulled out from the kerb. 'How long until your train leaves?'

'About half an hour, but it would have been pushing it to wait for a taxi. Thanks. What are you doing when you get your headache?'

'Just shut up about the headache will you? I can forget about it if someone isn't twittering on about it.'

130

Sally concentrated on driving. The traffic down Leman Road to the station was thankfully light and Sally pulled into the station turnaround. She hoped out of the car and unlocked the boot.

Mike hauled his bags out. He settled the backpack over his shoulder and turned to go.

'This isn't right,' Sally said. She rubbed her head again. 'Something's really out of kilter here.'

Mike looked at her, a very puzzled light in his eyes. He dropped the suitcase and leant in. He wrapped his arms around her and rested his head on her hair.

'You're right. Something is very wrong, these headaches shouldn't have happened,' he whispered. 'Try and forget that something is wrong and I'll find out how to cure it.'

Sally tried to struggle out of his arms, but he held her. She gave in. 'If you're going to talk nonsense…'

He slid a thumb over her lips silencing her. 'Please, trust me. I'll sort it.'

She turned her face aside. 'We didn't fight last night—' Pain jabbed her eyes.

Mike ran a cool hand over her head. 'Forget about it please.'

'Will I see you again?'

Mike lowered his eyes, and then he lifted them back to hers. 'No. I'll get someone else to sort out the problem if necessary. It would be best if you stayed at Gail's until the full moon is over.'

Very gently he touched his lips to her forehead. The kiss felt like a patch of sunlight on her brow. The headache faded, and even her stiff neck loosened. He hesitated then lowered his mouth to hers, just the brush of a butterfly's wing. Sally breathed in his breath. He released her and checked his watch.

'I've got to go, my train's here.'

Sally watched him go. She had this double image, like she was seeing him off at the station 12 years ago but this time knowing he wouldn't return.

The mobile in her pocket trilled. Turning away from her watch on Mike's back, Sally lifted it out of her pocket. The caller ID told her that it was Gail. She opened the car door as she hit the answer key.

'Hi Gail,' she said. 'I've just left Mike at the station. I'm on my way back to your place now.'

'Don't hurry,' Gail said. 'Mum fetched her car, and since you said you were taking Timmy to the fast food place, she's taken him off along with my two. Then she and my dad are taking all three of them to the fun fair—since Mike said your visit was interrupted. That okay?'

Sally leaned forwards on her steering wheel. 'Thanks for that Gail. I'll go back by my house and finish off a few things before I come over to yours.'

'Remember to get some lunch,' Gail said as she signed off.

A taxi driver tapped his horn at her to remind her to move her car.

Hissing imprecations at the oblivious taxi driver, after all she couldn't move before she had ended her phone call, Sally let out her clutch and pulled away.

Sally parked her car in front of her house. She did not want to take it down the drive to her garage, because then she'd have to look at the boarded over back door again. For a moment she just leant her head against the steering wheel, then, taking a fortifying deep breath, she climbed out on the pavement. Trying to be brisk, she stepped over to the front door holding the key ready.

With one foot on the front doorstep, she halted. She had no reason to go inside. None of the paperwork for the insurance was here, nor would it arrive until Monday. She didn't feel like eating anything. What she really needed was a walk in the fresh air to clear her head.

She took her foot off the step and walked back up her garden path, carefully closing the iron gate behind her. Now why had she done that? She shook her head. The answer was stuck behind the Great Wall of China that stood between her and her memories of Thursday evening.

She left her car standing at the curbside and strode off towards the River Ouse. A walk along the riverbank would do her the world of good. Feeding the ducks and geese would be fun. She stopped and would have turned back to fetch some bread, but knew if she returned to her house she would find something to do, and not have her walk.

Right now she felt so stuffed up that she needed to get a clear head. Perhaps she was coming down with something. Mike had said… What had Mike just said? Oh nothing important she was sure. Her feet crunched the leaves fallen from the local beech hedges. Sally preferred privet, for a year round green, but at this time of year the browny-orange leaves were quite beautiful.

A left onto the main road, and Sally felt quite light-hearted for the first time since she had started this nonsense with the Internet dating. All the weirdness would end and she could get on with enjoying her life.

132

Her headache started to lift. She had been right. All she needed was to be away from the stuffiness in her house. It was that smell of burnt plastic that was causing the headache.

Halfway to the river, Sally walked past a high hedge. She knew it surrounded some allotments with the railway track on the other side. A glance through the gate showed her obsessively neat rows of vegetables and some sheds in need of paint. There was a fine display of dahlias on one of the strips of land.

About a third of the way down on the right, Sally noticed the police tape marking off an overgrown area. Curiously, she halted in her tracks. Glancing round to see that no one was about she trod the hardcore road down the middle of the allotments.

There were no police around, just the tape. When they had visited her house, earlier, the police officers had said that her belongings had been dumped on some allotments beside the railway. Sally stretched her nose over the tape and tried to image how the ground would have looked with her mother's pearl necklace draped over the weeds.

'Goodness,' a voice behind her said. 'It's Sally Cartwright.'

Sally spun around. Her shoes slipped in the mud and she had to catch her fall on the metal spike that the police had dug into the ground to hold the tape.

A thin man with salt and pepper hair stood watching her from the gravel path. Sally recognized him from her first Internet date.

'You're not supposed to be over there,' Pete said. 'The police were digging there this morning.'

To Sally he sounded overly smug at catching her in wrongdoing, but she smiled a greeting anyway. He had been the one normal man she had met in this last week. She carefully stepped through the mud to join him on the path.

'Hi, Pete,' she said. 'It's my stuff the police found here. I had a break in. They stole my jewelry.'

'How foul for you.' He looked at the damage, then back at Sally. 'You're looking a bit paler than last Saturday. Have you been ill?'

Sally thought she must look awful since everyone was commenting on it today.

'Not really,' she said. 'I've just had a headache all morning. I'm going down to the river to try and walk it off.'

'Where's Timmy?' He looked around as if he expected to see Timmy hiding in Sally's shadow.

'He's with my friend's family today.'

'Would you like a cup of tea or coffee? Before you continue on, fortify you for the rest of your walk. I've got electricity in my shed,' Pete said. He gestured down to the next strip of land. 'I installed a solar panel. I'm very Green.'

Sally nodded. It would be pleasant to have a drink, so she let him lead her to his shed, one of the few that was neatly painted. Now that Mike was not within comparison distance, he seemed a comfortable man.

Sally looked at his neat rows of flowers. The path led down to a wooden shed with a glass lean-to greenhouse attached on the side. His solar panel looked like it could provide enough electricity to power this section of the electric lines for the railway at the bottom of the allotments.

'This looks very fine.' Sally said. 'Did you say you won prizes? Do you take them to the agricultural shows?'

'Thank you,' Pete said. 'It's all organically grown you know.'

Sally nodded and smiled at that as he opened his shed door. Inside Pete had a computer. Neatly labeled discs were stacked on one side.

'Do you keep track of the seed lines on this?' asked Sally, stroking a finger over the flat screen.

'No.' Pete turned on the kettle. 'I run my online magazine from here.'

'About Dahlias?'

'About unexplained phenomena.'

'Pardon?'

'Sit, I'll tell you all about it.' He unfolded a deck chair for Sally to sit on and pulled his wooden kitchen chair out from under the potting bench.

The bright light shone through the window straight into her eyes.

Pete had the kettle boiling in moment. 'I was just getting myself a brew when I saw a trespasser too close to the police line. I came out to run you off. How about some herb tea? I've grown them fresh in my garden here. It's a little remedy of my gran's. It's a tonic to build you up after illness, you look like you need it.'

'Really I'm not that ill,' Sally said. 'It won't taste nasty will it?'

'Oh no, I have some local honey I add to the mix, to make it taste better than the stuff my gran used to force down mine and my sister's throats.'

'Thank you, that sounds lovely.'

Sally watched as he poured hot water over a metal ball full of crushed leaves. He made up a second ball and added water to that. Pete added honey to the mix and handed a mug over to Sally.

He watched her to see her reaction. Sally sipped, cautiously. She blinked in surprise and took a bigger sip.

'This is good.' She gulped it down. 'You said you were a journalist, is that what your magazine is for?'

'That's right.' Pete put his cup down. He rubbed his finger down the side of his watch. 'I write about … odd things. Have odd things been happening to you, Sally?'

'Oh haven't they just.' She stopped. She blinked. 'No actually, I don't think they have. I…'

Pete frowned and looked at Sally's cup. Sally glanced down the honey drink was almost gone. 'That was good. What's the recipe?'

'It's a secret,' Pete said. 'Nothing odd or strange has happened?'

'Pardon?' Sally said. She looked down at her cup. 'Well thank you for the drink I need to get on.'

'No wait!' Pete dived across the shed and slammed the door shut. He stood with his back against it. 'I need to know, people need to know what happens on those dating sites.'

'Nothing happened. I met a bunch of odd men, not saving your presence, and I deleted my profile.' *Not another weirdo,* thought Sally. *I thought he was normal.*

'Are you sure?' Pete said. 'I need to know what's been going on. Did the Church set you out as bait? What?'

'I don't know what you're talking about. Let me out.' Sally glanced around the shed, looking for some other way out, but the window was fixed.

'Did that Church man alter your memory?' Pete's eyes lit up triumphantly. 'That must be it. I can get the memory out with hypnosis. You want to get your memory back don't you?'

'What Church man?'

He must have turned the heating up in the shed, because the stuffy warmth was making her feel really queasy.

'The man who was with you at the amusement park.'

'Oh Mike Rider? He's just my best friend's little brother. I've known him since primary school. Is he with the Church? What church?' Sally giggled slightly and scrubbed at her forehead. She was so hot. 'That's wrong.'

'Come on, Sally, give me my story.' Pete took her arm and tried to lead her back to the chair. 'There are people who need warning what is happening.'

'There isn't a story.' Sally remembered saying something like that to Mike, but again the memory fled.

'There has to be,' said Pete. 'I thought the drink would let you tell me, but I can see that the spell the Church Officer put on you is too strong for that.'

'Spell?' Sally said. 'Magic is for kids' stories.'

'Don't tell me I've got it wrong?' Pete slammed his fist into his shed wall. 'Your profile read like it was written to attract the Creatures of the Night. You've got to be bait?'

'I'm sorry Pete, I've no idea what you are talking about.'

Pete sagged. 'I thought that you were there to help the Church Officers capture rogue Creatures of the Night who were using the site to lure in people who subsequently go missing. I can't be wrong. It's all a big cover-up you know.' His eyes glittered as he explained.

Sally smiled in what she hoped was a soothing way. 'Honestly Pete, I've no idea what you're saying here. I need to go.'

Pete stood aside. 'I'm sorry Sally. Thanks for everything.'

Sally slid out of the shed. Was no man in York normal?

Chapter Nineteen

A frog, no a toad, hopped drunkenly across her path. Sally frowned—it was an odd time of year for toads.

A crunch behind her, and another toad crawled along. A third toad landed next to it.

Sally looked around to see who was throwing toads.

No one was about, while amphibians continued dropping to the ground around her. She hunched her shoulders and ran.

Next to the entrance gate of the allotments was a bus shelter. Sally ducked underneath as a toad plonked down on the Perspex roof. Looking up, she saw three toads crawling over the cover.

On the road, people had stopped their cars to watch toads falling from the sky. One woman lowered her window and snapped a falling toad on her mobile phone camera. Another couple was scooping toads into their car. Yerk!

Here was a supernatural happening just on Pete's doorstep. She glanced over the fence to Pete's shed, and saw him hunched over his computer.

'I hear,' said a lady, who joined her under the shelter. 'That the frogspawn gets sucked up from ponds as the water evaporates. When the frogs get too big they fall.'

Sally nodded absently. She saw her crows landing on the ground, snapping up toads for their dinner.

She waved at Pete, but his eyes remained glued to his screen as the rain of toads stopped as suddenly as it had started.

I wonder if I ought to move, thought Sally. *If outlandish things keep happening to me, then I might be a danger to my neighbors.*

She hurried home before anything else could happen. Walking along her street she saw a telephone repair van sitting outside her house. She nearly ran, but her appointment was arranged for next week.

However, as she opened her gate a man climbed out of the van. 'Mrs. Cartwright?'

She halted. 'But the appointment is Tuesday.'

The man shrugged. 'You're on my job sheet for today. I can always go away and you can see if you're on the job sheet for Tuesday.'

'No! That's okay, I'm sorry. I ... never mind.' She glanced at the photo ID clipped to the man's shirt. 'Come in.'

She opened up the house. The smell of burnt plastic rolled over them. 'Sorry, I've had such an odd week.' She stopped, now why had she told Pete that nothing had happened? She shook her head. 'The phone jack is down here. I wasn't expecting you so nothing's ready.'

'That's all right, Mrs. Cartwright. I'll just go and get my tools while you're getting the space clear for me.' After a moment she could hear the van open and the clattering of tools from behind the hedge, where the even the October sun sharply delineated the shadows.

Ignoring all that, she heaved the coats off their pegs and out of the way over the banister. 'Goodness! There's Timmy's scooter, he was looking for that.' She picked it up and leaned it against the opposite wall. With the door open she saw the repairman walking back through the gate. Now where had she seen him before?

She cleared the last of the coats as he returned with a toolbox. He dumped a cloth bag on the doormat. Looking over the area he said, 'That's fine, Mrs. Cartwright.'

'Would you like a cup of tea, I'm just about to make one for myself.'

White teeth gleamed. 'That would be just great, thanks. With milk, please.'

Sally tossed her coat over the top of the others on the banister and headed into the kitchen.

She was sure she had seen him before.

While the kettle boiled, Sally stared out of the window. There were even more crows out there. She could no longer count how many were in the roost. At least they stayed away from the house. In those numbers they would come through roof. Sally wondered if the tufts of cat fur on the posts were still there keeping out the crows.

What? She tried to figure out why she had just thought that piece of nonsense

She set out the cups and a teapot and considered whether she should walk back to the allotments and tell Pete Granger about the odd happenings she had forgotten, but the kettle boiled so she made tea.

She really needed to return home soon, she thought as she bent to scoop out the cat litter while the tea brewed in the pot. She took the mess to the downstairs toilet and took another look at the telephone repairman. He had tied his long hair away from his face to work. It looked like a cat tail down his back.

138

Where had she seen him before? Was he someone famous, masquerading as a telephone repairman for charity? Perhaps if she looked close enough she'd see the candid camera he wore. She shook her head and smiled—now she was being ridiculous. She wandered back to the kitchen, washed her hands and poured the tea.

She brought a cup through to the hall, just as Firey deigned to notice she was home. He trotted down the stairs and halted on the third step. Taking one look at the repairman, Firey fluffed up his tail and cat-swore at him. He meowled. His claws dug into the stair carpet.

'That's no way to talk to me, little brother,' the man purred as he confronted Firey.

Sally recognized the stance. It was just how he stood to face over-the-road's dog. 'You're the postman,' she blurted.

She regretted it immediately. She should have backed away before he saw her, got out the kitchen window and called the police on her mobile—which was in the pocket of her coat over the banister.

The man looked at her and blinked, slowly. He smiled—it was pure Cheshire cat. 'You noticed. That's good.'

From his toolbox he whisked out a carnival mask like a jaguar and held it over his face.

The shadows under the hedge congealed into a large panther that stalked towards the open front door.

Firey tossed more cat curses at the creature.

It flicked him a glanced then ignored him, pacing over the threshold to sit next to its master, and then curling its tail over front paws.

Sally took a step back. She felt an itching on her throat from the cat's eyes. She kept her eyes focus on the beast. *Never show fear,* that's what they were told. *Make the animal know you are the boss.* The commanding voice they were taught to use hid in her throat.

Animals could smell fear.

Now where had she seen that cat before? Mike had fought a large cat in the street? But that had been a dream. The back of her mind had a small voice saying, *'Yawn, not another uncanny happening.'*

'You needn't worry. I'm not here to hurt you,' the man said.

Sally found her voice. 'You put my postman in hospital. Why would I believe you?'

'Because I recognized you immediately from your profile.'

'We have never met before.'

Firey leapt over the banister and scampered into the kitchen, the coward; Sally wished she could do the same but the back door was blocked.

'Not in this life,' said the cat man. He held the mask away from his face. 'But in a previous life we knew one another… intimately.'

Sally opened her mouth, but closed it again when she realized there was nothing to say. She slid another step backwards, thinking fondly of the rolling pin.

'We walked the banks of the Nile at Bubastis, you were Lady Cat, the high priestess of Bast, and I was the son of the Pharaoh. It was under the full moon, the symbol of Bast in the sky. I knew we would meet again after I found this mask that links me to Bastet, the form the Goddess currently takes.'

He laid his hand on the head of the panther. It sat unmoving.

'I don't remember any of this.'

The man refocused on her from his idyllic vision of the past. 'It took hypnosis to bring my past life to the surface. I needed treatment for my depression and discovered the misery from my previous incarnation is blighting this life. You can do the same and we can finally be together.'

Sally forced the sneer off her face. 'No, thank you. I'm quite happy as Sally Cartwright.'

'But you must. It's the only way for us to be truly happy.' He frowned. 'Do you want to live a miserable existence? Never knowing bliss?'

Sally tried to smile. 'Actually, I'll stick with how I am. Bliss would get a bit wearing after a while. I deleted my profile for a reason. I want nothing more to do with any dates from the website. Now, leave this house.'

'You dare defy the will of the Goddess Bastet?'

Sally flicked a glance at the passive cat. 'Do you have a license to keep a dangerous animal as a pet?'

'A pet?' the man raised an eyebrow. 'The Goddess is not a pet.'

She had to keep him talking. Even if his talking was angry at least he it kept him from acting, while she thought of a way out of this situation. 'Why did you break in and steal my Victorian brooch?'

He scowled at her. 'What are you talking about?'

'It must have been you,' Sally said. 'You mugged the postman to scout the road and—'

'This is nonsense. We have no need for Victorian frippery. Once we are together, I will drape you in the correct attire.' Lifting the carnival cat mask to his face, he pointed at her. 'Great Goddess, she defies you.'

The panther stood. It paced forwards a step, then another.

The man followed. 'You will obey the Goddess.'

Firey chose that moment to trot out of the kitchen, with a toy mouse in his teeth. He laid this at the feet of the panther.

Both cat and man looked at the toy.

Sally took her chance. She lobbed the mug of tea she carried at the man.

It hit his head and hot tea split over his face and hands. He staggered backwards.

'Bitch!' the cat-man shouted.

She spun to flee into the kitchen and tripped over the scooter that stood against the wall.

Unable to catch her fall, she cracked her head on the lounge door. She dropped to floor. Liquid dripped on her as the cat man leaned to whisper in her ear.

'We're going to do that wedding now.' He wrenched an arm behind her back.

The room spun as he hauled her to her feet.

'Stop it!' Sally whispered. She blinked as he shoved her out into the sun. The privacy hedges blocked her neighbors' view—even if any of them had been at home at this time of day.

The panther paced back to the hedge. Momentarily, it blended into the shadows and then returned with a writhing sack in its teeth. It hauled the bag down the path that ran along the side of her house as if it were a cheetah hauling a downed antelope.

The sun out here stabbed into her eyes, adding to her headache. Where was Mike when she needed rescuing—again? A train whistle sounded from the tracks that ran near her house. Oh yes! He was gone.

'We're going to get married,' the cat man hissed in her ear. 'Right now.'

Sally stumbled as the man shoved her on. They rounded the house and onto the back patio.

The panther dropped its burden next to the barbecue. The sack wriggled.

The cat man pushed Sally down onto the wall of the raised flowerbeds. 'Watch her! Keep her there.' He looked at the panther.

The cat sat. It stared at her with unblinking eyes.

141

Vanessa Knipe

Sally darted at glance at the cat-man, then back at the panther.

The man laid a fire in the barbecue pan. He twisted a letter from his pocket into a spill and lighted it from his a lighter.

'Hear me great Bastet, as I honor you this day by doing your will.'

The panther sat and watched Sally.

She rubbed her forehead, prodding the developing bruise.

The man slid a black knife from a pocket. Sally's mouth dropped open as he slit open the sack and the Jack Russell terrier from across the road slid out. It struggled against the tight ropes. Its muzzle had been bound with duct tape.

'What are you doing? Untie that dog!' Sally pushed up, but the panther stood and yawned.

Eyeing the keen teeth, she slowly sat again.

She glanced up at where the cat-man stood. The sticks he had set on the fire were smoking badly. He muttered to himself—all the while wearing the jaguar carnival mask.

'Look—'

'Shut up, woman.' He turned to her, the knife held in his right hand. 'Your part will come shortly. You and I will be one, as we were destined to be.'

'I don't see how you can mistake me for an Egyptian priestess,' Sally said desperately. 'I'm blonde. Don't Egyptians have black hair?'

He clenched his fist around the knife, but didn't bother to turn. 'The Great Goddess Bast is often pictured with fair hair.'

Sally flicked a glance at the panther. It sat where it had been directed to sit.

The man started chanting in a language Sally had never learned.

Behind the hedge, the murder of crows cawed a dreadful plainsong accompaniment. Some of them swooped down towards the hedge but they always veered away before reaching the privet.

The chanting at the barbecue became more urgent.

A pattern emerged to the cawing, as if they sang the responses in a church service.

The man bent and hoisted the dog up to the barbecue. Surely he didn't intend to cook the dog!

'Stop!' Sally said.

The black knife slid over the dog's throat.

Its back legs kicked feebly before stilling.

The man shouted a word, and the 'amen' from the crows was raucous.

142

'No!' Sally grabbed a handful of dirt from the flowerbed. Ignoring the panther she flung the powdery soil into the man face.

Spitting dirt from his mouth, he staggered back into the barbecue. He screamed as his hand dropped into the open flame. Jerking away from the pain he tripped over a flowerpot.

Launching forwards, Sally grabbed the pot and lobbed it at him.

He coughed as the missile landed on his stomach and the begonias spilled out onto his chest and face.

She prepared to escape but remembered the cat. It sat with its tail curled over its front paws, just as it had in the hall, before the man had put the mask on.

Glancing back at the man, she saw him groggily turning over. He groped around, apparently seeking his fallen mask. It lay among the barbecue tools at the bottom of the barbecue. She darted forward and snatched the mask and one of the spikes.

The panther looked at the mask in her hands. The man groaned. 'Where…? Give that here!'

He looked at the panther. 'Get my mask back!'

Sally lifted the spike ready to stab. The panther passively watched Sally.

The cat man stared between Sally and the cat. 'Give it here, quickly before the cat goes wild.'

Sally frowned. The mask seemed important in some way. 'No. Get him.' She pointed to the cat-man.

Hand on the back wall, he scrambled to his feet and started to back up.

The panther remained impassive.

The cat-man smiled, the smile of a jaguar. He took one step towards Sally. 'I will have you. You are destined to be mine.'

Sally remembered how he had lifted the mask over his face when he commanded the panther. Hesitantly, she did the same. Seen through the eye slits of the mask, the man's eyes widened in terror.

She felt something tearing away from the man.

The man keened. His body jerked as if the ripping were a physical thing. The something flailed around then wrapped gently around her.

And she knew the mask was made of cat skin.

She felt the cat spirit. The strength of its muscle twitched at her arms. Scents of mold and the musk of fallen leaves wafted over the garden.

And then there was the man.

The cat hated the man. It awaited the order to kill.

'Chase him off,' Sally said.

The cat-man fled. Sally followed the cat. He leapt over her gate and sprinted down the street. The cat bounded after him gathering its muscle for the chase, to sink its fangs into this throat, to lap up the blood.

She could feel blood running down her throat. It was warm in her stomach.

'No!' Sally said.

The cat fought the bidding—it *always* killed the old master for the new one. Pictures of a thousand killings, rippings, satings ran through her head.

Sally shuddered. 'No!'

She saw herself being ripped open by the cat, the mask in the hand of a new master. The cat wanted to be free. Sally pulled the evil thing away from her face.

Panting as if she had done the running, muscles aching, she noticed she now stood in the front garden. She took two steps backward and slumped down onto the doorstep.

When she raised her head, the panther sat in front of her, tail over front paws, waiting.

She felt blind with the mask away from her face. She wanted to lift the mask over her eyes and feel the scent of the moldering autumn leaves, The scent of the catnip mouse that Firey had left in the hall made her want to roll over and have her tummy tickled.

Desire to wear the mask tugged at her. 'Go away.'

The cat stared at her.

'GO AWAY!' She buried her head in her knees. 'You're free.'

The panther sat in front of her, waiting with its tail tucked over its front paws.

It wanted to be free, why wouldn't it go?

Firey rubbed up against her and purred. She caught Firey in her arms and cuddled him. 'Tell it to go away, Firey, this is your house.'

Firey purred. He smelled of the sunlight he had been lying in. She remembered the freedom of running that the panther had somehow shared with her. But then there was the anger, the fear. If anyone took this mask from her she would be killed.

As long as she had the mask she would want to put it on. Sally stood up. Determined, she walked down the side of the house, to the wheelie bin, and lifted the lid.

She hesitated with the mask in her hand. Both cats followed her and sat in identical postures watching her. A drift fragrant of smoke from the fire on the barbecue wafted over the bin.

No! Someone else would find the mask. It needed a more permanent disposal. She hesitated, remembering how it had felt to run with the wind in her fur. The hunger.

And just how was she to feed something that big? Well just look at it—cat food alone would be a nightmare expense.

The carcass of the Jack Russell terrier lay on the patio. Blood puddled around its head. She pressed her hand against her mouth. How was she going to get rid of the body? She had an image of prizing up the patio slabs to hide the Jack Russell.

The frantic cawing of the crows roused her. They circled the hedge, trying to reach the fresh meat.

The mask drove people to terrible actions. She tossed the beautiful piece of art into the flames.

The carnival paint peeled.

The panther stared at her.

'Go!' she said. 'You're free.'

It prowled over to the barbecue. With troubled green eyes, it studied the burning mask.

Her face burnt.

She pressed cool hands to her cheeks, but there were no flames.

Thick black smoke coiled into the air, Sally choked. Something was strangling her. She dropped to her knees.

The panther licked her face, cooling the burns.

Firey watched from the garage roof.

As the flames died, the panther gave her one last look. Snatching the sacrificed dog in its jaws, it bounded down the garden. It grew bigger and bigger, yet more diffuse like smoke. By the time it reached the hedge, it faded into the shadows.

The crows dropped from the trees like a black snowstorm, disappearing below her hedge.

Despite the cat's first aid, Sally knew she had torn something from her soul in the act of freeing the cat. She ought to feel curiosity about what had happened but she ached. Dimly she could feel the wall in her head shift to suck up the memory of the cat priest. It will be all right, a voice whispered in her head. It sounded like Mike.

Trying to cling to what had happened, she crawled to the front of the house. It slid out of her memory like clutching at sunbeams. With the help of the front step, she got to her feet and locked the door. Dizzy and nearly fainting Sally stumbled to Gail's front door. The doorbell was almost beyond reach, but with concentration she managed a quick pat.

Gail flung the door open and caught Sally as she fell into the front hall.

'You're burning up,' Gail said, her hand stroking Sally's forehead. 'What's happened?'

Shivers ran through her body. Gail might say she was burning, but Sally was freezing. Her teeth chattered uncontrollably.

'I'm putting you to bed,' Gail said. 'I'll get you some medicine.'

'Timmy…?' Sally managed to get out the word between rattling teeth.

'Don't worry about Timmy. You know he's looked after here. You've had so much going on recently that you've forgotten to look after yourself. Now into bed.'

Gail helped Sally into her pajamas and into bed. Gail left briefly but returned with a glass of water and some tablets.

'Swallow these down,' Gail ordered.

Just drinking the water helped settle Sally's stomach.

Gail drew the blackout curtains across as Sally drifted off to sleep.

Chapter Twenty

Mike slams his hiking stick into the face of a wolf. Lightning crackles through the creature's body. It convulses. 'Get out of here, wolf.'

Sally draws her curtains over the scene. Turning, she sees a clawed hand reach through the cat flap. Paralyzed, Sally watches it turn the key. The wolf steps in. He reaches out with his clawed hand and hands her a blood red cloak. 'Join me, Sally.' He turns to gesture at an altar. 'I've got dinner ready.'

Timmy sleeps on the stone. Sally opens her eyes to scream.

The cloak turns into a shadow. Like night it covers the scene. The shadow purrs. She closes her eyes and listens to the cat song.

* * * *

She still felt washed out the next morning, but the early night, and having Timmy looked after by Gail's mum, sorted the headache.

Gail's car remained with the stumped mechanic and breakfast threatened to turn into one long family wail.

'But we must see the Grand Turk. I'm doing sailing ships this term,' Dan said. 'Uncle Mike said we ought to see it before it is sold. It might be moved.'

'Can't help it, we have no car,' Gail said. 'And Grandma and Granddad need their car today.'

Sally looked up from her small helping of cereal. 'My car is insured for all drivers. You could take my car. In fact, we can all go if we squeeze, even with the booster seats for Timmy and Sophie.'

'That's brilliant, Auntie Sally.'

The children piled off to get ready.

'Are you feeling well enough?' asked Gail. 'If you're not, don't martyr yourself for the sake of my kids.'

'I'm fine. A bit of sea air would do me good,' Sally said. 'And I can martyr myself for Timmy's fun can't I?'

'You're just hopeless.' Gail slapped her shoulder.

'So where is the Grand Turk docked?' asked Sally.

'It's at Whitby,' Gail said. 'Fancy you not knowing that.'

'Like I keep up with sailing ships! Whitby? This isn't a plot on your part to see a bit of that Necromancer concert is it?'

Gail grinned. 'You know we'll be well home before the concert starts.'

'Only teasing,' Sally said. 'I'll just have a gentle walk round to my house and pick up the car.'

'No!' Gail said. 'We'll all walk around together.'

Sally lifted an eyebrow. 'Why?'

'Oh nothing,' Gail said. 'I just thought let's not spoil the kids. They can walk as well, in fact at the moment they'll walk better than you.'

'That's not the answer. I'm not finding my keys until you spill.'

'You're a nuisance, you know. Mike thinks you're in still in danger from those lunatics that kidnapped you on Thursday night. He asked me to look out for you.'

'This is the person who got distracted so easily that I got taken off the street under her nose.' Sally laughed, trying to ignore the nagging itch of a headache that sprang up thinking about Mike. 'Oh sure, we'll all walk around to my house together, even if Timmy wails about the hike.'

'There, you're turning into a strict mum already. And do you know the worst of that situation? I still don't have a ticket for the concert.'

Sally looked sharply at Gail and realized her friend was still grinning.

Instead of moaning, Timmy raced Dan to get there first, despite Gail and Sally shouting after them.

'Dan cheated,' Timmy shouted.

'Didn't so,' Dan said. 'I'm taller than you.'

'Stop shouting,' Sally said. 'I'll back my car out, Gail. Then you can take over.'

'Yeah, thanks. Your drive is a bit tight.'

Sally walked down the drive. She gripped her keys with the ends pointing out between her knuckles. She glanced at the back door and stopped dead. The plywood board screwed over the gap had eight deep gouges along the edges, as if something had tried, with huge claws, to rip off the paneling.

With white eyes, Sally darted a glance at the trees. There were no crows.

They had all gone.

For a moment Sally felt bereft. Her personal murder of crows had flown. Laughing at her silliness, she lifted her garage door and jumped into the car. She straightened her shoulders. Even with these new claw marks, it was over.

Though, she hoped she could keep Timmy from seeing those markings, and how was she going to explain them to the double glazing people.

She started the engine and reversed the car before Gail came down to see for herself. Gail looked at Sally suspiciously.

'Why don't you stay at my house for the day?' Gail said. 'Timmy will be fine with me and the kids.'

'Actually,' Sally said, as she climbed out of the car. The air in garden smelled sweet, almost like it had with the cat mask. 'I think I'd like to get out of York for today.'

Gail glanced down the drive, but accepted the driving seat.

Sally strapped Timmy into his booster seat. Sophie's seat was added, and Dan squashed in the middle. The drinks were stowed away in the boot.

'Why can't we have a picnic?' Timmy said.

'It'd be fun to eat on the beach,' Sophie said.

'You like *sand*-witches,' Dan said, grinning.

Gail shook her head. 'End of October's too cold for a picnic, and that's final.'

Sophie and Dan subsided, but Timmy opened his mouth to continue.

Gail folded her arms. 'We're not going to even start. Until all children have stopped whining.'

Timmy's mouth dropped open and he stared at his mother.

Sally climbed into the passenger seat. 'I'm not the one driving.'

Timmy hunched back in his seat muttering.

Gail waited.

Dan nudged Timmy. 'Mum's not gonna move 'til you shut it.'

Timmy glowered but fell silent.

Gail adjusted the mirrors and set off. Sally tried not to twitch about looking for the dog-man that had attacked her house three nights ago.

It's full moon tonight, thought Sally. *Mike said it should all stop after the full moon, and look it's already happening.*

Sally smiled as she stared out of the car window. She had nothing more to worry about, so she started a game of I Spy, to Gail's groans.

'If I hear I Spy something beginning with R, I'm dumping the lot of you on the R and going home,' Gail said.

'I Spy something beginning with … T,' Sally said with a malicious grin at Gail.

'Tree,' shouted Sophie.

'No'

'What is it, mum?'

'The point is you've got to guess, Timmy.'

'Timmy,' Dan said.

149

'No.'

Gail laughingly moaned at the poor quality of modern education at every wrong answer given as she drove Sally's car to Scarborough. On the dual carriageway section Sally saw a crow lift off from some road kill.

Ignoring them it landed on the concrete parapet of a bridge and ripped apart its meal.

It paid her no attention.

They turned off at Pickering and crossed the moor, past Fylingdales listening station. And down the great hill into Whitby.

Whitby was full of people dressed in black. Sally shrank into her seat, and watched as the car passed through streets full of people that she had come to dread.

Oblivious, Gail negotiated her way to a car park near the quay where the Grand Turk was docked.

'Oh! Wow! Look at that dress!' Sophie stood awed by the fancy costumes.

It took all Sally's nerve to open the car door and get out. Only the fact that Timmy had already jumped out got Sally out of the car. Dan and Timmy were pointing toward the masts of the ship.

'Do you think it has cannons, mummy?' Timmy asked as she opened the door.

'I bet it does,' Sophie said. 'It's been used in a lot of films and TV shows you know.'

Gail got them all parceled together.

'Right, it's just gone twelve, let's have lunch in that café over there and then we'll pile onto the ship. Is that fine with you, Sally?'

'That sounds good.'

Sally hovered at Timmy's side with this congregation of the black-clothed. As she glanced nervously around, Sally saw that no one was paying them any attention. Mostly the looks they got were looks from people in a herd to people outside the herd. It felt really odd to be thought an outsider by a bunch of Goths. Some of the women wore startling clothes that would have suited Queen Victoria. Yet others wore ball gowns or wedding dresses.

What it really was, was an excuse to wear the fancy clothes and feel normal, Sally decided. Even when she had been married to Timothy she had never worn pretty dresses. With a wry smile, she remembered the properly discrete dresses worn to the University dinners. For a moment she wished she were Sophie, awe-struck by a red lacy wedding gown.

A Date with Darkness

After lunch Sally noticed more of what she considered *normal* people about, and began to relax. They wandered about gawping at the Goth Festival attendees.

Once on the ship, Timmy ran straight for the cannons. Sally charged after him—the cannons were on the edge of the ship, where a small boy might fall in the water if he was too engrossed in cannons to pay attention. From the corner of her eyes, she saw Gail shaking her head in dismay at her over-protectiveness. All three children chased around, exploring everywhere on the ship.

After a while, Sally noticed that Timmy started to drift around the exhibits in a cursory way.

'Are you all right, Timmy?'

'I need the toilet.'

Sally translated this.

'Gail,' Sally walked over to her friend. 'I think Timmy has had enough. He says he needs the toilet so I'll take him out to the one in the car park. We can sit in the car and wait for you lot.'

'Why not go back to the café?' Gail pointed to the café, now a distant landmark on the shore. 'You and Timmy can have a drink and a sit down while you wait instead of you having him bounce at you in the car. We'll join you shortly. When I've got Dan a few more photos for the school project.'

'That's a good idea. Don't hurry, we'll be fine.'

As Timmy and Sally emerged from the toilets, they were hailed. 'Sally! I didn't know you had Gothic inclinations.'

Considering she was wearing her usual pale blue anorak, this surprised Sally. Turning, she saw David Grenill. He was dressed with an eye to the local dress code, but not in a threatening way.

It was pleasant to see a face she recognized, but even with her coat zipped, she felt his x-ray eyes. Then she remembered what the police had said, but Timmy ran over before she could catch him. David took Timmy's offered hand.

'Hi David,' Timmy said. 'That was a brill daytrip to the water park.'

'Hello David. We're just here to see the Grand Turk. My friend's son has a school project or something like that.' Sally walked over, trying to smile.

David frowned at her. 'You're not looking well. Why don't I buy you a drink or something so you can have a sit down?'

He waved a hand, vaguely towards the town. The sunlight glinted off his watch.

151

Sally blinked, trying to look away from the flickering beams and say no.

Timmy jumped in. 'Mummy was just taking us to that café over there. Can I have another milkshake?'

Sally smiled as gratefully as she could manage. Since the cat-man had told her that he had no interest in the brooch, and that left David as the only suspect. Although why he would steal back a present, she had no idea. Anyway, she could dump him after Gail arrived and then she could phone the York police. Over on the ship, she could see Gail waving. She waved back.

'That's the friend I'm with today, she'll be meeting us in the café as soon as she can get her kids together so it can't be a long drink I'm afraid.'

'That's not a problem,' said David. 'I'm meeting some people shortly as well. It's good to see you again.'

They crossed the road and entered the café.

'You sit there, Sally. I really think you're not looking well. Timmy if you'll sit with your mother, I'll see if I can get a milkshake for you.'

Sally sank into the plastic chair, eager to get the weight off her feet. She really did feel tired after following Timmy around the ship with all the climbing up and down those steps that were a wicked cross between stairs and ladders.

She watched David go to the counter and order drinks. She had to admit it was comfortable just to sit with the sun shining through the window. Surely this kind man had nothing to do with the break-in at her house.

Timmy, with a milkshake on the way, was recovering nicely. He started to fiddle with the leaflets in the center of the table. The top one had a steam train on it, probably advertising the North York Moors steam railway, Sally guessed.

'Put those back,' Sally said, taking them out of his hands.

His busy fingers were soon playing with the packets of ketchup and then he knocked the salt over.

'Oh Timmy stop it,' Sally said. 'Your drink will be here shortly.'

'Here we go.' David put a tray on the table. As it crunched in the salt he grinned. 'I took a bit too long did I? I forgot to ask what you wanted Sally. I hope you don't mind coffee?'

'Coffee is just fine,' Sally said.

Timmy grabbed for his milkshake.

Sally caught it first. 'What do you say?'

152

'Thank you,' he grunted.

Sally released her hold.

The milkshake spilt into the salt pile. Sally grabbed a napkin and started to mop.

As she was dealing with Timmy, David said, 'You said you took sugar in coffee, that's right?'

'Yes thanks, two please.'

David look at his watch then stirred the coffee.

'Am I making you late?' asked Sally.

'What? Oh no, it was just a compulsive check of the time, sorry, didn't mean to worry you. Here's your coffee. Let me mop that up and you get that coffee down you.'

It was really nice to be looked after like that. The mix up over the brooch must be all a mistake, she thought as she sipped her coffee. Once the police had talked to him, it would all be sorted. Sally knew she was making nothing out of the broach nonsense.

David looked straight into her eyes. 'You look like you need to sit still for a good long time.'

Sally nodded. She felt warm and day dreamy in the sunshine.

'That's good. Why don't I take Timmy to show him the museum? He shouldn't miss that.'

Dreamily, Sally nodded again.

'Yippee!' Timmy jumped up, delighted for the extra treat. He trotted off happily, holding on to David Grenill's hand.

Trapped inside her mind Sally screamed, but all she could do was sit in the sunshine, smiling and watching the crows circle above Whitby Abbey.

Chapter Twenty One

She felt Gail shaking her. Dreamily, she smiled out the window.

'The sunshine's nice isn't it?' she said. A bright bubble of sound left her lips and floated to the ceiling, where it burst scattering rainbows.

'Sally, Sally what's happened? Where's Timmy?'

Who was Sally? Oh yes, *I* am. She giggled.

Gail tugged at her arm. 'Sally get up!'

Sally looked down from a great height at the hand tugging on her arm. She sat and smiled.

'What's wrong with Auntie Sally?' Sophie said. 'Where's Timmy?'

'Shut up, and sit with your brother,' Gail said. She grabbed Sally by both shoulders and shook her. 'Hang on, Sally. I've phoned for Mike. He'll be here soon.'

'That's nice.'

Gail's hands clenched on Sally's shoulders. 'Stop that stupid smiling.'

'Look lady.' The man who served behind the counter came out. 'You're making a fuss. If the lady don't want to go with you, she don't go.'

Sally smiled up at him. 'The sunshine's nice today.'

'Can't you see she's been drugged?' Gail said. 'He drugged her and you let that man walk off with her son.'

'They came in together, course I let him walk away with the boy. I thought he was the kid's dad.'

'Museum,' Sally said. Trying to break through sunlight in her head, she remembered that one thing.'

Gail swung around. 'What was that?'

'They've gone to the museum.' The sun called to her: the warmth sank into her bones making her feel well again. She gave up and looked out of the window.

'Which museum?' Gail had grabbed her shoulders again for another shake.

Mike burst into the café. He was panting. Sally smiled at him. With all the black he wore, he fitted into Whitby's Goth Festival.

'Your brother is very handsome.' Sally giggled again.

Mike ignored her. 'Gail! What's happened to Sally? Where's Timmy?'

'I don't know. Sally managed to tell me he was at a museum.'

154

'Who with?'

'I was watching Sally from the ship, because she was so ill yesterday and I could see she was flagging. I saw her meet my bastard ex. He brought her in here. I had to get my kids before I could come over here and rescue her. She must have been seeing him as one of her dates.'

Mike leaned closer to her. Sally wondered if he was going to kiss her. He lifted an eyelid and Sally smiled at him. She turned back to the sunlight. It was warm in the window, so she just wanted to sit here and feel well.

Mike tossed his wallet to Gail. 'See if you can get some chamomile tea would you, Gail? Horlicks or hot chocolate otherwise. Get some drinks for your kids as well.'

Gail shrugged at his request and turned away.

'Could you kids sit over at that table until your mother gets your drinks?'

He shifted his body to block his actions from the rest of the room. 'Sally look at me.'

Sally turned her head and smiled. He had a penknife out.

'I'm going to prick your finger. Hold out your hand.'

Obediently, Sally proffered her hand to Mike. She didn't even flinch when he drew a drop of blood on her left ring finger. He did the same to himself. He pressed their fingers together.

'It's the same finger,' Sally said.

'Huh?'

'But not the same knife,' she added. 'This one's clean.'

Mike frowned then shook his head. 'I need to see what happened, so I can counter it.' He paused and sighed. 'Because of how close we are, you might see things too.'

'That's nice.'

'Oh you're holding hands again. That's sweet,' Gail said. 'You two really should forget your differences. I'd like Sally as my sister-in-law, I always did. Here's the chamomile tea.' She dumped the tea on the table between them, along with Mike's wallet, and went to feed her children a substantial snack.

Mike looked like he wanted to strangle his sister; Sally giggled.

'And it would be a help if you quit the inane laughter.'

Sally tried to feel serious but there was a blanket of warmth inside that made her want to laugh. She looked straight into the open sky of his eyes.

She felt ill again and struggled to pull the blanket back over her head. Dizziness curbed her desire to laugh. She was falling through the red plastic chair and there was nothing beneath...

* * * *

David checks his watch, and then stirs the sugar into her coffee.

'Am I making you late?' Sally asks.

David smiles, it doesn't reach his anxious eyes. 'What? Oh no, it was just a compulsive check of the time, sorry, didn't mean to worry you. Here's your coffee. Let me mop that up and you get that coffee down you.'

David stares into her eyes, like Mike did, but she hasn't seen Mike yet. 'You look like you need to sit still for a good long time.'

Sally feels warm and day dreamy in the sunshine.

'That's good. Why don't I take Timmy to show him the museum? He shouldn't miss that.'

* * * *

Sally is falling, falling, falling...

* * * *

'Sir, I did what you said,' Mike says with gritted teeth. 'But something's gone really wrong. My sister called, Sally's been attacked again. And I don't want to hear anymore muttering about it being her fault.'

'I wouldn't dream of saying anything like that,' Nathan says. 'I can't say that I've ever approved of that particular pact, but as I've always refused a post on the Council then I can't complain. Didn't the forgetting take then?'

'The anti-coffee left Sally with a god-awful headache. She didn't look well when I left. It's like she knows she's forgotten something and is trying to remember.'

'That's very unusual.' Nathan runs a hand through his blond hair. 'All our people know that spell back to front. You share a blood bond, that is clear from your comments. If I had known that I would have argued more strongly against the trickery performed on you.'

'Because you hate to deal with broken-hearted young men.'

'I've dealt with them for many years, Mike. You can't teach teenagers without facing that trial. No, I would have suggested letting the infatuation run its course and helped you through with the inevitable broken heart.'

'If she had received my letters Sally would have remained true. Half of her trouble is that she feels she betrayed me by not waiting.'

'You wanted to be a witch finder, Michael. At any point you could have taken a trip home to see your True Love, but you chose not to.' Nathan makes a soothing gesture. 'These childhood affairs rarely last, and if they do they are less of an impediment than the Council believes. The Council members fear that *they* would use your wife as a lever on you. They don't realize that more often a woman brings an unmarried man low.'

Sally hears the bitterness underlying Nathan's tone but Mike fails to notice.

'What relevance has this to Sally's illness?'

'So focused on your love? Have you had sex with her? That would strengthen the blood marriage you performed as children.'

Mike flushes. 'Not recently. Only kisses, and wishes. Would that do it?'

'If wishes were horses... no Michael, wishing doesn't count.' Nathan frowns.

'So how do I help Sally,' demands Mike.

'As long as you are not close, it'll fade again. She'll only be this ill for a day or two.'

* * * *

Sally landed in the seat with a jolt. She looked up with tears running down her cheeks, but the sunshine still wrapped her head around. What had she just seen?

Mike picked up a packet of sugar and tipped it into the chamomile tea. Taking the spoon in his left hand he checked his watch then stirred the tea. He lifted it to her mouth.

Looking straight into her eyes he ordered, 'Drink the tea, Sally.'

Sally obediently sipped at the cup. The part of her that had been pounding on the feather duvet in her head came screaming to the front.

'Timmy! He's got Timmy!' She jumped to her feet.

Mike grabbed her and pushed her back into the seat. 'I know. Gail told me. What were you doing going anywhere near Gail's ex-husband?'

'Who? That was David Grenill. I've never met Dave Green, she'd divorced by the time she moved back to York.'

'Didn't you tell her the names of the men you were going out with? Drink the rest of that please.'

Sally scrunched up her face as she glugged the rest of the disgusting brew. 'No of course not! I haven't even told her you were stalking me like a jealous ex-boyfriend. Why did I just do what you told me without thinking?'

Then suddenly Sally remembered Thursday evening. Mike had done something. Her mind shrank away from admitting that he had cast a spell on her, to make her forget his explanation. She had felt ill from that moment trying to remember what she had forgot. Her eyes blazed up.

Realizing from her expression where she had got to in her memory return, Mike held up a hand. 'Instead of getting cross with me could we concentrate on getting Timmy back.'

Sally looked around as if she expected to see Timmy nearby. 'Where did he take him?'

'That's what we've got to find out. Can you remember what Dave Green said and did?'

'He called himself David Grenill, so anyway Gail wouldn't recognize it.'

'You'd be surprised,' Mike said. 'Grenill is an ancient derivation of Green hill.'

Sally took that in as she looked at Gail talking to Sophie. They were discussing the pamphlet from the center of the table. 'Why is she sitting over there? She's usually in my face about everything.'

'Gail has had enough of my world from when she was married to Dave Green. She wants to keep her kids safe,' Mike said. 'Can you blame her?'

Sally looked over at her friend, who was desperately trying to keep her children occupied and not talking about what happened. She shook her head.

'No, I don't blame her at all.'

'Was he the one who gave you the brooch?'

'Yes, after the date at the Water Park.'

She saw Mike's fight with jealousy written over his face. Despite the dire situation, she smiled. 'I spent the time trying not to wonder what you'd look like stripped down. It's not polite to think about one man while on a date with another.'

Mike laughed. Then he sobered again. 'The brooch had two spells on it. One a location identifier, which is why I wanted you at Gail's, the other was a calling spell. I'd thought I'd cancelled them both, but obviously not, since you came here.'

'We came here so that Dan could see the Grand Turk for a school project,' Sally objected.

158

'Spells work in ways that seem like coincidence, or there would be no way to hide their effects from the general public. For instance, it was me who put the idea into Dan's head. I can't guard against every coincidence.'

'Why is it that you both looked at your watch before you do the drinks spell?'

Mike blinked. 'Do I? My goodness I'd no idea. To make a drink an *anti*-spell it has to have something stirred in anti-clockwise. I imagine I'm checking which way is anti-clockwise.'

'David did it too, in exactly the same way. So he is a witch finder like you?'

'Not like me,' Mike said, stuffily. 'He consorts with the Creatures of the Night. The same people trained us. He failed the fifth year exams, so he had to drop out.'

'What does he want with Timmy? Is he like Jack Harper?'

'He's not a Creature himself. Dave acts as a daylight broker for Those who Walk in Darkness.'

'You sound like a bad b-movie sword and sorcery epic. This isn't real. None of this is real. I'm going to the police.'

Mike straightened. 'Actually, that's not a bad idea. He wanted you in Whitby for a reason, so I expect his client is waiting for him here. Police would give us manpower, which might just find Timmy, because Dave is blocking magical methods of finding him.'

Mike pushed to his feet. Gail, hearing the scrape of chair legs, turned.

'So what have you decided?' Gail asked.

'We're going to the police,' Sally said.

Gail looked at her brother.

He nodded.

Sally took pity on Gail.

'Why don't you take my car and go home? If I don't phone to tell you we've found Timmy, could you feed Firey?'

'We'll go home on the train,' Gail said. 'We just saw an advert for a steam train. It's leaving at four so we just have time to catch it. You might need the car.'

Gail gave Sally a quick hug and gathered her children. She almost ran away from the abnormal situation. It would have been comical if Sally felt like laughing.

'We've got to check the museum first,' Sally said, suddenly remembering. 'He said he was taking Timmy to the museum.'

'I doubt he's taken Timmy there.'

159

Vanessa Knipe

Sally frowned. 'What are you doing in Whitby? I thought I'd taken you to the station to go to a conference.'

'I'm working. Don't ask any more.'

'I'm getting well sick of you telling me not to ask,' Sally said. They left the café following the direction Gail and her children had taken.

'Not like I can help that,' Mike said. 'I wasn't even cleared to help you just then. I ran out on a conversation with my tutor. I hope he's going to be more amused than angry. Nathan usually is, some of the others would get uppity.'

'I dreamt about them.' Sally charged along the pavement to the museum.

'You would,' Mike said.

Sally reached the ticket booth. 'Has a man come in here with a little boy?' Sally fished in her pocket and brought out a wallet. She pulled out a passport photo of Timmy. 'This little boy?'

'I don't remember them, but I see a lot of people.'

Mike pulled Sally away before she exploded at the ticket taker.

'Come on Sally,' Mike said. 'Let's go to the police station. He'd be using an aversion spell anyway. No one is going to remember him unless they are really looking for him. We just need to get him distracted enough hiding from the police, splitting his power so much that I can get through his blocks and get a location.'

'Why didn't you say?'

'I thought I did. I agreed to the police.'

'Try and remember that some of us aren't totally up on this magic.' Sally spat the word out.

Chapter Twenty Two

The reaction at the police station was all Sally could have hoped for. The beginning explanations were a bit hairy. The police were all attention when they realized a little boy had been kidnapped in broad daylight in Whitby.

'So you just sat there and let him take your boy?' asked the desk sergeant, a bit bewildered.

Mike smiled coldly. 'I expect he used one of the fast metabolizing date rape drugs, you know they make a person very compliant. All the women in London have to guard their drinks against them. I used a technique I learned through living there to bring her out of the daze.'

Sally wondered if Mike was doing a mind control thing.

'Oh yes.' The sergeant smiled. 'We don't have much of that in Whitby, but I imagine you're correct with all these people coming from everywhere.' He looked down at his notes. 'Let's get this straight. You'd been on one date with him, an Internet date… that's dodgy to do I'd heard. So your little boy, Timothy Cartwright known as Timmy, went off with this David Green or Grenill happily when the man drugged you.'

'That's right,' Sally said. She was nervous now, maybe she was wrong to bring it to the police, but Mike had said it was a good idea.

'And you are, sir?'

'I'm Michael Rider. My sister, who came to Whitby with Mrs. Cartwright, asked me to help because she had to take her children home. I'm registered at the hotel.' Mike gestured towards the top of the cliffs.

The policeman nodded. 'I'll take this picture and get it photocopied. As soon as that's done we'll have people out looking for your little boy.'

Sally and Mike were shown into a private room and given tea. Sally paced around the room.

'Why did I do the Internet thing?'

Mike watched her as she walked over and pounded a fist on the wall. It jarred her aching wrist from where she now remembered being bound and gagged by a Vampire.

'What does Dave Green want with Timmy?' She swung around to face him. 'I need to be out there looking for him.'

'You need to sit down and drink your tea.'

'This isn't helping!' screamed Sally. 'Why are you here? You should be out there looking for Timmy.'

'We'll go out shortly.'

A knock on the door heralded a policewoman. 'Mrs. Cartwright, we've got people out on the streets now, showing pictures of Timmy to locals and festival goers—someone is going to remember seeing Timmy.'

Sally clenched her fists as Mike stood. 'Thank you.' He said. 'I'm going to take Sally up to my hotel and give her dinner. You'll find us at the hotel restaurant, or on our mobiles.'

'I can't I've got to—'

'Mrs. Cartwright, what you've got to do is keep well. Eating diner is a good idea. You come back to the station afterwards and ask for me. I can give you an update on how our investigation is progressing.'

Mike tucked his arm through. 'Come on, Sal.'

Sally could feel herself going all obedient again. She pushed his hand off her arm. 'Don't do that!'

'Then walk out of here with no more fuss, please.'

Darkness was creeping through the streets of Whitby as they left the police station, even though it was only 4.30 PM.

She looked into the sunset holding back the tears with a fierce determination. 'I'm not having dinner when I could be looking for Timmy.'

Mike held up his hands in a gesture of surrender. 'Okay, we'll go down to the beach. I'll have a go now but after that I'll need a promise.'

Sally studied him suspiciously. 'What's the promise?'

'That we can go and have dinner. I need some food before I start a proper hunt for Timmy.'

Sally frowned. 'Why—'

Mike interrupted. 'We're setting up a distraction for Green. Once he spreads his power thin enough, trying to stop the police and other people from finding him, I can break through and locate Timmy. But, I need a lot of extra energy before I start hunting by magic, which I will get from eating, so come with me and keep me company, please.'

Sally sighed. 'Fine, we'll do it that way.'

Mike stared in her eyes for a moment, then accepting her word, he led the way through Whitby to a secluded section of the beach.

'Why here?' asked Sally.

'I want some peace and quiet where I can concentrate on finding Dave.'

162

'You sound like you know him well?'

'I do,' Mike said coldly. 'We trained together. He was an apprentice too and three years older than me. How do you think he met Gail?'

'I never asked. I wonder why?'

'Because Gail has a spell on her so that no one does ask about Dave Green, unless she brings it up first. Now, if you don't mind I need some quiet.'

Sally almost bit her tongue as Mike led her down some slippery steps to the sheltered beach. The sun was dropping below the horizon, turning the sand to blood; it crunched under her feet like ice.

Mike stood there. He seemed to be studying the way the rising moon reflected on the incoming tide.

Sally wanted to scream at him to do something, but didn't know enough about what he did for a living to know if he was already at work. She dropped onto the sand and scrunched up in a tight ball. The air was cold, she had no idea where Timmy was, and no one seemed to be able to help. It was like the bleak days, a few weeks after her husband's death, when everyone had gone home to their lives and she was left with no one to help her with this new baby that just screamed all the time.

She bit into her hand to stop herself from crying. That wouldn't help anyone.

Mike shifted his weight and looked around. He scanned the beach as if he expected that she might have walked off.

With an impatient noise, he strode towards the steps and nearly tripped over Sally on the ground.

'Oh there you are. I've got a vague impression.'

He held out a hand to her.

She grasped it. He was warm, almost feverish to the touch.

He wrapped his fingers around her icy cold hand.

'God you're freezing here.' He tugged her into his coat.

Bodies touching, she could feel how cold she had become.

'Sorry, I tend not to notice how long it takes to work that sort of spell. No don't move yet.'

He wrapped the leather coat around her back and she realized that he was passing her some of the heat he had generated.

Sally leaned into him, face burrowed into his shoulder.

'Warm enough yet?'

Sally nodded, though she really just wanted to stay there.

He unfolded his arms and grabbed her hand. With long strides he led her from the beach and into town.

'Right, now we get dinner.'

'But you said—'

'Sally you promised,' Mike said. 'And I really do need some food before looking any further.'

Mike tucked an arm around her as they walked up the hill to his hotel. His black leather trench coat was high fashion in Whitby today.

Sally in her blue jeans, blonde hair and blue anorak felt really out of place. But no one was paying them any attention.

The streets were crowded with festival goers. The clubs and pubs advertised drinks with Goths in mind. The closest challenged them to drink all the Seven Deadly Sins in one night. Another board offered Transfusion and Afterlife as refreshments.

From everywhere her ears were assaulted with dark rock music.

Struggling for something neutral, that didn't sound inane, Sally said, 'You seem to be doing nothing but looking after me these days.'

Mike shrugged. 'At first I was doing so because the Council told me to find out why the Creatures of the Night had congregated in York. I continued with my protection, even after they ordered me to stop, because it was you. Despite all I thought was between us, I couldn't let anything happen to you.'

'I was so furious to keep finding you in my garden. I kept coming up with odd ideas about what you were doing. Then I discovered you were protecting me.'

'Well, hell, what did you think I was doing in your garden at past midnight? Indulging in some weird flagellation ritual?'

'You have turned out to be a Goth!'

Mike raised his eyes to the heavens. 'The witch finders police this festival the way we police all alternative lifestyles festivals, music festivals, rock concerts, because alternative lifestyles are a good place to hang out if your lifestyle is slightly more alternative than most and you want to hide from the mainstream. I'm just as likely to be found lying in a muddy ditch, watching witches on hillsides as in a comfy hotel. A Goth Festival is the perfect place for the Creatures of the Night to hide. We just want to make sure no one notices anything odd.'

'Watching witches dance naked!'

Mike sighed. 'You have some remarkably shallow notions in that pretty head of yours.'

The climb up the hill to Mike's cliff top hotel was tiring.

'Pete Granger tried to break your spell,' Sally said. 'So he could report on what he called odd happenings in his paranormal magazine, about the dating agency.'

'He's one of many,' Mike said. 'No one in the mainstream believes cranks like him. Here we are.'

He took Sally through the outside door to the restaurant. 'Most of the witch finders are going to be a bit stuffy about a woman with me.'

'Yes,' Sally said coldly, 'You explained.'

'Michael Rider, room 45,' he said to the major domo. 'And guest.'

He shrugged out of his coat to hand to a waiting assistant, and Sally got a proper look at what he was wearing. He had coupled his black jeans with a black velvet smoking jacket and black shirt with a spider-lace collar.

She sniggered.

Looking her up and down he said, 'you wear much too plain clothing. You ought to show off more.'

She hid her smiles by turning away to take off her own anorak.

It was handled as if it was radioactive. Perversely, Sally wished it were printed in orange and yellow flowers too. She'd feel more apologetic for being underdressed if everyone wasn't busy rubbing her nose in it.

'He's not dressed up fancy.' Sally nodded at a young man in ripping jeans and a well-washed tee shirt. She frowned, she was sure she had seen that whip-like red pigtail before. But where?

Mike looked up and nodded. 'How you dress depends on what section of the festival you're working. Hi Josh.'

Josh walked over and grinned at him. 'Still disobeying everyone? That's not like you.'

'I just have to.' Mike shifted his feet. 'Is Mr. Dunkley here yet?'

'Naw, he's got held up at Avesbury.' Josh's eyes went blind.

Sally clutched at Mike's arm and glanced up at him.

Josh blinked and refocused on Mike. 'And when you get into a fight with him, try not to hurt him. I'll be there as soon as I can. See you round.' Josh wandered out, his red plait swinging between his shoulder blades.

Sally uncoiled. 'And what was that about?'

'He sees things, like I do.' Mike shrugged. 'If he could have told me more, he would.'

'Well what use is that?' Sally asked. 'Don't you like him?'

Mike turned back to her. 'Josh is great. Why?'

'You seem to be a bit wary of him, that's all.'

Mike rubbed the back of his neck. 'Josh is… well he's very powerful. I once watched him take out my tutor, deliberately…' He trailed off.

Sally opened her mouth to demand an explanation, but the waiter returned. 'This way, Mr. Rider.'

Sally huddled close to Mike. The room was filled with people in black. No one else was dressed out of the current fashion statement—blue jeans were just not the in-thing.

As Mike, rather formally, helped her to sit, a smartly dressed man lifted an eyebrow at Mike. The man's waistcoat was a riot of dark colors under a frockcoat and Sally recognized him from her dreams as Nathaniel Trewithick, the man whose opinion was indispensable to Mike. His face clearly said, there had better be a good explanation for this woman. Mike nodded at the older man, who continued his journey out of the dining room.

As he sat down next to Sally she said, 'Do you really want me here? I'm causing trouble.'

'Don't worry about Nathan,' Mike said. 'He's a little off women at the moment.'

'I thought you were all "off women",' Sally said tartly.

'Nathan is a bit of a rule breaker,' Mike said. 'But he's gone all rigid since his last mistress dumped him.'

'Oh so it's the proper way around for the man to dump the woman is it?'

Mike made calm down gestures with his hands. 'From Nathan's point of view, yes.'

'And do you share his opinion?'

'Can we argue later, please?' Mike lifted a hand to call the waiter.

Sally sagged in her chair. 'If I don't stay angry, I'll just collapse in the vapors like some useless Victorian melodrama heroine. Timmy's all I've got left.'

Sally felt that at this point Mike should be wrapping her in his arms, stroking her hair and telling her it would be all right, but instead he brightened and snapped his fingers.

'Victorian, that's it, you're a genius Sally.'

Sally decided he was mad. 'What are you talking about?'

'The Victorian brooch was the link. What arrived in Whitby in the Victorian Era?'

'Go on enlighten me.' Sally sighed.

'Dracula!'

'Don't be silly,' Sally said. 'That's just a story.'

Mike looked heavenwards. 'The lack of belief is the reason we let the story out. Fictionalized accounts of magic are the best way of covering our activities. I wonder if it is possible to lure the creature through time so that it didn't die back in Victoriana?'

'By offering it my son!'

'You are partly right, I suspect, but there has to be more to it than that. Now I really need some advice. I wish Dunkley were here, but Nathan should know.'

The waiter arrived at the table. Mike ordered dinner for them.

Sally eyed the formal surroundings with distaste, but she let Mike do all the talking with no argument for now. Sally had to admit that his time living in London had put a lot of polish on his manners. She had moved in academic circles with Timothy where manners had been less formal.

Watching the men walking in and out, she leaned closer to Mike. 'Which are the witch finders then?'

Mike opened his eyes wide then smothered a laugh with his napkin. 'The dyspeptic-looking ones.' He leant conspiratorially close. 'Energy for the magic we do comes from within ourselves. It's the ultimate in diets. I have to rely on glucose tablets. Most of us have our little tricks.'

Sally looked around at the people, she actually didn't see any difference between people in the restaurant, but guessed the ones with women were probably not Mike's colleagues. Her mind drifted.

'Why couldn't Pete Granger break your spell?'

Mike blinked. 'I have had access to a centuries old tradition of education. Most people either start from scratch with experimentation or they join one of the official UK covens. I would guess that your Pete Granger is one of the former. Look, I shouldn't really be discussing this.'

'I know, you can't tell me anymore,' Sally said. She toyed with her meal a little more, and then put her knife and fork down. 'Could we hurry so we can find Timmy?'

'I'm finished. Let's see if the police search has caused a thinning of Green's magic so I can follow up on my idea.'

Mike signed the bill the waiter presented him with. There was no pretense of equality here. Under other circumstances it would have grated up Sally's spine, but right now she wanted Timmy back so she squashed the irritation.

Chapter Twenty Three

Sally followed Mike as he charged across the lobby, energized by his meal.

'Mr. Rider!'

The authoritative voice brought Mike to a stop. He turned to face the man who was walking down the stairs.

'Ah! Hello, Mr. Marishes,' Mike said. 'Have you seen Trewithick about?'

Mr. Marishes had his eyes fixed firmly on Sally. His nostrils flared as if at some noxious stench.

'What have you brought a woman with you for? You are as aware of the rules as I am. After all, I was the one who drummed them into you.'

Sally stared at the man. It was hard to believe Mike's tale that these people hated women, but it seemed that this man embodied that dislike.

'Never mind that,' Mike said. 'There's going to be a big breakthrough tonight. I need to talk to Trewithick so we can work out how to contain it.'

'Nonsense,' Mr. Marishes said. 'If a breakthrough were happening, the alarm wards for the Council would be sounding. Nothing major will happen tonight. No one would be stupid enough to do any Dark Working with such a gathering of Church Officials here.'

'It hasn't started yet,' Mike said. 'We can get the jump on *them*.'

The man permitted himself a smug smile. 'None of the other seers have predicted a breakthrough. How would you have prior knowledge of this activity?'

'They've kidnapped my son,' Sally burst out. 'They're going to sacrifice him.'

Mr. Marishes almost jumped as a *woman* spoke to him.

'Ah, yes. This must be the woman who has advertised her offspring on the Internet for *them* to find. I don't think you can complain now, if *they* take you up on the offer. Michael you need to return to your duties.'

There was an odd intensity to Mr. Marishes's voice. An image of David Green trying to get her to have sugar in her tea at the water park, what seemed an age ago, popped into her head. He had used the same compelling voice.

Mike just ignored it.

'No really, Mr. Marishes,' he continued. 'I'm absolutely sure they have found a way to drag the elemental that formed *Dracula* forward to this century so that We cannot kill it back in the 1890s.'

'Michael return to your duties.'

This time Mike caught the intonation. He lifted his head, and then he frowned.

'Dear me, Marishes.' Sally recognized the rich voice sounding from the shadows from the dreams. 'Haven't you figured out that the link to Michael has failed? You're usually so quick on the uptake too.'

Nathaniel sat in one of the leather-covered seats in the lobby, shrouded in shadows. A silver-topped, black cane leaned on the chair arm. Carefully, the man stood.

Nathaniel Trewithick now wore a leather trench coat over the formal clothes, suggesting that he was already on his way out. He tucked his cane under one arm and walked out of the shadows, in one hand he held a cigarette and in the other a brandy glass. By his careful walk, Sally thought that this might not be the first filling for the glass.

'Trewithick! You are smoking... this is a non-smoking hotel,' Mr. Marishes said, His hot color rose in his face, almost like a Victorian apoplexy.

Nathaniel flicked him a sneering look. Sally thought that Mike had yet to learn the full sneer if he had copied the art from Nathaniel Trewithick. He had certainly copied the ponytail and the leather trench coat from his master.

Nathaniel's coat hung open, revealing the full glory of the waistcoat that had dazzled Sally from a distance. A design of peacock feathers displayed a rainbow of dark colors, which were woven into the black material. He looked every inch a successful stage magician, right down to the cane he had tucked under his arm.

'Yes, Mrs. Cartwright,' Nathaniel Trewithick said, in a creamy coffee voice that matched his clothes. The dreams had failed to convey that full richness. 'There is a certain sort of righteousness that always looks dyspeptic.'

Transferring the glass to his cigarette hand, he bowed over her hand, like an old time gentleman. Under the courtesy onslaught, Sally had to force herself to remember that this man had admitted to separating her from Mike.

'Come, Michael, let us take our filthy habits outside. There we may indulge in them without upsetting poor Marishes's digestion further.'

169

His expansive gesture took in Sally.

Mr. Marishes looked very offended by all three of the people in the lobby.

'But sir…' Mike tried to interrupt, but a faintly weaving Nathaniel ushered him out.

Outside the door, Nathaniel put his glass in a plant pot and became less drunk. He waved them to a terrace at the side of the hotel, which in summer would provide *al fresco* dining for the hotel guest but was deserted on this October evening.

'There are things I can say drunk, which would offend more if I said them sober,' Trewithick said. He leaned on the terrace wall and look out at the sea, taking a drag on his cigarette.

At least, Sally thought, *Mike hadn't copied that habit from his teacher.*

Mike politely awaited his master's next words. Sally had no such scruples.

'Can you help me with rescuing my son?' she demanded.

'No,' Nathaniel said. 'Even Mike is not supposed to be involved, but there seems to be a prior blood contract between you that means, by our rules, he has to intervene. Isn't paradox marvelous?'

'If you can't help, then I'm going to hunt for him myself,' Sally said.

Mike waggled his hands behind Trewithick's back in a furious calm down gesture. Sally gritted her teeth.

Trewithick smiled at her then flicked an eye towards Mike so that she knew that he was aware of what was going on behind his back.

'I've often thought,' Trewithick said. 'That swimming out into the sea as far as one can, until exhaustion sets in, then just stopping fighting would be the nicest way to die.' He stared at the moon-scarred sea.

'But you're Religious, like Mike.'

'You see a lot, Mrs. Cartwright. Lapsed, definitely lapsed.'

'I saw you fiddling with a crucifix in one of the funny dreams I've been having,' Sally said. 'You know I've been having Mike's dreams?'

'Yes, he told me. You must have the tightest link between two people that I've seen.' He lapsed into silence contemplation of the moonlit sea again.

Sally cast a look at Mike, telling him to hurry this up.

Mike nodded. 'Nathan, I need some advice. I wasn't joking when I said I think there is a major breakthrough happening here in Whitby, tonight.'

'A Halloween under a full moon, would be a major belief focus for *them*. So you think *they* are bringing the Dracula entity forwards...' Trewithick shook his head but Mike looked ready to argue.

Trewithick lifted a hand. 'What do our records from the 1890's show?'

'The killing of the Dracula entity,' Mike said. 'But can't they bring it forwards from before it was killed?'

'Whatever it is that they are doing it will not include bringing something to our time that we have records of its demise. That is not possible.'

Mike looked unconvinced and prepared to argue his point.

Sally interrupted. 'I'm sick of this talking around the subject and getting all b-movie horror flick talking about *them*. Would someone please explain?'

Trewithick lifted an eyebrow at her impatience.

'Sally isn't like other women Nathan,' Mike said.

'All women want the same thing,' Trewithick said bitterly. 'To bring a man so low he will rejoice that all she wants is for him to stuff her full of babies.'

Mike's face went darker under the light of the full moon. Sally nearly giggled at him.

He's blushing, she thought.

Trewithick smiled. 'Ah well, there's no hope for you then if she's convinced you that you want that too. I request you consider again, before you turn in your license.'

'I like this career, so I am thinking, very hard,' Mike said.

Trewithick sighed. 'I wish that were true. Very well, Mrs. Cartwright, let me tell you about *them*.'

Sally had a qualm. She looked down at Whitby, with its streetlights shining below them. Somewhere Timmy was being held. She imagined him terrified and cowering away from his captors.

'Do we have time for this?' she asked.

Mike jumped in before Trewithick had done more than let his sneer cross his face. 'It's part of *their* belief system that the denouement of any sacrifice must be at exactly midnight, and it's only just past nine. Don't worry about Timmy being scared. Green will be keeping him in a Xanadu spell. He won't want to deal with a hysterical child.'

'But we have still to find where he is hidden.'

Mike made a *calm down* gesture. 'I'm pretty sure I'll be able to find him shortly. I nearly broke through before we had the police search to distract Dave.'

Sally pursed her lips. 'Fine, tell me about *them.*'

Trewithick continued gazing at the sea. 'Imagine a war that has been going on for so long that most people have forgotten what started it, or indeed that it is going on at all. Christianity sees the nature spirits as demons, but nature spirits eat belief. They started to act like demons and they demanded that their ceremonies of worship become increasingly dark. Some of the Druids became dark priests, now called sorcerers, to dark powers.

'We allied ourselves with Rome against the evils of human sacrifice, and we have steadily tried to wipe out the nature spirits, which we now call demons. It's a never-ending war. At the forefront are the Demon hunters like, your Michael, Marishes and myself.'

'So your people just joined up with the winners, to write the history.' Sally's nostrils flared in distaste as she looked at Mike. 'And you are a part of this... this genocide?'

Mike flicked a frantic glance at Trewithick.

'It happened a long time ago.' Trewithick grimaced. 'We cannot be forever regretting the past: we'd never have the time to correct the failings around us now. And that is what we do. We work to protect the people—normal people—from a problem caused by our ancestors. Surely twenty centuries of continuous penance is enough even for you.'

Sally plastered a smile on her face at the absurdity of this conversation. *He seems to think he's in a hall lecturing students,* she thought. But he continued.

'They only become really dangerous when they incarnate. It is possible that Timmy will be used for incarnation, or he could be a sacrifice to draw favor. All you need to find out is who.'

Mike jumped in to restart his previous argument but Nathan held up a hand to stop him. He continued with his lecture.

'I'm not saying they are not reaching for a vampiric entity. You see Mrs. Cartwright, everything you have heard about a Creature of the Night is an incarnation of one of these Nature Spirits turned demon. Discarnate spirits can demand worship, and they can grant their priests extra power by infesting them. I don't know if this is considered a privilege or not—the priests seem more inclined to offer others than themselves as potential vessels for demonic infestation.'

'You keep going on about *infestation* as if it's nothing more dangerous that the fleas on my cat,' Sally said.

'And what caused the bubonic plague?'

'You are not going to convince me that was caused by these demons.'

'I wasn't going to try,' said Trewithick. 'As it was caused by *harmless* fleas.'

Sally opened her mouth to speak, and then closed it slowly as she thought about what he had said. To cover her confusion she turned disbelieving eyes on Mike. 'Are you telling me all this because you are going to wipe my brain clean again?'

Trewithick laughed. 'The trouble with young people is that when they get agitated they tend to do things too enthusiastically. Michael is one of our most powerful practitioners, so when he gets excited and does a magic canceling spell he has cancelled any magic on you for the next month or so. By then the memory will be in long term storage and no spell on Earth will wipe it.' He turned to look straight into her eyes. 'No, Sally I'm telling you as one of a very few women who become a witch finder's wife.'

'I'm not sure I want to join this mad world that you belong to,' Sally said. 'Does the other side have similar archaic rules about women?'

'I believe that sorcery is an equal opportunity career option.' Nathaniel sighed. 'Your son will remain in danger from *them* even if he does survive this encounter. And that is my why advice to you both has to be, go and mourn your little boy and breed replacements by the score.'

Sally slapped him across the face. She turned and walked away.

Mike hovered between staying with his master and following Sally. She turned and stood at the edge of the terrace waiting to see which way Mike would jump. She tried not to care if Mike chose to stay with his colleagues.

Chapter Twenty Four

Mike hung back, standing between Sally and his old tutor. 'Nathan I need help, please?'

Trewithick leaned back on the terrace wall. 'The Council has issued a statement deploring your actions.'

'Help me, Nathan.'

'I can't help you. The Council has sent me out to call my puppy into its kennel. They want you to return to your duties.'

'I am doing my duties!' He stared at Trewithick. 'And what do you think I should do?'

'I never think for anybody else. Do what you think is correct and pay the price demanded.'

Trewithick straightened. He took a last draw on his cigarette and flicked the stub into a nearby bin.

'Nathan, help me, please.'

'I can't,' Trewithick whispered, his eyes dying. Hesitantly, he walked towards the hotel.

'Nathan, how can you just leave?'

Sally could see the hero worship falling from Mike's eyes. It was painful to watch.

Mike extended his staff and planted it in a crack in the terrace paving.

'Nathan help me! Thrice I ask and bind you to it!' His voice thundered in the darkness.

Trewithick stopped. His face screwed up, as if he was fighting himself. Turning to face Mike, he planted his cane into the paving. The two witch finders stood staring at each other and straining. They seemed to grow tall, blocking out the moonlight.

Sally shrank back against the terrace balustrade. She realized that some sort of power struggle was going on. Mike suddenly bowed his head. He leaned exhausted on the hiking stick. If it had been a power struggle then Mike had lost for Nathan still stood tall.

Mike stepped forwards. 'You've got to help us. Who else could?'

Nathan stared him in the face again. A sneer fastened onto his lips

'Come, then.' From the cane, Nathan slid out a sword. It flashed silver in the moonlight as he saluted Mike. 'Make me.'

Mike ran a nervous hand over his hair tucking some strands behind his ears. Then he lifted his staff. 'I have to.'

Nathan nodded, then dropped into an *en guard* stance, which Sally recognized from the fencers at Helmsley. Mike rushed in, lifting his staff high and using the tactics he had used against the dog-man. No! She should accept its real name: werewolf.

Nathan dodged under the falling staff. He pricked Mike's shoulder, but the leather coat held the blade back.

His staff crackled with the blue lightning again as Mike brought it towards Nathan.

Lifting his sword, Nathan took the full blow of the lightning into the sword and with a laugh snapped the blade to the ground. The lightning earthed out.

Shaking his head mockingly, Nathan flicked his blade at Mike.

Sally got the feeling that Nathan was playing with Mike. Clearly Mike had noticed this as well. He leaned on his staff to shorten it. Then he started to fence properly with Nathan, just like the show fighters had.

The smile faded from Nathan's face. Mike was well trained; Sally could see it in the concentration that both men put into their fencing.

She wondered at the life they must lead that would mean that they had to learn these ancient skills for their job. She was not suited to the lifestyle of witch finder's wife. She was a young widow already, it was not something she wanted to repeat.

Both men were so focused on their fight that they did not see other members of this witch finders's guild emerge from the dining room to watch the contest. Neither man was panting.

They must be supremely fit, Sally thought. She'd seen Mike fight these Creatures of the Night and still be fine the next morning.

Nathan had Mike on the retreat. He had backed as far as the balustrade. Nathan came in for a throat thrust.

For one moment, Sally believed that the man was going to kill Mike, and then Mike extended his hiking stick to full, blue lightning surging down the shaft.

The force of the two together hit Nathan on the chest and sent him flying. The sword flew out of Nathan's hand and skittered across the terrace.

Mike stepped forward holding his crackling staff above Nathan's throat.

The young man with the red plait of hair stepped out onto the terrace. 'Stop this now.' His voice rang with confidence.

Mike jumped away, panting, and Nathaniel got up from the ground.

Josh looked between then. 'Mike, I need to talk to you. Mr. Trewithick, I believe I'll leave Mr. Dunkley to talk to you.'

Trewithick bowed stiffly and walked to the hotel entrance, past where Sally huddled against the balustrade.

As he passed Sally he said, 'Say a prayer for a fallen angel.'

Then he stalked into the hotel. From his other pocket he produced a flask, identical to Mike's, from which he took a swig, indicating his intention to get as drunk as he had pretended to be earlier.

Under the gaze of all his colleagues Mike had defeated his master.

The shocked witch finders slunk away from where Josh stalked towards Mike. The three of them were left alone on the terrace.

Josh shrugged. 'Mike go and get on with it. If there really is a breakthrough, call me. I can help. Have you got your prayer book? You'll need this to hold them off until I get there.' He slid a hand into his pocket. He held out a slip of paper with a series of number ratios on it. 'You might need to get inventive to fight them. While I respect your vision, I still have to follow my ordained tasks.'

Mike lifted a slim black volume from his pocket and slipped the paper inside before returning it to his pocket. 'Thanks. I—'

Josh shook his head. 'If you are wrong, you'll answer to Mr. Dunkley. You know that.'

'I know.'

Josh looked through them. 'Have you tried the Dark Web yet?'

'I'll do that next.' Mike grabbed Sally's hand and dragged her off the terrace, his face a picture of betrayal.

'What did Nathan say to you?'

'"Say a prayer for a fallen angel".'

'I wonder what he meant by that?'

'Obviously a reference to his being lapsed. Now what's with the book?'

'Nathan has never missed a mass in all the time I've known him,' Mike said. He stared at the hotel entrance as if he thought he ought to go after his one-time tutor. 'Whatever else he is, he's not lapsed.'

'The book,' Sally said trying to drag him out of his abstraction.

Mike slid a hand into his pocket as if reassuring himself the book was still there. 'It's the *Book of Common Prayer*. It helps us focus.'

'And how did that young man get to order the lot of you about. How did he know about the fight beforehand?'

'Josh? He's in training to be the next Watcher. The one who keeps us all in line and following the rules. Mr. Dunkley is the current Watcher.' He looked down at Sally and he smiled. 'He's promised his help. That's good. I can't believe I won against Nathan!'

'Why didn't he use magic against you? Even when you used it.'

Mike shrugged. 'Knowing Nathan it will be some obscure point of honor that a teacher may not harm his student with magic or something like that, which he has forgotten to mention to me.' He took out the prayer book and opened it, checking it against the numbers on Josh's list. 'If I need *these* passages, it's time for serious thought.'

Sally peered over his shoulder but the printing was tiny. 'How did he know?

'Because he has Sight, like me. It's not a common ability.' Mike frowned. 'I need better light, but I don't think going to my hotel room is a good idea at the moment. Ah over there.' He took Sally absently by the hand and returned the book to his pocket. 'Don't worry Sally. Now that I've got this, we'll stand a much better chance of getting Timmy back.'

He led her to another café. She was trying hard not to ask questions but she saw neither Dave Green nor Timmy in the room. 'What do we need in here?'

'It's an Internet café,' Mike said. He sat at a computer; lifting a hand he ordered two coffees.

Sally dragged up an extra chair and watched his hands flicker over the keyboard.

Two coffees were dumped beside him.

Still watching the screen he unfolded his wallet and got out some money. The waiter took it and went away.

Sally sipped her coffee, being very careful to get to it before Mike did. He grinned at her, and tossed her the sugar and a spoon.

'I have to crawl the Deep Web,' he said. 'The Dark Web is the other name for it. It's the part of the Internet not registered with search engines. It's vast, bigger than the web you can access by normal methods. That means you can hide things in here.'

Typing rapidly, he brought up a list, canceled it, and brought up another. Finally, he scrolled down the screen and stopped.

'Ha! That's it.' He took a sip of his black coffee.

A website appeared on screen 'It's been heavily coded but luckily I already know Dave Green's fingerprint. Okay, they're in Whitby still. That's a good start. See here, he's insisting that the purchaser be at the Festival.' He tutted. 'He's raised the price on Timmy—because they were trying to go around him and diddle him out of his fee—and he's insisting on them hiring himself as sorcerer for any ritual necessary.'

'What? How much does he want? I'll give him anything.'

'No,' Mike said. 'We can't do it that way. It would reinforce the belief that Timmy is property to be bought, sold and used. And in my world, belief is very important. The bidding's nearly over.'

Mike kept one hand on the edge of the screen—with the other he sipped his coffee.

Sally drank hers—a full mouth prevented her from screaming at him to put in a bid. She took a deep breath. She needed to trust that Mike knew more about this situation than she did. Okay he'd been tricked into leaving all those years ago, but he did mesh with this weird world of shadows.

Mike swigged the last of the coffee and logged out. He stood and stretched. Sally followed him as he walked to the door to pay for his time.

Once in the street, Sally clenched her fists. 'Well?'

Mike looked down at her. 'Oh God Sally, I'm sorry I'm not used to working with someone who has no idea what's going on. Okay, Timmy has been sold to the band Megachiroptera, for the World Premier of their single Innocent's Sacrifice. Maybe I was wrong as to why.'

'No one's sacrificing my son as the highlight of their silly little Goth Festival,' Sally said. She stopped dead in the middle of the pavement and glared at him.

Mike pulled her out of the main street where some Goths were within hearing distance of Sally's outburst.

'Healthy skepticism is fine in its place—but you're taking your sarcasm too far and too loud.'

Sally pressed her fists against her mouth, and Mike nodded.

'Try and remember your manners, please. You're the guest here,' Mike said. 'There's only so much misdirection I can perform before it's obvious I'm doing magic.'

Sally looked around and saw people staring at her. They lost interest when she remained silent and turned away.

Mike leaned closer and nodded at one woman. 'I have to say, you'd look good in that.'

Looking at the dress Mike mentioned, Sally flushed and turned away. 'I would not. Stop trying to distract me. Don't tell me you have tickets for the concert?'

'Unfortunately not,' Mike said. 'And as it's taking place here, it means that I can't just wave any old bit of paper at the ticket taker and go in. They'll have wards up to stop that sort of thing. The Goth community is a hotbed of Cræft practitioners of both sorts.'

Mike stopped at a streetlight. He leant against the post and flicked open his book at Josh's next number. Sally paced around the street not just to keep warm, but also to work off the nervous energy that wanted to run somewhere, anywhere, just to keep looking for Timmy. These slow, but sure searches didn't suit her need.

Sally jumped as more Goths approached down the street. They gave her a funny look. Her pale anorak stood out here and she wanted to blend in a bit more. She paced back to Mike to see how he was doing.

'I think *they*'re going to have to make a channel down time with the dead contacting the dead,' Mike said looking up as she arrived.

Sally sat bolt upright. 'Are they going to mur… use Timmy to start it off?'

Mike looked surprised. 'Oh no, Timmy is going to be used to provide the demon with a place to live, didn't I explain that. Only the dead can talk to dead, they need half-dead people, Zombies who can talk to both the living and the dead, to kick off the tunnel. I wonder how they will do that.'

'This isn't an academic exercise. This is Timmy we're talking about,' Sally said, trying her hardest not to be shrill. She unclenched her fists and took a deep breath. 'Living dead? Perhaps they're going to recreate the work environment of the modern office.'

Mike smiled slightly to acknowledge the feeble joke. 'Actually the modern, boring lifestyle is why there's so much interest in the paranormal at the moment.' He checked his watch. 'We've got an hour to go.'

'I can see that you want to watch their ritual, but do you think we might go looking to see if we can find Timmy before they drag him up on the stage to kill him?'

'Okay,' Mike said. 'If it makes you feel better to be running around in circles when we know where he will be in an hour.'

Sally managed not to strangle Mike. 'What else *can* we do?'

'Nothing,' Mike said. 'I suppose running around will at least keep us warm.' He got up and tucked his arm around Sally in a very proprietary way.

Sally remembered her doubts back on the terrace as she had watched the two men fighting. 'You're getting very free with that arm lock.'

Mike grinned ruefully. 'Well, as Nathan said, they forced a contract on someone with a prior contract, theirs is invalid—in this instance.'

'Huh! I told you that ages ago. I'll bet that after your fight against your Nathan, they won't even try to enforce their decree. Anyway we can talk about that once we get Timmy back,' Sally added as she remembered her resolve not to be involved in this world.

Mike looked down his nose at her. 'So in return for rescuing your son, you'll think about getting back together with me, is that right? What are the other two out of three impossible tasks that I have to do to win your hand?'

'Don't be like that,' Sally snapped. 'All I meant was that I can't think about anything else right now.'

Mike lifted his arm from around her shoulder and stalked on. She regretted the loss of the arm—aside from everything else, she was cold now.

'You know they are going to need an army of Zombies,' Mike said suddenly. 'To open a tunnel that far back. I wonder what they are going to do?'

Sally waited for more. 'Can you find anything about where Timmy is being held? With that magical sight of yours.'

'Actually yes,' Mike said. 'While I was in the café, I saw they have Timmy in the back stage tent at the concert in the park.'

'Let's go then,' Sally said heading off.

'Well I suppose we can scout the area to see how we get in.' He strode alongside her, easily keeping pace.

'No,' Sally said. 'I know how we are getting in. We're going to tell the police where Timmy is. Or at least that we heard a rumor that Timmy is being held there. They have to let the police in and we can just happen to follow to stop the sorcerers from stopping the police from seeing Timmy. That's what we are going to do.'

Chapter Twenty Five

'**Wait.**' Mike caught her arm again before she ran off. 'That worked as a distraction. But there are rules that both sides stick to about not involving the ordinary community. If I break them then they will be free to break them too.

'This isn't a game,' Sally said. 'They kidnapped an ordinary boy. I'm not part of your world—I don't care about your rules.'

'But you see you advertised him,' Mike said.

'No I didn't!' Sally nearly screamed. 'I advertised *myself* as a possible partner, oh and yes I have a little boy. I did not say come and eat my son. You agreed to use the police earlier, what the difference now?'

'I used them as a smoke screen,' Mike said. 'To hide what I was doing. I did not use them for a full frontal assault on a Dark Citadel, which is what you are suggesting.'

'Fine,' Sally said. 'Even if you stand aside, I'm going to the police.'

Sally shucked off his arm and stormed off in the direction of the police station. She didn't look back to see if he followed.

Mike caught up with her halfway down the street, but he remained silent.

Even as she pushed open the door, she could tell something was happening. People crowded into the front office; busy, like an anteater had run its sticky tongue through a termite mound.

'Mrs. Cartwright,' said the desk sergeant, catching sight of her hovering in the entrance looking surprised. 'We've got a lead, you'll never believe this…'

Pete Granger jumped up from where he sat in the front office. 'Sally, I saw Timmy. A man led him into the tents back stage at the Megachiroptera concert.'

Sally nearly fainted with relief. 'Corroboration. Thank you Pete! I'd heard a rumor that the band are going to use Timmy as part of their stage show of their World Premier Innocent's Sacrifice.'

'You've been out asking questions too,' said the policeman. 'We are keeping the kidnapping of your son from the press at the moment, but we found this journalist who brought us the information.'

Pete Granger glanced at her, but Sally had no intention of undermining his credibility as a police witness by outing him as a crank, seeking paranormal stories.

'I'm covering a ceremony at a mystic well up near the Abbey ruins and saw them.'

Sally opened her mouth to tell him about this *Dracula* thing when Mike smiled at Pete. 'We've got a number of people covering that ceremony, you know. I'm a bit put out that I've got to help Sally instead of going myself.'

Sally glanced at Mike then back at Pete, who looked like someone had given him a cream bun. He was very nearly licking his lips.

She opened mouth again, but Mike put a hand on her shoulder and directed her to the desk. 'The sergeant is wanting to tell us all about it.'

Looking over her shoulder she saw Pete slink out of the door. Before the door shut he was running up the street.

People shouted out orders; someone had a map of Whitby Abbey pinned to the wall.

She turned on Mike. 'Why did you tell Pete that? Covering the Megachiroptera gig would have been the scoop of his career!'

'If he ever got proof...!' Mike shook his head. 'You've got to trust me on this one, time and again it's said, "but people ought be able to protect themselves", and all that happens is a lot of innocent people get killed. We need cranks like him to prove we don't exist.'

'Mrs. Cartwright!' The desk sergeant waved to catch her attention. She walked across. 'With the information we received from... Oh he's gone. We've got his address. Anyway we have enough to raid the concert.'

'I promise, I'll never say another bad thing about journalists.' Sally sagged against the desk. 'So let's go and get Timmy.'

'We're organizing that right now. If you'd like to come, sit down and have a coffee...'

'No! I don't want to sit.' Sally almost screamed. 'I want to pace about and follow after you to grab Timmy when you get him back, and never let go of his hand again.'

A quick nod from the desk sergeant and the WPC came out to calm the hysterical mother.

Sally felt like there was a volcano in her head about to erupt. She clenched her fists and stalked out of the police station and into the street before she thumped the poor WPC.

'Sally,' Mike called. He chased after her.

'Go away.' Sally stalked down the road. Not noticing her direction, she found she was crossing the bridge. Ahead, she saw the steps that led up to the Abbey ruins. She could go and get Timmy back, right now!

Trotting Mike caught up with her. He grabbed her and spun her to face him. 'You are not going up there now.'

'Get. Your. Hands. Off. Me.'

'You would ruin everything, and maybe get Timmy killed.'

'They're just sitting there!'

'Sally, they're just doing their job,' he said. 'You were the one who wanted to call them in.'

Sally stared at the steps that wound their way up through the houses to Whitby Abby on the cliff top.

'I'm not going to let you walk up there.'

She spun around and stalked towards the bridge. Through gritted teeth she added, 'I want to kick and bite and thump, and if you don't stay away from me you are going to be the punch bag.'

Mike fell back, but he still followed her.

Sally turned and ran back across the bridge. It wasn't far to her car—it stood in the car park, near the Grand Turk. She was glad now Gail hadn't taken it: there was no way he could stop her from driving up there. She could hear him pick up speed as he guessed her intent.

A flag fluttered on the windscreen. Sally fumbled for her keys as she sprinted over the car park.

She stopped dead and stared.

Tucked under the windscreen wiper was a plastic bag containing a summons notice; she'd got a parking ticket for not paying the right amount of money for the length of stay.

She felt someone fishing in her pocket and spun around. Mike had her keys out. He slid them into his pocket and shook his head.

Icily calm, Sally snatched the notice. Flinging it on the ground she stamped on it. She jumped on it. She danced a furious tarantella on the offending plastic bag, grinding the words into oblivion in the tarmac of the car park. How could she have been so stupid as to forget something as simple as the metered parking?

Under the nearest streetlight, Sally could see Mike. He quietly requested a fascinated Goth couple to move away.

Sally sagged against the car. Leaning on the car roof, she could see the pattern her tears made in the dust and dirt she hadn't had time to wash off her car.

Mike returned from interference duty. He unlocked the car, sat on the passenger seat with his feet on the tarmac, and patted his knee.

Weakly, Sally sagged onto his lap and buried her face into his leather-clad shoulder. Warm arms came around her, but he didn't say a thing.

She wasn't sure how long she sat there, but she felt Mike move his arm, checking his watch around her head.

Sally sat up and rubbed at her eyes.

Mike looked at her critically. 'You can still cry without making yourself hideous,' he said. He nodded over at the toilets in the car park. 'But I'd say washing your face was in order. We have about ten minutes before the police are going to storm the concert.'

'What?' Sally said. She scrambled off his knee. Looking at her own watch told her it was nearly half past eleven.

'That's why I came after you, to tell when we needed to be in place. Now you've had a good cry, maybe you can function better.'

'I wasn't crying,' Sally said, as she ran over to the toilet block. Splashing some water over her face made her feel a little better. She ran back over to Mike who had her car locked again. The plastic bag containing the summons was no longer in sight.

'Why are they leaving it so late?' demanded Sally. 'They could have sacri… done something dreadful to Timmy by now.'

'I think,' Mike said, charging after her, but not as out of breath. 'They needed to bring in some back-up. Whitby isn't provided with the quantities of staff they need for a raid on a rock concert. And there is this, they decided that it was better to see what other charges they could bring against the band in the hopes that the more they throw maybe something will stick once the band gets their expensive lawyers on the case.'

Sally didn't have the breath to argue against this reasoning. In her opinion, anyone kidnapping Timmy deserved to spend the rest of their life rotting a Victorian-style jail.

Up at the police station they were waiting for her. True to Mike's prediction, a number of police from Scarborough seemed to have been drafted according to the painting on the side of the riot vans.

The liaison policewoman greeted them with a smile. 'There you are Mrs. Cartwright. We're just setting off. If you and Mr. Rider would like, you're sitting in this van. You can be ready to calm Timmy down when we have him back for you.'

Mike hung back a little and talked to the desk sergeant. From the corner of her eye Sally saw him pass over a battered plastic bag, but she was too involved in Timmy's rescue to get embarrassed just now. She'd save that for later.

Sally climbed into the middle front seat but Mike had to go in the rear.

The vans were nearly silent as they drove along the winding streets up to the concert on the cliff top.

Sally picked up a level of nervous excitement from the young men around her. She got the impression that this sort of thing didn't happen very much in Whitby and they were getting a thrill. She didn't care, as long as Timmy got back safely.

The vans drove through the streets of Whitby and up to the ruined abbey that stood on the other cliff. They parked outside the wall to the ancient cemetery. Young men in their best riot uniforms filed out of the vans

'Please could you stay with me, Mrs. Cartwright,' said the WPC.

Sally perched on her seat, sitting on her hands to stop them lifting to open the catch on the van door.

Mike leaned across from the back of the van and touched the constable on her shoulder.

She started to turn, and then she nodded forwards, restrained in a sitting position by her seat belt.

'Right Sally, we'll give them two minutes, then we follow,' Mike said.

'What did you do to her?' Sally stared in horror at the WPC.

'She's just asleep. Hopefully we'll get back and in our seats before she gets a reprimand for falling asleep on duty.'

As she looked closer, Sally could see, by the rise and fall of her coat buttons, that the woman was still breathing, but it was scary to see someone just drop to sleep at a touch. She looked at Mike with awe in her eyes. If only she could do that to get Timmy to sleep at bedtime.

'Do you really think that Megachiroptera will use this magic stuff on the police?' asked Sally. 'Isn't it a bit dangerous?'

Above the racket coming from the concert venue, a loud ripping noise sounded. The noise was a bit, Sally thought, like a huge zip being undone at speed.

Unearthly, purple light flickered out over the hedges making the Abbey ruins look like a supernatural slug had crept over the walls. Perched among the Abbey ruins, crows protested too early a daybreak.

'That's our cue,' Mike said. 'I don't think we can wait any longer.'

'What's happening?'

'They've started to vortex their time tunnel. I bet the alarm wards at the hotel have triggered now.'

185

Sally and Mike jumped out of the van, leaving the sleeping WPC behind. Just behind Mike, Sally ran towards the entrance across the uneven grass. She was feeling a little put out at how fit Mike was when she had spent so much money on her gym membership and was still out of breath at the speed everything was happening in this odd world that Mike belonged to.

Mike halted before the makeshift ticket booth and held out a hand to catch Sally before she ran past him. The police had gone through the entranceway but no further. Now they stood staring at the stage with blank eyes chanting along with the rest of the audience.

The crowd did a shuffling dance, spiraling around the central stage. In their fluorescent riot gear, the police looked out of place among the crow-clothed fans of Megachiroptera. From out of the stage, dry ice fog misted the air turning the whole picture dreamlike. Standing at the base of the stage, tough looking ushers wore black balaclavas, only their eyes were visible through the slit.

'They've got their army,' Mike said. 'They've turned everyone at the concert into zombies. How I wonder?'

Sally struggled against his restraining hand.

'Let me go,' Sally said. 'Can't you see Timmy on that stage?'

The stage hung above the mist, like the isle of Avalon about the lake. The stage set didn't need any extra lighting—nature provided the perfect illumination as the light of the full moon lighted up the set.

A huge bat formed the backdrop to the set. A dais, in the exact center of the stage that rose up so everyone could see, hung before the open mouth.

Mist swirled in the spiral pattern set up by the dancing crowd up and around the dais and linked up with the unearthly purple light that went deeper and deeper until it looked like it entered a black hole pinpointed on the bat's mouth.

Timmy stood at the front of the dais, as blank eyed as the rest of the crowd and dressed in a white toga with a black circle over his heart.

Mike turned Sally so that she faced away from the stage. He lifted her chin with a cupped hand and forced eye contact.

'If you pass that gate you will be a part of the Zombie audience. You will be helping them to harm Timmy.'

Sally stopped her struggles as he pulled her into the shadow of the ticket stall. 'Get into thinking mode and quickly,' she said. 'I want Timmy back before they bring that demon here and put it in him.'

'So do I,' Mike said. 'Once it has a human host it will be that much harder to eliminate. What do we know about Megachiroptera?'

'I know nothing about any Goth band.'

'All right, I'll rephrase that. What has Gail been telling you about Megachiroptera? There's something in Gail's twittering that is nagging at my mind. I sure something she said can tell me how this zombie effect is created. So give me what Gail has said about the concert?'

Sally closed her eyes. 'It's like the night club.'

'What?'

Sally opened her eyes. 'The people at the night club drank Zombie cocktails and they danced just like that.'

'There's no way they've given everyone a drink,' Mike said. 'The police wouldn't have taken it.'

Sally nodded. 'I heard the bartender say that the drinks were taking too long. They'd have to think of something different.'

Mike frowned. 'There's something in the conversation last Sunday, something important Gail said—however unlikely that is.'

She tried to remember back to Sunday, batting into oblivion the part where she and Mike were arguing about the Internet dating, and concentrated on Gail.

'She said something like "Megachiroptera are playing at the Whitby Goth Festival after all, I thought they were on tour in Haiti."'

'Stop. That's it—Haiti,' Mike said. 'They are using a voodoo ritual which involves dancing.' He waved a hand at the crowd's circling. 'And drugs. As far as I remember—though I've not really studied Haitian magic in any depth, you understand—a *coup de poudre* has things like puffer fish toxin and toads.'

'Well that's odd,' Sally said. 'There was a rain of toads in York after you left.'

Mike nodded. 'They must be administered very quickly to have caught the police as they rushed in. It has to touch the mucus membranes.'

'I don't know much about drugs but aren't some breathed in as smoke?' Sally pointed to the fog vents.

'I should work with you more often,' Mike said. 'I wish I'd known sooner, it's too late now to get some salt.'

'Pardon?'

Mike grinned briefly. 'Haitian-style zombies can be freed from domination by salt in their mouths. Hush now.'

He lifted his staff and his eyes unfocused again. With his free left hand, Mike reached for her hand. He brought it to his lips and Sally felt something invisible wrap around her.

'Right let's go and get Timmy.'

Chapter Twenty Six

Mike edged forward to peer around the ticket booth into the Abbey cemetery. The full moon sharply delineated the shadows of the wall. The sea breeze blew the clouds in, setting the shadows twitching like an impatient cat's tail.

Sally had a look over his shoulder at the shuffling, chanting dancers. Their shadows mingled into one. As she watched, one of the police officers collapsed.

An usher wearing a balaclava pushed through the other dancers. Bending over the fallen man, he forced open his mouth and stuffed something in.

'They did that at the club too,' Sally whispered. 'And look he's back on his feet.'

'That will be the Zombie Cucumber. It lets the bokor control them all.' He waved a finger at the lead singer of Megachiroptera.

'Like on Pete's website?'

Mike nodded as the rest of the police raid began keeling over. Other masked ushers joined the first to administer Zombie Cucumber to all the fallen.

When all the police were back on their feet, Mike pulled Sally through the wrought iron gateway into the Abbey cemetery hand. Beyond the gate the audience shuffled in their voodoo zombie dance, which Mike said would open the time tunnel. Sally searched the crowd for a way through to Timmy.

A scuffle at the edge of the stage drew her attention. She saw Jack Harper career onto the stage as the bouncers scrambled after him. He was in his dog-man form but Sally recognized him. Shuffling forwards on his awkward back legs, using his heavily clawed front hands for balance, he made straight for the make lead singer of Megachiroptera.

With gaping jaws, he went for the throat.

The lead singer swung his heavy, old-fashioned microphone stand at the werewolf, knocking him flying.

Jack's claws skidded along the stage then gripped the edge. Kicking off bouncers, he clambered back on.

Vanessa Knipe

Sally winced as the lead singer swung the iron stand again. 'But those singers!' she whispered to Mike. 'They're the one who had the fight with Jack on the log ride.'

Mike eyed her, and then he smiled. 'I forgot you're not part of this crowd. Yes, they are the lead singers of Megachiroptera. They usually toe the line.'

She gritted her teeth and returned her attention to the stage. From the corner of her eye she saw David Green hanging out by a tent near the ruined Abbey walls, which shadowed him. He held what looked to be a fire-blackened curtain pole. Sally jerked her head up, but she lost sight of him.

'You're not having the boy,' Jack howled. 'He's mine. I need him for my cure.'

The words snapped Sally's attention back to the stage, again straining to push a way through the mass of people. And again in the corner of her eye, she saw David Green. He stood in the exactly same place.

'Mike, I'm seeing that Dave of yours,' Sally said. She looked straight on but he had vanished again.

Mike squinted in the direction Sally was looking. 'Well spotted Sally.'

'But he's gone again.'

'It's just an aversion spell.'

Mike waved his hiking stick. '*Let mine enemies be seen,*' he said, and David came all the way visible. The sorcerer jerked around as if he had been hit and faced Mike. With a snarl on his face he launched a black shadow from the end of his pole. The murder of crows could be heard over the band music.

'Behind me, Sal, but keep close,' Mike said. He lifted his fully extended hiking staff. '*I go hence like the shadow that departeth.*'

Sally ducked behind Mike, almost hugging the hem of his trench coat.

The shadow swooped towards them. Mike stood tall. The tip of his stick drew in the moonlight. Silver dripped down the stick and flowed like a waterfall around both Mike and Sally. Where it touched the ground, the dry ice jerked away like a sea anemone's tentacle. The Shadow faded into nothing under the glow of the moon. Mike gathered his silver light into a vortex by twisting his staff three times clockwise. He pointed the tip at David. '*Let mine adversaries be clothed with their own confusion as a cloak.*'

David's face grew strained as he gathered the black of a moonless night over his head. Mike's moonlight drained away, but far slower than David's shadow had dissipated.

'Very good,' whispered David, but his voice carried to their ears. Sally guessed it was more of this magic. 'So this *is* the Sally you kept going on about in your first year at college. I did wonder when I found she was protected. Did you set her out as bait?'

Mike declined to respond but David continued, 'Was *Mr.* Dunkley very shocked when he learned of my perfidy?'

'None of us were that surprised,' Mike said. 'Nathan was the most disturbed by your becoming a daylight broker, I think.

'Ah yes! The great Nathaniel Trewithick. I was never good enough to be his apprentice. I was a second rate apprentice to a second rate demon hunter. Well, it's good that Trewithick's replacement has learnt all his lessons.'

'Nathan doesn't need me to replace him,' Mike said. 'He's the greatest hunter of demon spawn ever.'

'Seen him hunting recently, have you?'

'*He cast forth lightnings and destroyed them.*' Delivered by his rage, Mike sent a bolt of his trademark blue lightning flying across the park to where David stood.

One look at the power behind the incoming spell made Dave duck behind a sturdier portion of Abbey wall.

Blue lightning crackled up the slime-covered walls. In the clear white light the crows awoke fully and dropped from their perches.

Dave emerged from the protection of the walls. As he gathered more shadow on his staff end the first crow dived him, pecking at his face.

Dave dropped his staff and covered his face—the next crow pecked at his ear. Then he was covered in crows pecking and tearing at his flesh. He screamed, a high weak note.

Sally stared in horror as the crows mobbed the sorcerer. She winced and turned her face away, to see that on the stage, Timmy stood blinking, as if he too were awakening.

Mike lowered his staff.

'I said they were looking for the one who sacrificed the crow at Toowich Park. They can smell the crow blood on him.'

'Help him,' Sally said. She kept her face turned away from where the mass of black crows was getting closer to the ground.

Mike turned to the main action. 'No.'

Jack Harper dodged about the platform as the lead singer of Megachiroptera tried to perform and fend off the enraged werewolf.

'Mummy!' Timmy screamed. The little boy looked around and saw how high he was. He shrank down onto his knees and tucked his hands over his head.

Seeing the sacrifice no longer in thrall, the band faltered in their playing. The lead singer waved a hand to the rest of the band. 'Keep going,' he shouted. 'Or we'll lose control of the spirit.'

The musicians picked up the chord they had dropped, but the damage was done; the crowd stopped their circling dance and turned blank eyes to the stage, awaiting further instructions.

Behind her son, the black hole flickered with life. Long strands of the unearthly purple lightning splayed out over the stage.

She cupped her hands to her mouth 'Timmy! Jump!'

Timmy heard his mother and searched the crowd below him. Finally, he saw her, struggling to reach him through zombie fans. On his chest, the black pattern flickered in time with purple light. Now that she was closer, the black circle looked familiar.

Timmy crawled to the edge of the high dais and peered down. He clung to the frame. 'Mummy!'

Something was crawling up the time hole towards Timmy.

Mike's face blanched in the pulsating purple light as he stared into the abyss. He grabbed Sally's hand and dragged at her, trying to get Sally and himself back through the wrought iron gate and away from the Abbey.

Sally struggled to free herself from Mike's grip.

'Turn it back, don't let it get to Timmy,' she shouted.

He yanked at her hand to jerk her along. 'It's nearly here. I can't fight it. It's too big.' Mike's eyes were wide with terror. 'We've got to wait until Josh and the other witch finders get here.'

Sally stopped her struggles.

Ever since Mike had said he thought Dracula was coming through, Sally had half expected a gothic gentleman with a fake foreign accent sauntering down this time tunnel thing. All she would have to do was stop the creature from biting Timmy on the neck and draining his blood. Or if, disembodiment was necessary for time travel, then it should be something along the lines of an animated sheet making 'whoooooing' noises.

She looked at the dais where her little boy clung crying, with this *thing* almost crawling over his shoulders.

'There's nothing you can do?' she said, quietly.

'Sally I can't. I've seen it now. I had to take on Dave, that's reduced me. And anyway, it will take us all of us to bring this one down.'

Sally nodded. 'I see.'

She nodded calmly and extracted her hand from his slackened grasp.

'I'm sorry, Sally.'

As he turned to leave, her hand lashed out. She clenched her fist into his crucifix chain and wrenched it off his neck.

Blood leaked from his neck as the chain cut his skin before it broke.

'Then it's up to me.'

Sally pushed through the crowd to the stage. She shoved zombie fans from out of her path. A face she half-remembered stood in her way. Mike's friend, the woman who had directed Mike after her at the fun fair, stood among the zombies, but Sally rushed past her. She had a little boy, just like Timmy.

Then more zombies clawed and grabbed at her pulling her out of the abstraction.

Punching out with half-remembered blows from her women's defense classes at university, she fought her way to the stage.

'Sally! Come back.'

She ignored Mike's call.

Zombies grabbed the hood of her anorak, holding her back from climbing onto the stage.

She shrugged out of the sleeves, leaving the pale garment looking incongruous among all the black clad revelers.

With no resistance to their tugs, those holding the anorak fell.

Zombies around them trampled them as the next wave tried to stop her.

She hauled herself up onto the temporary stage.

Jack Harper still fought with the bandleader.

Ignoring them both, Sally sprinted across the stage to the scaffolding holding up the central dais.

Seeing Sally struggle up onto the stage, Jack tried to disengage, but the lead singer gave him another whack with the microphone stand.

Jack went flying. The blow flipped him over and he skidded along the stage on his back, tail and paws thrashing wildly. The lead singer pounded after him.

Sally started her climb to where Timmy sat, a statue of a terrified boy. What was coming down the tunnel nearly paralyzed her with terror. Only Timmy's danger forced her to move her hands to grasp the rungs of the scaffolding.

With a howl, Jack clawed at the lead singer. He bounded over the stage to the dais scaffolding. He started climbing up the side opposite to

Sally, hindered by the claws and the way his legs bent in the wrong places as a dog-man. In his desperation, he was faster than Sally.

'He's mine,' Jack howled.

Already Jack was halfway up the tower towards this *thing* and Timmy. Sally's hand grasped the cold iron scaffolding. Its very normality felt reassuring in the face of the *monstrosity* crawling out of the anomaly. If a hermit crab had tentacles, it would have appeared like this as it exchanged shells. Which, Sally supposed, the *thing* was actually doing. It pulsated like a cuttlefish, in colors from a starling's wing. Or, thought Sally as her mind blanked out the impossibility of this vast mutant *thing*, like the dark colors of the peacock feathers on Nathan Trewithick's waistcoat.

The metal rungs clanged as the soles of her shoes hit them. The iron was cold and slippery as the condensate from the mist machines clung to it. She concentrated on now.

She had to save Timmy.

Jack clawed his way onto the dais. Just behind him, Sally grabbed the last rung and got a knee up onto the top stage. Under her hand the scaffolding pole shifted. Sally got her top half resting on the wooden platform at the tower's height. Gently she pushed on the pole with her foot to wriggle the rest of her body onto the platform. The pole rolled under the sole of her trainer but stayed put.

The stench of the *creature* assaulted her nose. A hundred times worse than any male toilets that she had ever smelt. Taking small gasps of air through her mouth, Sally was grateful that it was the end of October, midnight and close to freezing—any warmer and she'd be helpless with retching.

Timmy burrowed into her side, holding the hem of his toga over his nose.

Below, Mike smashed his way through the zombied fans, clobbering any that got in his way with the weighted end of his hiking stick.

This close, she saw that the black circle on Timmy's chest was the brooch that David Green had given her. So that's why he'd stolen it back—they had needed it for their ritual. The inset marcasite stones flashed in time with the music and the pulsating light.

Jack took up a station between the *thing* and Timmy. In a demented frenzy, the dog-man grappled with the *thing*.

As Sally watched, tentacles grabbed and strangled Jack. Other appendages stretched out for Timmy. One tentacle lovingly stroked the brooch with its tip.

Sally bludgeoned the nearest part of the *thing* with the fist still clutching Mike's crucifix.

The tentacle shrank away. She thwacked another tentacle, regretting the lack of her rolling pin that had worked so well on Jack.

Below them Mike had climbed onto the stage, lashing at the band with his blue lightning whip. The mist coming out from the dry ice machines began a roiling climb up onto the stage. Then it oozed up the dais scaffolding that both Jack and Sally had climbed earlier. The mist thickened and blocked out Sally's view of the stage.

On the other side of the *thing*, Jack's Alsatian jaws grimly bit into one globulous eye. Jelly spurted out over the dais. Sally's trainers skidded on the soapy surface as she tried to stand. Her knees thudded onto the wooden planks, sending spikes of pain up her spine and into her head. The purple light strobed over the Abbey in a victory shout as an enemy of the *thing* went down.

The goo smelt even worse than the *creature. Appropriate to the location,* thought the part of Sally that had to remain distant from this horror or she would not be able to function and rescue Timmy, *that the creature reeks of seaside bins, that odd mixture of rotting fish, chip wrappers and vomit.*

Mist surged up the scaffolding and writhed around the dais. The light of the moon thinned as the mist edged up to form a dome over the stage set.

She tried not to gag on the fetid odor. The goo was on her hands and soaking through the knees of her blue jeans.

Kneeling on the edge of the platform, clinging to the edge Sally felt for the scaffolding pole that had shifted as she tried to stand. That would be better than her rolling pin. She tugged at it.

The pole rattled in its clamps.

She pulled again.

The foul stench from the creature rolled over her again. How Jack Harper could keep standing after releasing the toxic smell into the air, was beyond her understanding—unless, being demon-infested himself, he just couldn't smell it.

Trying to breathe through her mouth, she hauled on the scaffolding pipe.

'Please be loose.' She whispered her plea though she believed that nothing could hear.

The shadows around her sharpened and a vibration, like a purr, ran the length of the pipe. It came loose. She had a weapon.

She forced one foot and then the other under her. Then she stepped forwards and pounded at the appendage reaching for her son.

Timmy shrank into his mother's side.

Wrapping the silver crucifix around the pipe she flailed at the *thing* again and again. Even with the reluctant help of Jack Harper, she was only just keeping the *thing* away from Timmy and herself.

Every tentacle not attacking Jack reached out to the brooch. She had to get it off Timmy. She switched to holding the pole with one hand, with the other she clenched the brooch. A tentacle coiled around her ankle.

She released her grasp and hit down hard. Sparing a glance at her son she shouted, 'Timmy, unpin that brooch.'

Timmy huddled at her side, too gone in fear to hear his mother.

Then words thundered off the cliffs surrounding Whitby.

'*In my trouble I will call upon the Lord.*'

The tentacle around her leg shivered. It slowly uncoiled.

The pipe thunked onto the wooden platform as Sally clamped her hands over her ears. The words beat against her eardrums. Timmy's eyes rolled back in his head and he collapsed against her leg. Sally dropped to her knees. Looking around, she tried to see through the dry ice fog.

'*He sent out his arrows and scattered them: he cast forth lightnings and destroyed them.*'

The words continued on in a rhythmic cycle.

'*The way of the Lord is an undefiled way.*'

Jack's body lurched with each proclamation. The words pounded into him until he could no longer stand. He fell to his knees and hands. The claws began to retract, and she could see the terrible pain on his face as muscles and flesh turned from wolf to man. A sickly yellow aura formed around his body.

'*Upon the ungodly he shall rain snares, fire and brimstone, storm and tempest.*'

A crack of thunder sounded in the clear night. Without Jack attacking on the other side the *thing* could concentrate on Timmy.

Even though the creature's appendages were taking a beating from the words, enough of them were still creeping towards Timmy.

Bracing herself Sally forced her hands away from her ears and reached for the brooch.

'*The words of the Lord are pure words, even as silver which from the earth is tried and purified seven times in the fire.*'

With her brain barely able to formulate instructions under the onslaught of the words, Sally knew she would be unable to use fine motor skills to undo the pin. Clenching her fist around the jewelry, she heaved.

The pin bent under her attack.

Tugging again, this time harder, she ripped it off the front of the toga. A gaping hole appeared in Timmy's only garment.

The tentacles started reaching for her, now.

In absolute terror, Sally flung the brooch into the time tunnel. Let *it* look for the summons back in *its* own time.

To Sally it felt like she was looking at a mirror, watching as the broach fell towards its own image. Like it was dropping down a deep well.

Sally counted the seconds by the beating of her heart to see how deep it was.

The brooch reached the image. The mirror shattered.

Sally flung herself over Timmy to stop the shards from reaching him.

'They are brought down and fallen, but we are risen and stand upright.'

The tentacles fell away from Sally and Timmy.

Moonlight broke through the mist and began to illuminate the scene. The drug-laden fog fell back to the ground, away from the time tunnel. The tunnel began to fold in on itself.

The *thing* screamed a horrible scream. Its tentacles lashed out, trying to a grab hold of this new time.

Holding Timmy to her heart, Sally scooped up the scaffolding pipe and hammered away a searching tentacle, grinding down with the crucifix.

The summons on the brooch pulled the *creature* back into tunnel.

Exhausted by his fight against the words, Jack crept to the edge of the platform. A thrashing tentacle caught in his aura. It clung to it, drawing the sickly yellow out of his body as the creature fell into the tunnel.

'No!' Jack screamed. With totally human hands he lashed out, trying to catch the insubstantial yellow mist being pulled out of him.

'Let us break their bonds asunder and cast away their cords from us.'

The words pounded harder and harder into her head. Excruciating pain pushed behind her eyes until she wished she could pass out, like Timmy had done. Jack collapsed on the edge of the turret, crying like a lost child.

'We will remember the Name of the Lord.'

The zombie-making fog oozed back into the dry ice machines. Sally could finally see properly down to the stage.

The Zombies stared around, as if wondering what was happening.

Megachiroptera lay across their instruments, blood pouring out of their ears. The leader singer had fallen as he was trying to crawl to where Mike stood, tall and bright.

He had the microphone in one hand. In the other he held the small black Book of Common Prayer from which he read out loud. The words that forced the *creature* back to *its* own time poured out of Mike like a fountain.

Sally sat and stared at him. His hair had fallen from its ponytail. It lifted in a brown shock around his head. Unearthly winds lashed his coat around his ankles, and a light so pure it was blinding, fell from the moon to wrap a halo around Mike's body.

For a heartbeat everything stopped. A vast calm filled the sea and sky. In absolute silence the unearthly purple light sputtered out. The tunnel no longer existed.

Mike sank into an exhausted crouch, clutching at the microphone as if it was the only thing keeping him from fainting.

Jack lifted his head. Sally saw his eyes, dead to any hope as he stared at his human hands. He lifted them to the moon in a silent appeal. His body drooped, as he got no answer. He started to turn, but his feet slipped in the slime.

Hampered by Timmy's body across her lap, Sally couldn't reach him. He made no attempt to catch himself and fell without a cry down the cliff. The image of the moon on the calm sea shattered as his body hit the water.

Sally turned away, numbed by the horror of the night. From her vantage point on top of the world, Sally saw witch finders swarming through the streets of Whitby. Their alarms must have finally rung out the warning of a demon incursion.

The moonlight halo surrounding Mike drifted up past the dais in a cloud of silver breath.

Sally and Timmy sat alone on the top of the stage. Sheltering her son in her arms like the Madonna.

And then the audience started to clap and cheer.

Chapter Twenty Seven

Sally woke up gradually, aware of being warm and in bed. After the horror of last night, that was all she wanted to know… at first.

She began hearing voices in the background. Waking up a bit more she realized that she was listening to the radio turned on low.

'And the Goth Band Megachiroptera was arrested last night for kidnapping a young boy to use in the stage effects for their new single Innocent's Sacrifice. A spokesman for the band said that the band had been unaware that the mother was not in on the deal. They thought that the child, who cannot be named for legal reasons, was the child they had arranged to mock-kidnap as part of their show. They had assumed that the mother, who was in Whitby with the child, during the Festival was also a Goth and would understand.'

Yeah right, thought Sally, *a Goth in a pale blue anorak.*

'Other charges being brought before the band, include the releasing of large quantities of hallucinogenic chemicals into the air around their stage set.

'On a brighter note for the band, they say they hope to negotiate with the mother of the child. The whole stage set was being filmed for the upcoming video and the scene where the mother fights the animatronic creatures makes very good cinema.'

'Oh like I'd negotiate with them,' Sally said. 'They can rot in hell for all I care.'

An arm tightened around her shoulder. 'You'd be better off doing a deal,' Mike answered. 'It'll be a decent amount, and you won't get vengeful fans after you. Believe me, you've only touched the surface of my world. I can be the go-between for you.'

She noticed that she was wrapped around Mike. 'You were great last night, Mike,' she murmured, returning the squeeze and snuggling closer.

'Uncle Mike? Where are we? And why are you in bed with Mummy?' Timmy said.

Sally jumped up—scrabbling for the blanket to cover her chest—then she noticed that she was fully dressed in last night's filthy clothes.

Mike grinned at her confusion. He lay next to her but on top of the covers, fully clothed, except that he was no longer wearing his long coat. It lay over him like a blanket.

'After we got you back from the people who took you, it was very late so I brought you and your mother up here to sleep for the rest of the night, instead of driving home when we were all so tired. As you got the sofa, I curled up here next to your mother. Bathroom's through that door Tim. Go and have a bit of a wash, please.'

Grumbling, Timmy did as he was told. Mike turned back to Sally. From the bathroom came a whoop of delight and shower water began to run and switch off and run and switch off.

'Don't worry. I didn't even consider undressing you, which I think is very virtuous of me.' Mike sat up. 'I ordered breakfast up here. We can eat, and then I'll drive you home, as I traveled on the train. I've had your car brought up to the hotel car park.'

'We didn't get that poor WPC into trouble did we?'

'No. Everything was so confused last night that no one has any idea of who was supposed to be where. At least the other witch finders helped out there. Josh made them cover it all up.' His mouth thinned into a stern line.

'What did they do?' asked Sally.

'They removed the remaining parts of the zombie spell. I was totally out of it by the time that creature was gone. I couldn't have lit a candle. At least I could leave it to them to explain all the zombies to the police. Hallucinogenic drugs.' Mike snorted.

Sally snickered. 'They're Goths, Mike. Who would have noticed the Zombiedom when they went back to work on Monday.'

Mike slid his arm around her shoulders again and sighed. 'Those are my friends you are talking about, Sal.'

Sally remembered the woman who had helped her at the fun fair. The one she had seen among the zombies. She tried to pull away, but Mike held her close.

'Sorry,' she whispered.

'You need an attitude adjustment. And I still think you'd look great in that dress from last night.'

She looked up indignantly. 'That wasn't a dress! There wasn't enough material—'

He angled in for a kiss. With his lips against hers he said, 'Okay, I rescued Timmy and you, so now I'm claiming the reward you promised.'

With a nervous glance at the bathroom, where the shower water was still stop/starting to the accompaniment of giggles, Sally gave Mike a peck on the lips.

He shook his head, hair brushing her face. His hand moved to hold her face still and his lips brushed hers. He lay back on the pillows, guiding her down with him. Sally tried not to listen to the shower as she slid her hands under his shirt to touch his skin.

A knock sounded on the outer door. Mike muttered a curse. Sally tried not to giggle as Mike flung his coat from his legs and stalked to the open the door.

It was room service with the breakfast he had ordered.

Mike dredged up enough manners to smile at the waiter. Now that he was standing Sally noticed that he had shed the velvet jacket and the lace collared shirt and wore only a black tee shirt. He dug in his trouser pocket for his wallet and passed over a folded banknote. With a wry smile he brought the tray to the bed.

Sally sat up cross-legged, her blonde ringlets hanging in tangled knots around her face.

'What is your job?' Sally asked as he put the wallet away. 'Or is that stuffed with magical money.'

'I'd lose any standing at all around here if I tried to pass off illusionary money,' Mike said. 'The job of witch finder actually pays quite well and there's a huge reserve for expenses. I'll have to find a real job now.'

Sally bit her tongue to stop her mouth dropping open.

Mike tucked his head around the bathroom door. 'Tim, if you want food you'd better stop playing with that shower.'

He fidgeted with something in the bathroom and tossed Sally a comb. Then he joined her, sprawling on the bed like a Roman at a feast.

Timmy charged back in wearing only a towel and dripping over the hotel carpet.

Sally threw back the covers on the rented bed and started to rub Timmy dry as he tried to pile toast into his mouth.

Mike shook his head. 'Give it up Sally. Ignore Timmy for two minutes and eat some breakfast. No wonder you're so skinny. Tim, wrap up in that towel and let your mum get something to eat.'

Timmy followed Mike's orders to Sally's indignation, but Mike stopped her protests by popping some fruit into her open mouth.

With everyone fed, Mike stuffed his clothes into his backpack. He quelled Timmy's complaints and got them out the door so he could check out.

'I didn't need to wash. My clothes are dirty.' Timmy said as Mike locked the door.

'At least you have clothes to wear, we had to find them last night,' Mike said.

In spite of his hurry, there was still a delegation waiting for them in the lobby. About ten men stood, looking ready to carry Mike in a victory ride on their shoulders. Even sour Mr. Marishes looked pleased.

Mike ignored them. The group opened a corridor between them in the face of his forbidding expression so he could walk to the reception desk to sign out. When one of the younger ones started a cheer, he turned to face them.

'Hypocrites, the lot of you,' he hissed. 'Who was willing to listen to my warnings last night? Who was at my side when the Demon broke through? All of you vowed to fight *them* wherever you find *them* and not one of you turned out to help.'

'And we were supposed to respect your judgment.' Marishes's expression returned to its customary sourness. 'When you appeared so under the thumb of that female.'

'Fine!' Mike dug out his wallet and slid out a card. He ripped the card in two and dropped it on the floor. He turned back to the reception desk.

Sally had never seen Mike so angry. Not even during their arguments. Timmy cowered into his mother's side.

She dropped an arm around him as she glared at the gathered men.

Mr. Marishes took two steps back.

One person refused to be quelled by Mike's display of temper. As Trewithick came forward, Sally noticed he was wearing glasses. He hadn't worn those last night. He was dressed in plain black jeans and T-shirt, no peacock displaying this time under the ankle-length, leather trench coat that Mike copied.

'Well done, Michael. Keep up that attitude whenever you deal with the Council.'

'I'll have no more dealings with the Council.' He waved an impatient hand at the ripped card on the floor.

'You too?' Trewithick said.

'What?' Mike said. 'You're the best there is. You can't be leaving Council Service.'

'I'm retiring. I trained you to be my replacement.' Trewithick touched the card on the floor with his toe. 'Reconsider. After last night's display, you surpass me. You are needed more than ever.'

Mike shook his head. 'Never! Not after the way they blindly followed the rules. If Mr. Dunkley had been here, everyone would have been at the concert. He recognizes vision.'

'And you're giving all that up, for a woman?' Trewithick shrugged.

Josh pushed through the crowd and picked up the ripped license. 'No you don't. Mr. Dunkley's going to kill me, you know, two of his top demon hunters retiring on my Watch. Think again, Mike.' He held out the torn up license.

Mike shook his head. 'I can't.'

Josh jerked his head at the gathered witch finders. 'Lots of them have regular girlfriends, you know that.'

Marishes snorted, looking totally affronted. Some of the men smiled wryly.

'Sally's different.' Mike waved that aside. 'But it's not that. My brothers betrayed me—following their stupid bloody rules to the letter. I can't do this job without back-up, no one can.'

Josh sighed. He looked at Trewithick. 'And Mr. Dunkley's gonna want to talk to you. So don't be rushing off like this.'

Trewithick ignored him. Picking up a black overnight bag, he walked out of the hotel.

The congregation stood in a stunned silence.

Grabbing his own bags, Mike charged after him, leaving Josh and the license behind.

Sally got hold of Timmy's hand and followed. Trewithick was unlocking a black vanette when Mike caught at his wrist to stop him opening the door.

'Nathan what are you talking about?'

Trewithick sighed. 'You've just ruined my dramatic exit, Michael.'

'Sod your dramatic exit. What are you doing? You can't be retiring; you're not even fifty. Baring Dunkley, you're the Council's top demon hunter.'

Trewithick leaned his head on the top of his van. He puffed out a sighing breath. 'Has it ever occurred to you what it's like to get out of bed every morning, God it's thirty years now, and think "I've got to face another demon today?"' Well, have you?'

Mike was silent.

'Michael, I'm just scared.' Trewithick shook off Mike's hand. 'Something's switched off in my head—like maybe courage.'

'Or maybe your common sense got switch on,' Sally said.

Trewithick flicked her a glance and turned away without answering.

'You can't be scared,' Mike said. 'I've seen you laugh at demons.'

Trewithick shrugged.

'Mike,' Sally said. 'This is the man who would have left Timmy to rot.'

Mike noticed that Sally had walked up behind them. He flicked a finger at Timmy. The boy trotted off to sit on the terrace wall and stare at the sea.

Sally looked at Mike then at Timmy. 'Oh you're using magic to control him.'

'Actually, that's the first time.' Then he turned back to Trewithick who had slung his overnight bag in the back of his van and strapped it in. He refused to look at either of them, but leaned back on the roof of his van to join Timmy in staring at the sea.

'Nathan, I don't know what to believe here.'

'Believe this, I am going to retire.'

'How did they know?' Mike demanded. 'Green, and the Goths I fought in York, they both told me I was your replacement. How did they know you were going to retire?'

Trewithick shook his head. His ponytail slithered over the weathered leather of his coat. 'We have spies among them, I would expect they return the favor.'

Mike dug his staff into the tarmac. Using that compelling voice he said, 'You've not gone over to *them* have you?'

Trewithick looked Mike straight in the eyes. 'I will fight against the Darkness for as long as I live.'

Sally glanced between them as Trewithick dropped his eyes and both men relaxed again.

'I suppose that you've found another woman you're going to share this *retirement* with, more like,' Mike said

'I'm retiring from a lot of things. I'm forty six, about time to start thinking about my life now.'

'You're not becoming a monk, are you?' Mike looked horrified.

'No, I'm not that far gone.' Trewithick's smile was brittle.

Mike shrugged. 'I'm just surprised that a woman dumping you has hit so hard.'

'That depends on what you think she hit,' Trewithick growled.

'You haven't got a heart to break,' Mike said, grinning. 'That's what you've always told me'

A Date with Darkness

'I have some more books I want to finish writing.' Trewithick didn't smile back. 'Did I ever tell you how I got my reputation of being the foremost demon hunter of this generation?'

'No.'

'During my year five exams, my tutor took me along to show me how to get the big ones. He was eaten, right in front of me. Digesting my tutor distracted the demon, so I coolly destroyed it.' He smiled ruefully. 'Mind, I threw up afterwards.

'By some miracle I'm still alive. I've too much imagination not to be able to guess how it's going to go if I stay in this business much longer.'

'Why didn't you use your magic against me last night?' Mike asked.

Trewithick blinked at the sudden change of direction. To Sally he seemed to be thinking on the fly.

Mike added, 'Green said something last night about that.'

Shut up, Sally thought, *you're giving him extra thinking time.* If that was the case, Mike had given him enough.

'How did you feel after fighting that demon?' Trewithick asked.

'Totally drained.'

'And do you think you could have taken on the demon after a real fight with me?'

'No, sir!' Mike said. 'In fact if those crows hadn't taken out Dave for me, I would have failed. As it was I only just made it through the text.'

'You've answered your question, then.'

'So what would have happened,' Sally asked. 'If Mike couldn't win?'

Trewithick looked round at Sally. 'Then Marishes, Josh and I—if I'd managed to crawl out from under my bed—would have taken it on.'

'You mean that you'd have jumped in and saved Mike at the last minute?'

'No,' Trewithick said sadly. 'If Michael had failed, he'd be dead. This demon would have eaten him.'

Sally frowned at even this level of social interaction with the man who had suggested that she not rescue Timmy. But she still had to know something.

'What happened to Jack Harper?' she asked. 'Was that *being eaten by a demon*?'

'Who?' Trewithick said.

'The Wolfman, from my Internet date. He thought that Timmy could cure him.'

Trewithick looked away from the sea to look at her. A tick twitched under one eye.

205

'The words Michael used ripped the demon loose from his soul. He was free of the curse. I imagine the larger demon ate the smaller one.'

'But he wanted to be cured,' Sally said. 'So why did he jump off the cliff?'

Mike grimaced. 'That's the problem with curing them. We can do it, but unless they are put into psychiatric care immediately, they tend to suicide. We have to cure them because a lot of those infected become serial killers. Quite a dilemma.'

Trewithick opened his van quickly. He flicked a glance at Timmy and whatever spell Mike had put on the boy failed, because Timmy looked round and saw the adults hanging around the van. He ran back over to his mum.

'I won't ask to be invited to the wedding,' Trewithick said, changing the subject. 'As the bride has good reason to hate me. But you have my amused and fond wishes.'

Nathan shook his head and slid into the van.

Timmy wrapped his arms around Sally. 'Mummy, does that mean you are finally going to marry Uncle Mike?'

Sally blushed and glanced at Mike, who lifted an enquiring eyebrow.

'Maybe. I'm willing to think about it.' She turned resolutely away from his smile. 'Have you really retired?'

'Yes,' Mike said.

'Good!' Sally glanced up. 'We can shut down that Internet dating site.'

Mike glanced warily at Timmy. 'I've still to keep those vows, people with my training can't just throw their weight around you know.' He nodded after Trewithick's van. 'He'd never break those rules.'

Feeling defeated, she looked over at the ruins of the Abbey. The huge murder of crows launched into the sky. She held her breath. The black cloud broke up into smaller groups that scattered. Three crows arrowed for the cliff where she stood.

Her nails dug into her palms as she watched them.

They veered off before they reached the hotel car park and flew over the black van.

www.ingramcontent.com/pod-product-compliance
Lightning Source LLC
Chambersburg PA
CBHW070124260626
47160CB00004B/1607